Forget the Night

To Mary:
Continue to build and
powerful dreams and to
reach out to others to
help them come true.

Leona S. Jockey

9-23-95

LEONA TOCKEY

DESIGNED AND ILLUSTRATED BY RICHARD MARTIN

Awakening in a memory of incest.

Dedicated to Jenny and Rich, and to all other children wounded by child abuse.

Forget the Night

Leona S. Tockey

Life Arrow
2464 El Camino Real
Santa Clara, Ca. 95051

Library of Congress Catalog Card Number: 95-77117

Tockey, Leona S.

Forget the Night: Awakening to a memory of incest

ISBN 0-9646921-0-4 "Hardcover"
ISBN 0-9646921-1-2 "Softcover"

Acknowledgements

To publish this book I had to let others support me, help me, laugh and cry with me, believe in me and most of all LOVE me. In the incestuous family the child learns that love literally means betrayal and abandonment. It can take a lifetime to relearn the distortions that develop around this painful experience.

Very special thanks to the friends who knew all this about me and did not let me run away or hide from my own truth. Each of them in their own way loved me and never betrayed me or abandoned me.

Richard Martin listened to Jenny's words chapter by chapter. He has walked with me in my darkest hours and unceasingly encouraged me to continue. In the gift of his art, the illustrations and the design of this book, he continues to heal his own abusive childhood. Anita Montero who held many tears and frustrations in her loving arms, contributed many hours of transcription and editorial time and offers her marketing skills to bring this publication into the world. To Kenne Zugman for his unfailing friendship and steadfast availability for both personal and professional support. Words are not adequate for the gratitude I feel toward the three of you.

My daughter Leslie worked many hours researching self-publishing and offered to all of us organizational management. She continues to have a continuous belief in who I am, personally and professionally. Her faith never wavered...To the Rev. Laurie Tockey, my son, a deep gratitude for his keen intellect, loving and understanding heart. It was Laurie who said to me, "If you need the money, ask for it!" Thank you to Bryan, my youngest son, whose reality is clouded with schizophrenia, for often keeping me in the day to day routines of my life. Three members of my family are not here in physical form to share this with us; my two oldest sons and my husband. They are with me daily however, in spirit, provoking me and fortifying me to heal myself and live my life to the fullest.

I am grateful to my brothers, their wives and children for supporting me to publish our family truth in the hope that it might help erase this sin against children from our society. To my mother who, in her nineties, struggles to comprehend how this tragedy could have been at the heart of our family. tells me, "You do, whatever you have to do to heal, dear". Incest is a family affair. Speaking and accepting the truth offers the family the opportunity to break the cycle of abuse, whether that abuse is alcohol, psychological, physical or sexual. This revealing has not been without pain for them and I am grateful that we have let that pain bring us closer and not distance us, as a family. I do not want my story to hurt anyone and because it is a painful story, there can be painful places. I felt loved in my family as a child and I still do. Each of us, in my family, must let the pain be transformed into growth and love.

My therapeutic healing has been unique, in that many both led and followed me on my pathway. To all of them I am grateful. During the painful places in the writing of this book I turned to four special people, therapists and friends: Carolyn Hutchins, Marilyn Luotto, Kenne Zugman and Dave Saxby. Special acknowledgement must go to the Giaretto Institute, (formerly *ICEF*) to *Parent's United, Daughter's and Son's United & Adult's Molested as Children United* where I found a therapeutic community to work and grow. For over ten years I facilitated adolescent and intermediate (8-12) age groups of sexually abused children and young people. To each child & adolescent I owe a debt of gratitude for the sharing of their lives.

Thank you to Margo Silk Forrest, Editor and Publisher of *The Healing Woman,* for challenging the writer in me and helping me confront the mountain of resistance and the canyons of fear about speaking the truth on paper. To Felicia Eth, literary agent, who said, "You have a market, publish it!". To Nancy Roberts, editor, who despite personal tragedies gave me supportive and positive feedback along with a lot of hard facts about the business end of publishing and to Martha Aarons. for continued editing and waiting to be paid as I could. To Debra Dake and Terri Music for saying, in the very beginning, "This is really good!". To Sue DelAra for edits in the manuscript and to Zann Erick for her brilliant final edit.

The actual printing of this story, the words on this very page, were made possible by the faith and generosity of each person who purchased an autographed, numbered, hard cover edition. I thank you for following my dream. Deep gratitude to those of you who extended your generosity way beyond my request: Kenny Zugman, Dick Seibert, Patrick Martin, Sue DelAra, Gene Kuehl, Dusty Miller, Bill Hallahan, Peggy Stoddard Womack, Jane Lewis and Nickoleus Reyes.

Lastly, it is impossible to mention everyone who supported this writing and publishing adventure. I am grateful to each of you.

I offer thanks for the Divine Guidance of this project. May the publication and distribution of *Forget the Night* be an act of power and an instrument of healing for each of you who have participated.

Introduction

Jenny's story begins in 1935, just before she turns 11. Her family had migrated from southern Idaho to the northern part of central Montana. The land was harsh, given over mostly to dryland wheat farming. Times were hard, and Jenny's father had re-entered the teaching profession to provide for his family. The family had moved a lot. Moving was always explained as economically necessary, but it is also true that Jenny's father harbored a basic restlessness and dissatisfaction with life.

Towns like Missoula and Helena were big towns, cities to Jenny and her brothers. They had no roots, no grandparents, no cousins. This made them dependent on each other. In many ways, they had a good family and a good life, but inside that good life, the child Jenny was sexually violated and physically abused. The extreme contradiction was part of the damage done to Jenny's soul as she struggled to make sense of what was happening to her.

The story of Jenny is the story of my family, the family in which I grew up. In that family, I learned about love and compassion, about integrity and fairness. I also learned about betrayal, hatred, and shame.

From my mother I learned about God, faith, hope, kindness, strength, and courage, and about being a good mother. Without her example and her constancy, I would not have been able to write this book. My fear is that the readers of this family tragedy will blame her, as I have, and not look beyond her to the society which still causes us to live in ignorance and prejudice. We can change our society only through openness and education, not through judgment and blame. My acknowledgment of this, however, had to come through living the pain of anger and shame, not through denial.

From my father, I learned about the gifts of nature and the gift of my mind. The mountains are my home because I followed his footsteps along miles of mountain streams where I waited silently for the rainbow trout to strike or to trick a wily cut-throat at dusk. From him I learned the meaning of antic-ipation, patience, and the excitement of success. Although my self-esteem suffered from his unrelenting academic standards, I have continued to accept those standards as a challenge. In my adult years, I knew he was proud of me and my accomplishments, even though he was disappointed when I abandoned my education for a traditional marriage.

On the day he died, at 84 years of age, I stood beside him in church as we sang "Rock of Ages" together for the last time. His voice had never been more clear, and when we sat down, he looked at me and smiled. I smiled back, acknowledging the elemental humor of life. For years I had believed I had disappointed him musically, when in truth, he still thought I had the greatest voice in the world! In some ways his love for me was truly blind. I don't suppose he would have wanted me to write this book and share our dark secret, but then again, maybe he would have. He did expect me to use the talents and gifts that were given to me. I suspect that he never fully used his own gifts, and his disappointment with himself was part of what caused him to abuse me.

I began my work with incestuous families in 1979, as a Marriage, Family and Child Counseling intern. In the years since, I have never heard a reason-able or rational explanation for childhood sexual abuse. Any sexual act against a child is evil. But the families, and therefore the people in the fam-ilies, are not evil. Most frequently, there is love somehow gone cockeyed. My family was and is no different from millions of other families: average American families where children are abused.

This has not been an easy book to write. Many times I wanted to make the words less painful, to leave parts out or pretend things weren't so bad. Each time I was tempted to change or deny the truth, the faces of the children I have worked with in therapy appeared before me. Their voices said, "How can I tell my truth if you will not tell yours?" This is not just my story; it is also theirs.

There is deep trauma and devastation for the child who is sexually molested. When the molestation is performed by a family member whom the child loves and trusts, there is also overwhelming betrayal. People who have not had these experiences do not understand how anyone can forget such atrocities. In fact, it is usually necessary to forget. Dissociation or Dissociative Disorder, to use its clinical name — is a miraculous phenomenon that allows the child to survive. I am frequently asked, "Do people really forget? How can you just forget?" My response to them is: It's a miracle, a blessing from the psyche. What cannot be tolerated must be denied until such time as the spirit can tolerate the memory. When you understand that, then you know how much courage it takes for a child to tell, whether she is 6 years old or 60.

I am indebted to Daughters and Sons United, the child and adolescent component of the *Child Sexual Abuse Treatment Program* in San Jose, California. They were the mirrors who helped me to understand my own survival. They taught me how important forgetting is. They also taught me that in order to remember, it is necessary to have a safe place of acceptance and love. All too frequently, our courts are unsafe places in which children are further victimized. Our society must work toward a better way of treating families so that children will feel safe enough to remember. The sharing of this story about Jenny is the sharing of that hope.

Chapter 1

"Jenny... Jenny, wake up."

Jenny stirred beneath the warm covers and she snuggled deeper, not wanting to waken.

"Jenny, it's Daddy, wake up. It's time for the eclipse. You don't want to miss it."

Jenny opened her eyes to the dark room and suddenly remembered her science report. The eclipse of the moon was tonight. She had been waiting all week for this important moment, when she would see, from her bedroom window, no more light on the moon, only darkness. She slipped out of the covers and walked toward the window. How amazing to look in the sky and see the moon turn dark, just as it was pictured in her science book.

"Daddy, will the whole moon be dark?"

"Yes, Sweetheart, but remember, the moon is not really turning dark; the earth is moving between the sun and the moon. There is no light on the moon. It's only the reflection of the sun that makes the moon bright."

"But, Daddy, how can we see the moon shining when we can't see the sun?"

"Here, Jenny, you stand on the stool and watch. Remember the picture you drew for your report, and you'll see that the earth will be like a great shadow."

"Oh, Daddy, what if it stayed there forever and ever and there was never a moon shining again? Night would always be dark!"

"Yes, I suppose so," said Daddy. "But it seems that's one thing we can count on. The planets keep moving, and the sun keeps coming up every day."

"But I love the moon. It's magic sometimes in the moonlight. I would never want it to be all dark every night." A frown crossed Jenny's face and a little shiver chilled her.

Daddy put his arms around her slender body and gave her a hug. "You don't worry your pretty head. In the morning the sunshine will be here, and tomorrow night the moon will be a tiny sliver with its promise to be full again."

Jenny's body suddenly stiffened. He didn't stop hugging her and his hand was under her nightie. Her mind raced as she kept staring at the moon.

Why is he touching me like this? Why is he touching my body? Is this a hug? Does he want me to hug him? Oh, maybe.

She turned and threw her arms around his neck and squeezed him. "Oh, thank you for waking me up, Daddy! Miss Snyder will be so pleased when I tell her that I woke up and saw the whole eclipse." But he didn't stop rubbing her body and touching her bottom.

"I guess I have to go to bed now," Jenny said.

Daddy lifted her off the stool and onto her bed. As he covered her up, he smoothed her nightie down, and it was not the same when he kissed her good night. He smelled different.

He said good night and shut the door. Jenny looked out the window at the shadowed moon. *What if Daddy's wrong? What if night is never, ever the same after tonight?*

Chapter 2

In the morning, Jenny heard her mother and baby brother, Jimmy, before her mother's voice called her, "Jenny, time to get up; you'll be late for school."

Somehow Jenny felt different today. She wanted to stay hidden under the warm covers. She lay on her side and looked at the little yellow stool beneath her window. Daddy had made that stool and painted it yellow just for her. Brother Adam had one, too. His was green. Her gaze went around the room to the yellow trunk with its lift-out tray. Everything special that Jenny had was in that trunk: paper dolls, books, and doll dishes; Orphan Annie secret decoder pins and rings; and things that grownups called "junk," like colored glass and special rocks. No one but Jenny had been allowed to open her trunk since her daddy had made it when she was six years old. That made her trunk about the oldest thing she had- five whole years! Older than Jimmy, but not as old as Adam. And they never, ever touched it.

Mom's voice came from the kitchen. "Jenny, you're poking 'round today. Daddy will be ready to leave, and you won't be ready."

Jenny hurried to dress, grabbed her books, and quickly slid behind her bowl of hot, steamy oatmeal. She didn't look at anyone, but just poured milk from the blue pitcher and started eating.

"Well, young lady, no more eclipses for you if you're going to be tardy to the table." Daddy's voice seemed to echo in the tiny kitchen.

Jenny looked up and saw her father across the table. He looked the same as yesterday. His smile and his words said that there really had been an eclipse, so Jenny wondered if that other thing had happened too. Maybe not.

Her mother's voice startled her. "Jenny, what's wrong with you this morning? Your father's right. We should never have let you wake up in the middle of the night, eclipse or no eclipse."

"Oh, I'm just thinking about my science paper. I wonder how many other kids in school woke up and saw it? I hope I'm not the only one. I'm going to stop at Lois's and see if she woke up. She said her big sister was going to watch it, too."

"Don't you want to wait for your father and Adam?" Mom asked.

"Uh-uh, not now; I have to go." She gave her mom a hug and a kiss, put her jacket on, and, with books under her arms, was out the door. "Good-bye, see you at lunch," she called. The night forgotten, Jenny was on her way.

The autumn air was brisk but the sun was warm as Jenny walked the familiar path to Lois' house. Jenny's world was wonderful, and she loved it. Everything about life felt good to her. She loved Miss Snyder, and she knew she was one of her favorite pupils. But the kids didn't care; they liked Jenny, too.

Jenny was smart, but she wasn't uppity about it; she was simply excited about knowing things. Not like Lois, for instance. No one helped her at home. Her dad was sick a lot of the time, and there were so many little kids at her house, Lois' mom didn't have time to help her and neither did any one else. Lois had a hard time remembering history, geography, or times tables, so she and Jenny made flash cards with all the questions and answers. They played school until Lois had all of the answers right.

When Jenny's dad didn't take Adam to his classroom, Jenny would. Everyone knew how good she was to her little brother. Adam was often shy and scared, so Jenny was the perfect big sister. Nobody pushed Jenny around; even the boys knew that. She loved Adam and knew in her heart that she was special to him. He made her feel important.

She was always chosen for the ball team and made sure that everyone else got a turn. She wasn't pretty or cute as one thinks of little girls, but she had a beauty all her own. She knew it, too; that was part of her confidence, part of her feeling good about herself and her world. The sun shone on her raven-black hair, and she swished it in the autumn breeze as she ran up the three steps to Lois' back porch.

"Lois, Jenny's here," she heard Lois' dad call. "C'mon in, Jenny. My good-ness, girl, you get prettier all the time! Those dark brown eyes of yours look like they got a secret this morning."

Lois' dad always said something like that about Jenny's eyes and usually she kind of liked it, but this morning, she looked down at her shoe tops and felt a strange flushing on her cheeks.

"Well, so you do have a secret," Mr. Taylor chided.

"W-w-well," Jenny stammered, "I did see the eclipse last night. Did Lois see it?" It felt good to get her voice back.

"Yes, I did!" Lois excitedly reported as she came into the kitchen. "Wasn't it just amazing? Do you think everyone in our class saw it? Ellen woke me up and we watched the whole thing. I could hardly wake up this morning, I was so sleepy." By now Lois had her jacket on, gave her father a quick good-bye kiss, and the two girls were off to school.

Outside, they silently took their time to enter their own world, walking quietly across the Taylor's front yard, past the garage and outhouse, to the path by the wheat field fence. There were wheat fields as far as you could see. There was always just enough breeze to gently move the heads of grain in a soft undulating movement. Far to the west, the Rockies rose majestically, and in the east were silhouettes of farm houses marking the section lines. Soon the thrashing crews would arrive with their noisy combines and rows of trucks taking grain to the waiting train cars.

Today, however, was sunny and quiet. The earth itself had a peaceful calm as the two girls walked side by side on the worn path to the school house. In winter, when the snow piled high, families ran a rope from each house to the fence beside the path. When the wind blew and the awful blizzards came, the children completely covered their faces with wool scarves so as not to freeze. No one talked then, of course, but one could tell by the tension on the rope when there was someone walking in front or in back. In such a little town, everyone knew where everyone else lived and who went to school from each house. When they got to school, there was a rope to hold onto that went into the schoolhouse.

As Jenny felt the autumn breeze, she wondered if it would be as cold as it was last winter. She broke the silence by asking, "Lois, will it get as cold this winter as it did last?"

"Oh, probably colder. My father says there will be snow over people's houses this winter. He says the eclipse is a sign of a bad winter. His back aches a lot now and that's a sign, too. Didn't you have snow where you lived before?"

"Oh, yes, a lot. But not the wind and cold. At least I don't remember it being so cold. I wonder if Dorothy saw the eclipse. I hope not."

"Me, too. Wouldn't it be wonderful if no one saw it but us? Then we'd have something very special, just the two of us."

"Well, we do. We talked about it first." Jenny wanted Lois to be a special friend, but she always felt funny when Lois didn't seem to want her to have other friends. Bernice was like that, too. One day when she was in the coat room with her, Bernice asked, "Why don't you be my best friend and not anyone else's friend?" Jenny told her that was dumb; she had lots of friends and so should Bernice.

Jenny gave Lois a hug and said, "You're the only one who lives by my house, and you're the only one who knows where my Little Orphan Annie secret decoder ring is. It doesn't matter about Dorothy. Her mother probably did get her up. Her parents bought her that globe with the moon to go around it like they have in the seventh grade science room. If you put a flashlight on the opposite side like the sun, it looks like a real eclipse. Tommy saw it. He does everything in science. He's the best in science in the whole room."

9

The sounds from the playground caught their attention, and they ran to meet their friends outside on the steps waiting for the school bell to ring. Jenny saw Tommy coming across the street from his house. It must be great to live directly across from the school, she thought as she hung back from joining the others to meet him. "Hi, Tommy, did you see the eclipse?"

"Sure, the whole thing. Allen stayed over and we watched it together. Did Lois stay over with you?"

"No," Jenny said and started to say that she watched it with her dad, but didn't. She felt strange and looked down again, remembering Mr. Taylor's words about a secret.

"No, but she saw it with her sister. Wasn't it great? We'll get to talk about it all day, and maybe Miss Snyder will forget the extra spelling words. I hate spelling!"

"Oh, you just hate it because you're not very good," Tommy taunted as the bell rang.

The long lines formed at the top of the stairs: first, second, and third graders in one line; fourth, fifth, and sixth graders in the other. Miss Johnson, Adam's teacher, had yard duty and was standing at the top of the stairs.

She won't open the door until everyone is in line. Oh, here comes Sam! He's always running across the school yard late, and we always wait for him, Jenny thought.

Once Jenny had been late. Although she was already at the fence, Miss Johnson didn't wait for her. She guessed Miss Johnson waited for Sam because Sam's father had left town with the lady who worked at the beauty shop, and Sam had to get his brothers and sisters ready for school while his mom opened up the post office. And Miss Johnson knew he couldn't stay after school because he had to get home right away to help out. Everyone must like Sam, since rules seemed to be bent for him.

As Sam slid in line in back of Tommy, Jenny felt glad she had a dad who took good care of her. She waved at Adam and smiled at him as his line started in the door first. "Wait here at lunch," she said in a loud whisper. "I'll pick you up, okay?"

Upstairs, the coat room was noisy and crowded. Jenny hurried to her seat in back of Lois and in front of Tommy. One time, Tommy had passed her a note and gotten caught. Jenny was afraid Miss Snyder would move him, but she didn't. The note was dumb anyhow. It said: "Do you like me?" Jenny figured he knew she did, better than any boy she knew. He was really smart, and he was always clean and smelled good. She liked him all right, but she wasn't going to tell him. Lois knew, but she wouldn't tell anyone. Jenny could count on that.

Miss Snyder didn't forget the extra spelling words, but she did give an extra hour to work on art projects to the children who had seen the eclipse and had written about it in their science papers. The children who hadn't seen the eclipse had to make a drawing of what the eclipse looked like and tell how it worked from beginning to end.

Jenny was excited about her art project. She wasn't very good at art, but she liked it a lot. They were making masks for a Halloween parade, and she was making an African dance mask. She brought a picture from a magazine she got at church. A visiting missionary had shown pictures of people from Africa. Jenny decided, right then and there, that she would be a missionary when she grew up and would go to Africa to teach school. She would teach reading, writing, and singing. She would teach the children of Africa all the songs she knew and maybe, just maybe, they would teach her how to dance as they did in the pictures. Next week, the mask would be dry, and she could paint it.

The bell rang, bringing Jenny back from the heart of Africa to the excitement of ending another day at school.

As she put on her coat and started down the hall, she wondered why it was so much fun to come to school every morning, and so much fun when school ended, too. How could both times feel good? Before she was able to figure it out, Lois was at her side.

"Can you come to my house to study our spelling?"

"I dunno. I think I have to go to the store or something. But come with me to get Adam. He'll be crying if I don't pick him up, and Miss Johnson will be cross."

"He could go home with my brother, Matthew. They're in the same class, and Matthew isn't afraid of anything. He'd rather die than walk to school with me. What's wrong with Adam, anyhow, that you have to pick him up?"

"Oh, I don't know, he's just a baby. He's always like that, and if he gets too scared and cries too much, he has asthma attacks and they make him really sick. I don't care; he's my brother. My dad says he should grow up, but my mother worries about him. If I don't pick him up, he has to wait for Daddy, and he doesn't like that."

"It's neat having your dad as a teacher. I wish my dad was a teacher. He doesn't go to work since he hurt his back, and I don't like it."

"I don't like my dad being a teacher. Mostly I don't like it because I feel like he's watching me all the time. You know, like at lunch time, the teachers talk. Once I had four 100's in a row in Spelling; Miss Snyder told my dad before he came home from school. I wanted to tell him! Then the teachers come over to our house, and it feels like there are two sets of rules — one set at home and one set at school. Like with Mr. and Mrs. Clark, for instance... I help Mrs. Clark with the baby and they're real nice to me and give me presents. At their house I call them Matthew and Lydia, but at school I have to remember to say, Mr. Clark. He acts different at school. I think it's because my dad is a teacher. When I was little, we had a paint

11

store and he painted houses and signs. I liked that better."

By now, Adam and the two girls were on their way home, but Lois wouldn't let it be. She wanted Jenny all to herself. She said to 8-year-old Adam, "I have a really good idea, Adam. Why don't you walk home with Matthew? He could even go all the way to your house with you. Then, you'd beat us home every day."

Adam listened but answered, "No, I don't wanna. I wanna go home with Jenny. My mommy wants me to come home with Jenny. I always go with Jenny, anyhow."

"It's okay, Lois. I'll let you know if we can study. Adam wants to come with me. C'mon, Adam." Jenny held his hand all the way home.

Jenny was disturbed by Lois' interference. Jenny's mother always told her that they had a really close family. The members of the family would always help each other because that's what families were for. Adam was okay. Jenny liked him and she liked being able to help him. She knew it pleased her mother, too, because she worried about Adam. Jenny figured that's what mothers did; they worried a lot. But Jenny didn't like her mother to worry. When she wasn't worried, she was gentle, kind, and lots of fun. But sometimes when she worried, she got cross and mean. Daddy would always say, "Now, Jenny, don't worry your mother," so Jenny tried very hard not to.

Home was nice and warm. Supper was already cooking on the stove. "Hi, Mom, we're home. Can we have a cookie?" Jenny called into the bedroom, where she heard her mother's sewing machine whirring away.

"Yes, and a glass of milk. Be careful pouring." Her mother left her corner of the bedroom and came into the kitchen. "I need you to go to the store to get crackers and milk, Jenny. You can pull Jimmy in the wagon. He hasn't been out all day. Change your clothes first, though."

She picked up Adam's papers off the table, "Why, Adam, what a wonderful Halloween picture. And is this your writing paper? What beautiful letters you are making."

Jenny's penmanship was terrible. She picked up her book and headed upstairs to change. She had written a poem for Halloween, but she guessed she would just put it in her trunk along with her other poems. She had put a lot of poems from last winter in a special book. "MY POEMS by JENNY

BENNETT," it said on the front. Her favorite was one she had written for Jimmy's birthday:

> *HAPPY BIRTHDAY, ONE YEAR OLD.*
> *You are so big today.*
> *You can walk and*
> *Say my name.*
> *I know it when you smile.*
> *You are fun.*
> *You are beautiful.*
> *I love to play with you.*
> *When you go to sleep*
> *And I put you*
> *In your bed*
> *I think you are*
> *An angel*
> *Come to live with me.*
> *Happy Birthday, Baby Brother.*

Jenny heard her mother calling, "Jenny, are you coming? Jimmy's getting too warm with his coat on."

"Yes, I'm almost ready," Jenny called. She knew her daydreaming bothered her mother. Too much make-believe wasn't good for you, she always said. You shouldn't have your head in the clouds.

Jenny carried Jimmy out to the wagon. She picked up the handle, reminded her passenger to hang on to the sides, and headed for town. Her mind drifted back to the warm kitchen and her mother's voice. Jenny truly loved her mother, but she felt as if she never did things quite right for her. That made Jenny sad, so she tried harder.

She thought her mother was sad sometimes, too, but she didn't know why. Every night her mother either brushed Jenny's hair or reminded her to brush it. Sometimes she got to brush her mother's hair, and she really liked that. However, the sound of her mother's words always made Jenny feel as if she was getting scolded,

"Always brush at night and in the morning, and use rainwater to wash when you can. Be sure you get the soap out and save enough water for a vinegar rinse. When it squeaks, it's rinsed clean." She would say the same thing over and over. Then she'd say, as if to herself, "Your father had hair this color when he was younger."

Jenny's mother had soft brown hair. To Jenny, it was beautiful. She wondered if her mother secretly wanted her to have hair like hers. Jenny's black hair and brown eyes were different from anyone else's in the family. Her brothers had blue eyes and blond hair. It made Jenny feel as though she didn't quite fit. When they lived in Idaho, someone once asked her if she got her hair and eyes from the milkman. After that, she watched the milkman with his wire rack and juggling bottles, but she never got to see his hair because he wore a white hat all the time.

"Hang on, Jimmy; we're going up on the sidewalk." Jenny liked to go to town. She went almost every day, except in the worst of winter. She waved at Dorothy's mother inside the bank. She was a very nice woman. Last winter, she had given Jenny a big stack of old ledgers to play school and make paper dolls with. Jenny, Lois, and Dorothy designed doll clothes. Sometimes when the snow was really deep, Rachel, who lived in the country, stayed at Jenny's house. It was great fun. Jenny thought she might go to New York one day, and design clothes like the ones in the *Lady's Home Journal*.

In the middle of her daydream, they reached The Mercantile. Jenny parked the wagon by the door, took Jimmy's hand, and went inside the store. After Mr. Larson had written her purchases on the charge slip and Jenny had it folded in her pocket, he said, "What, no penny today?"

"No," Jenny said looking at the jar of candy sticks. "I don't have any money today."

"Well, I guess you're too big to be giving away kisses for peppermint sticks, so why don't you just pick one out for you and one for little Jim there?"

This was a game Mr. Larson and Jenny played. If there were people in the store, he didn't offer her a candy stick. However, he always did when she was alone in the store, and she would thank him and take it. She would never kiss Mr. Larson, anyhow. It just seemed to be a joke. When her father paid the bill each month, Mr. Larson sent home a whole bag of candy. Free! Mother said it was because Jenny's dad had a regular paycheck. She guessed that was why he gave her candy sticks: because they paid their bill.

Jenny's family had sold their paint store and moved to Montana because of the Depression. A lot of people in town were very poor, too poor to have a charge account. By the train tracks on the edge of town there was a big hobo jungle with shacks and old cars where hobos and bums lived. Kids weren't allowed to go there, but the townspeople gave the hobos food and work when they could. Jenny's father talked about the economy a great deal at the dinner table and had voted for Franklin Roosevelt. There was a lot Jenny didn't understand yet, but she understood that her father's monthly check made her luckier than many of her friends in town; Lois, for example. Jenny had never seen Lois in a new dress, just in her sister's hand-me-downs, which were always too big.

Lois didn't like Mr. Larson because he gave her candy only if she was with Jenny. Once she had asked him for some, and he had scolded her for being a little beggar.

As Jenny took the candy and gave Jimmy his, she had the same funny feeling she had had that morning at Lois' house, and she knew she was blushing.

"Why, I declare," Mr. Larson said, "our little Jenny must be growing up."

Jenny just wanted to leave, so she said, "Good-bye, Mr. Larson, and thank you for the candy." She almost forgot to put the milk and crackers in the wagon. It was good to be outside and on the way home. Jimmy was all sticky, but it would be okay; she would bathe him when they got home and do her homework after supper.

Chapter 3

The crisp autumn days began to shorten; the night of the eclipse faded into the past. Tonight was Halloween and Jenny was invited to a party at Dorothy's house.

She decided not to wear her African mask, partly because in Africa it was worn by a man, and he had nothing else on but a cloth to cover his private parts; but mostly because she loved it, so she didn't want anything to happen to it. She hung it on the wall across from her bed, and imagined it would keep all evil spirits away from her.

She went to the party as a bum, like the bums in the old cars by the railroad. Jenny thought that some day she would sneak over there and see them, to see if they had real beds in the cars and if they really ate stray dogs and cats, as people said.

At the party they bobbed for apples and had a relay race with a marshmallow on a spoon. It was fun, but the most fun was waiting for the big bonfire outside. While they waited, they played kick-the-can. Danny was picked to be "it."

Jenny heard Tommy say, "Hey, Jenny, wanna hide with me?"

"Yeah," she replied, and off they ran into the alley and under the edge of the Johnson's woodshed.

"Let's climb up here and hide in the rafters, okay?"

They quickly climbed the steps made of boards across the two-by-fours. As they scrunched down together, they heard Danny's footsteps and Tommy whispered, "We won't run until he's clear down at the end. He always looks in the old Stoker house 'cause someone always hides there. He won't even suspect we're so close."

Jenny's heart beat faster and faster as Danny's steps walked back up the alley. She had a strange feeling in her body that had something to do with hiding in a close space with Tommy. Just excited, she guessed, but she was conscious of how close Tommy was to her. She could feel his breath by the side of her face, near her neck. It was warm and it kind of tickled.

"Let's go! Let's go now!" she said.

Tommy grabbed her jacket sleeve, holding her back. "No, not yet, he's in plain sight".

Jenny froze. *This is all very confusing. I like being here in the dark with Tommy and I like him taking charge. How strange!*

"Now, now!" Tommy said. "Run for it!"

Down the steps they flew, across the alley and through the yard. Tommy kicked the can clear into the next lot, and they both jubilantly hollered, "Kick the can!"

Poor Danny, he didn't have a chance in a race against Tommy, or, for that matter, Jenny. As they stood around the bonfire holding sticks loaded with sticky, gooey, often burned marshmallows, Jenny thought, Nothing in the world is as important as having fun with your very best friends...

She kept watching Tommy on the other side of the fire. She thought, "When I get home, I'll write in my diary about hiding with Tommy and the strange feelings I had, but I don't want to tell anyone else yet, not even Lois."

The fire was dying and Dorothy's mother announced it was time for every-one to go home: "Your parents are expecting you by nine o'clock."

After thanking Mrs. Baxter and Dorothy for the best time in her whole life, Jenny began skipping and running toward home, with Lois fast behind her.

"Oh, wasn't that a great party?" Lois exclaimed, and the girls chattered about every single moment they had just experienced. But Jenny didn't tell about hiding with Tommy or about watching him across the fire. She thought Lois might be mad at her for keeping a secret. Perhaps she'd tell her another time.

At home, Jenny's dad had all the lights on, hoping to frighten anyone who might want to trick him. He didn't like Halloween and all its pranksters. Jenny couldn't wait until she was in high school and could soap people's windows and push over outhouses. It would be all the talk at school tomor-row. Jenny almost hoped their outhouse would be tipped over. It would make her father very angry, but it would be worth it, just to be chosen.

Her mother had hot water ready for her to wash up. Her nightie was on a chair in the kitchen. She felt good and very special as she undressed and washed her body with the warm water. When she finished, her mother checked her ears and brushed her hair. She made Jenny a cup of warm tea with lots of milk and sugar, and they talked about the party.

"Now, off to bed with you," Jenny's mother said fondly. Jenny threw her arms around her mother's neck and said, "I love you, Mommy; I truly, truly do!"

"Yes, dear, I know. And don't go reading in bed tonight. Go right to sleep."

With all the excitement and the warm milk, it was no problem. Jenny fell right to sleep. Sometime later, her bedroom doorknob turned and Jenny awakened with a fright. *Oh, my gosh, it's a ghost!* Jenny thought. But no, it was Daddy come to check her. She decided to pretend she was sound asleep. She heard the door latch behind him. Then he was sitting on her bed.

20

"Shhhh, Jenny, it's Daddy. Don't make a sound." His hands were cold and heavy as he reached under her nightie and rubbed her buttocks gently. Jenny's whole body stiffened. She was scared without knowing why. Then he turned her over, and his big hand touched her nipples and moved as if to cup her tiny breasts...

Her mother had said, just last week, that they had to go to Great Falls, the next biggest town, and get brassieres for Jenny. "You're getting too big for undershirts," she had said. Jenny didn't like the idea. Only Dorothy and Bernice at school wore brassieres, and they were both fat. Jenny felt fine the way she was.

...the hand moved down her body, feeling heavier and heavier. *Oh, no! He's going to touch me down there!* She clenched her child thighs tighter and trembled at the sound of his voice.

"Don't be afraid, Jenny. Daddy won't hurt you. Just relax... relax. Daddy loves you. I won't hurt you. You are growing up, and Daddy wants you to feel good."

Jenny's mind whirled around like a merry-go-round out of control, colors going up and down, loud clanging music, around and around, too fast. *Why is he doing this to me? What am I supposed to do?*

"Don't be afraid Jenny. Just relax. Daddy won't hurt you. He loves you."
Finally he stopped. He pulled the covers up and tucked them under her
chin. "That's a good girl, Jenny. This is our little secret, our special love.
Go back to sleep." And he left.

Chapter 4

In the morning, Jenny heard her mother's footsteps coming up the stairs. She lay in bed, not moving.

The door burst open, and her mother's irritated voice filled the room. "Jenny, what on earth are you doing still in bed? Get up this instant and be at the table in two minutes. It's snowing and I want you to go to school with your father."

"I'm too cold, I guess."

"Are you okay?" Her mother touched Jenny's forehead with the palm of her hand. "Just get dressed. Warm oatmeal will take care of the chatters."

But when Jenny spooned the oatmeal into her mouth, it didn't feel warm. It had a chill, too. She didn't look at her father. *Last night must have been a dream. But why would anyone have a dream like that about her own father?*

"Jenny, don't eat so fast. You'll get sick. What's going on with you, anyhow? Did you turn the light on after we went to bed and read half the night?" her mother asked.

"No, Mommy. I guess the party was just too exciting. I like Halloween better when we don't have to go to school the next day."

Talking seemed to help. Jenny talked about their new school project: to make a real bank. They were going to save and borrow money and take turns being bankers. First, they had to paint the bank, which was made out of cardboard.

Jenny's father spoke for the first time. "Jenny, did Miss Snyder talk to you about the declamatory contest? I want you to enter. You can do real well. Maybe win first place. No reason why not."

"No, she didn't say anything, but probably she was busy," Jenny said, excusing Miss Snyder.

"There's plenty of time. Get your things on. It's time to go."

At school her father kissed her good-bye on the mouth. She didn't like him to kiss her on the mouth, especially in front of her friends.

His smell reminded her of last night. *He did come in my room and touch me, and I didn't like it. It wasn't a dream.*

It was one of those awful days at school when the kids made fun of Bernice. Jenny felt sorry for Bernice because she was fat and talked funny, but she liked her too. She especially liked Bernice's grandmother.

Jenny didn't have any grandparents, so sometimes she went to Bernice's house and her grandmother told them stories about living on the plantation in Louisiana. Bernice's grandmother said that Jenny had special powers; she could tell things about people that they didn't even know about them-selves. She also taught Jenny to wish off warts, and Jenny could wish warts off anyone. Her mother said, "Wishing off warts is good magic, but you leave that other stuff alone. Don't you pay too much attention to Bernice's grandmother. After all, they planted peanuts in their garden, and everyone knows peanuts won't grow this far north!"

Bernice's problem was that she would get bloody stains on the back of her dresses and no one would tell her. The other kids would just giggle and laugh, leaving Bernice standing by the wall of the school, ashamed and embarrassed. One day, Jenny told Bernice that Miss Snyder kept a sanitary napkin in her desk for Jenny. She guessed that Miss Snyder would keep one for Bernice, too. Bernice had never heard of a sanitary napkin. Her moth-er gave her old rags folded up and she had to put them in her underpants. She didn't have a belt with pins like Jenny's mother had given her. Worst of all, she had to save these rags and wash them for the next time!

25

Jenny thought the whole thing was disgusting. She took Bernice home and showed her the box of napkins and the elastic belt her mother had put in the closet for her. Nobody had told Bernice about growing up, so she shared the book that her mother had given her. They wrote down the address where Bernice could get one for herself. The book even told about having babies, but Jenny already knew about that from when Jimmy was born. Bernice did not even know that menstruating had anything to do with hav-ing babies! She wondered if this ignorance was because Bernice's family came from the South or because they were poor. She thought it would embarrass Bernice if she asked her.

It was beginning to seem to Jenny that growing up was not such a great thing. Her friend, Rachel, had two big brothers in high school, and Rachel talked about how much fun they had. So high school would be okay, and she would be old enough to baby-sit. Money would give her more independence. In light of Bernice's problems, growing up seemed to be more a bother than fun. Jenny hated the thought of wearing a bra and decided to put off menstruating as long as possible.

Bernice and Jenny didn't talk again, so Jenny didn't know if Bernice got sanitary napkins from her mother or not. Jenny knew she was Bernice's friend and so did everyone else. It seemed to Jenny that the other kids were nicer to Bernice now that she and Bernice were friends. She hated for anyone to be treated badly; and she didn't like teasing. Her father always said it was cruel to tease. He said we never know what someone else's life is like if we don't live it; we can know only our own. Jenny felt that hers was pretty lucky. And if she ever forgot it, her father was sure to remind her.

That winter, when snow covered the houses and school buses were stranded, Jenny's house was filled with kids sleeping over. Her mother baked bread and made big pots of soup.

Jenny did get brassieres and she also menstruated, even though she tried not to. She pretended for two days that it wasn't true, but then she remembered Bernice. She didn't want that to happen to her, so she started using sanitary napkins.

At night, she listened for the doorknob, hoping her father would not come in her room. But he did. She began to think that it would be easier and less scary if she relaxed as he kept urging her to do. Mostly she tried to forget about it. When she didn't forget, she couldn't stop thinking about it. One day, she didn't even hear Miss Snyder call her name, though she had spoken it three times. She got in trouble for daydreaming and had to stay after school. Miss Snyder asked if something was bothering her. "No, I don't think so," Jenny said. It never even entered her mind to tell about her father. That was a secret.

She won the declamatory contest, went to the county contest, and placed second. When school was out, she got to go Rachel's house for two weeks.

Chapter 5

Rachel's family owned a big dairy. They took milk and cream to the train station. Besides cows, they had horses and pigs. Jenny loved to go there. Rachel had a big sister, Ann, in the eighth grade and two brothers in high school, Charles and Emmett. Her older cousin, Bruce, who had just graduated from high school in Indiana, was also there. Everyone in the family worked hard, but it seemed like they had fun too, laughing and joking all the time. Rachel's father was a big man with red hair, and sometimes, Jenny thought he was kind of scary. He slapped people on the back and was always saying, "Great job, great job," to Rachel's brothers, even if it was just for a checkers game or a song on the harmonica.

The only time Jenny ever saw Rachel's parents get angry was when she and Rachel hid in the barn the day the neighbor's stallion was brought over to breed with Emmett's brown mare. The girls had asked Rachel's mom if they could watch, and she got really mad and turned around so they couldn't see her blush. "How could you even think such a thing? That's men's business. You just stay away from there. You ought to be ashamed; that's what you should be."

Neither Jenny nor Rachel could figure out why mating animals was "men's business". From what they knew, it took a male and a female to make a baby of anything, and hadn't they already seen dogs and rabbits and chickens mating? Once the bull had broken the fence and got in the pasture with the dairy herd. They knew they shouldn't have watched the results, but they had. So it didn't make any sense that they shouldn't watch the horses.

So they plotted to go watch. They packed a lunch and told Rachel's mom they were going to the pond in the east pasture. They knew they'd be in big trouble if they got caught lying, but they really wanted to watch. Jenny knew it was a terrible thing to tell a lie, and it always made her anxious. But grown-ups lied all the time, and they made it very hard for kids not to tell lies. A lot of time, there was no other alternative.

Jenny always kept track of her lies. When she went to church on Sunday, she told God about her lies and said how sorry she was, but she always told Him she had had good reasons to do so. The only way to keep from going crazy was to lie. Grownups seemed to believe lies a lot faster than they believed the truth. That's the way it was that day in the barn.

It was exciting and scary in the barn. The men laughed, shouted, and slapped each other. The horses pranced and kicked, bit each other and looked wild-eyed. For something that was obviously fun for the men, it didn't seem to Jenny that the horses were particularly happy. It took quite a while, too.

Suddenly Rachel sneezed. The girls were terrified, but when no one looked up, they assumed the sneeze hadn't been heard. They were wrong, though. At the dinner table, Rachel's father cleared his throat and in his big booming voice said, "Rachel, didn't your mother forbid you to go to the barn this afternoon?"

Both girls gulped and nearly choked on their food. Rachel whispered, "Yes, sir."

"Then what, may I ask, were you doing in the hayloft, being in places that don't concern you, places where no decent girl would be? I am ashamed! And taking Jenny there with you! What will her parents think? They may never let her stay again. Why, they're not even farmers!"

There was silence all around the table. Jenny noticed that all the men looked mad, but also amused. It was confusing, and it scared her.

"Excuse me, Mr. Bradford, but its not Rachel's fault that I went in the hayloft. It was partly my idea."

"Oh, it was, huh? Well, then, you can both go to your room and stay there until morning. And in the morning, you two are going to clean the chicken house for disobeying!"

Jenny hated the chicken house. She didn't even like chickens, but she didn't think Mr. Bradford knew that. The worst part was moving the hens so that fresh straw could be put in the nests. Rachel had explained that when the straw was clean, the eggs would be clean and wouldn't have to be washed before they were sold. Oh well, at least they didn't have to clean the barn!

Guiltily, the two girls went up the stairs to Rachel's room. They didn't talk about their lie and the trouble they were in, but about what had happened in the barn. They continued to wonder, Why was it okay for men and boys to watch but not for women and girls?

A few days later, Jenny and Rachel helped Mrs. Bradford in the kitchen all day, baking bread and cake and pies for the big auction at the Stintson farm on Sunday. Mr. Stintson had died, and Mrs. Stintson was going to California to live with their daughter. Although Jenny didn't know them, she was excited to be going to the auction because everyone for miles around would be there. They all went to bed early that night because all the chores had to be done before they left: cows milked; pigs and chickens fed; and the breakfast cooked, served, and cleaned up afterwards.

The girls were in bed but still talking when they saw the doorknob turn. They jumped simultaneously and closed their eyes as if they were asleep. The door closed and they heard the latch click shut. Someone walked stealthily across the room and then sat on the bed. Neither Rachel nor Jenny was brave enough to open her eyes. A voice said quietly, "Hey, you two, I know you're not asleep; I could hear you in the hall. I just wanted to lie down and talk a little."

Their eyes popped open as if with one set of lids, and they gasped, "Bruce!?" in one voice.

"Shhhh, keep it quiet," he said, and he slid under the covers.

This is really strange, but kind of exciting, too. Jenny felt her heart racing. She could hardly breathe.

"What do you want, Bruce? You should get out of here," Rachel whispered.

"Oh, I just thought we could play around a little." He leaned over and kissed Jenny on the ear, then on her neck. Jenny froze when she felt Bruce's bare leg against her as he pushed up her nightie with his hand.

"Jenny, don't do that! He's my cousin. Bruce, you get out of here," Rachel continued in a loud, scared whisper, but Bruce just reached over, pushed her down, and rubbed his other hand on her breasts.

"C'mon, Rach, you know you like it. We won't do anything just play. You can even touch me if you want."

He gently rubbed his fingers between Jenny's legs. She thought she might be sick to her stomach. She felt her face getting redder and redder.

She turned to her friend in terror, with tears were just beneath the surface of her lids. "Oh, Rachel, make him go away!" she pleaded.

"Jesus Christ!" Bruce exploded. "You guys have been asking for this all along. Be quiet and shut up! I'm leaving!"

Just like that, he was gone. The two girls lay shivering together under the covers. "Let's block the door, so he won't come back," Jenny suggested. "Or maybe we should tell your mom."

"Oh, no, we can't tell my mom. She'd tell Daddy and he'd kill him or send him back to Indiana. He said once that if any guy ever touched me, he'd kill him. And I like Bruce; I don't want my dad to kill him! Let's put the dresser and the chair against the door."

Once back in bed, they created a great scheme to get the long ladder out of the barn the next day and put it up to the window. If Bruce got in past the door, they would escape out the window. It was an exciting plan, but he never came back so they could try it out.

Jenny did not sleep for a long time. She felt confused again. Although she had been so scared of what Bruce did and said, something inside of her liked the feelings it gave her when he kissed her neck and when he first touched her "down there." And his leg had been so warm and strong against hers.

She thought about asking Rachel if her father touched too, but somehow, she knew better than to even mention it.

This all has something to do with "men's business." Like in the barn. That's why no one can say anything. And you can't tell your mother. I couldn't do anything, anyhow, because of it being "men's business." This major issue put to rest, Jenny slept.

Later that summer, Bruce went back to Indiana. Rachel told Jenny he had come to her room again and her brothers had heard him. Her dad had told him he could never return. Her brothers were mad, too, and said Bruce was no cousin of theirs. Jenny felt bad for Rachel but she couldn't help but wonder, *If this whole thing is "men's business," how come they get so mad about it?*

Chapter 6

The summer lazed along with lots of hide-and-seek and kick-the-can. Jenny's family moved out of the big house they were in to a smaller one on the other side of town. Jenny's mother said the big one cost too much to heat, and Jenny didn't question it. Her room was cold all winter, and lots of nights Adam would come sleep with her so they could keep warm.

Jenny made friends with the girl next door. Her name was Lucille and she was fifteen. Jenny learned a lot about sex from Lucille. She had magazines under her mattress: *True Story, True Confessions,* and one she snuck from her brothers that just had pictures. In one story, a girl did things with her father, and the girl liked it and thought it was okay. When Jenny asked Lucille what she thought about it, Lucille said it was positively sickening. The worst thing that could ever happen to anyone was for their own father to do anything sexual to them. She said one time one of her brothers came to her bedroom and touched her, and when her dad found out, he whipped her brother with a razor strap. Sex definitely did not belong in the family, according to Lucille.

Jenny kept wondering, *how come the girl in the story liked it?* Jenny's father thought she should like it, only she didn't. Maybe it was just like with boys; some of them you liked and some of them you didn't; like John Austin. He had kissed her once at a church party, and Jenny had slapped his face. She didn't like him, so she sure didn't want him to kiss her.

In August, Jenny's family went camping. They had been camping before, on the Salmon River in Idaho. Except for Christmas, camping was Jenny's favorite time. They had a special camping cupboard that fit on the side of the car. She and her mother would make a list and stock the cupboard every year. Her mother told the story of going to Yellowstone Park with this same cupboard and a bear chewed the corner off, trying to get in. Her dad had repaired it but you could see where it had been painted over. That had happened the summer before Jenny was born. As far as she knew, they had gone camping every summer after that.

Her parents had a big tent, but Jenny found her own special place in the trees to make herself a home in the forest. Her father helped cut pine boughs for a soft mattress and no one was allowed to go in her special place. Her dad chose the White River as the place he wanted to fish this year, almost a day's drive from home.

Jenny begged her mother to let Lucille come along. Lucille was a big help with Adam and Jimmy, who was now running all over, so her parents said yes. It was a wonderful, exciting time for Jenny. She loved the forest and all its animals, and most of all, she loved how happy her family was out of doors. Her father never touched her during the summer. She didn't know why. Maybe it was because he was happy, too.

Friends came on Sundays, the Forest Ranger came, and they had huge pans of fried fish, boiled potatoes, and pan fried bread. Her dad loved to fish and Jenny loved to follow after him with the can of grasshoppers and the fishing basket. He would spot a school of fish and tell Jenny, very quietly, where to stand so she wouldn't make a shadow. The reel would whir and a tiny ripple would appear as the hook and grasshopper hit the water. Jenny would clench her teeth to keep her mouth shut, so she wouldn't squeal if there was a strike. The biggest rule of fishing was to be very, very, quiet.

When a fish hit, she watched the silver body thrashing and tugging at the hook. While her father skillfully reeled in the fish, Jenny took the tape measure out to make sure the fish was at least eight inches long. They never kept anything smaller. Jenny held the little ones in the water "until they got their senses," as her dad would say. Pretty soon, they wiggled off, and in a shimmer, they were gone. For years to come, brook trout and boiled potatoes remained one of Jenny's favorite meals.

All too soon it was fall, and school started. It was great, though, to see all her friends, especially the ones who lived way out in the country. Some friends, she had not seen all summer. Jenny missed Miss Snyder and feeling special in her class, but she also liked not feeling like such a little kid. In the seventh grade, Miss Rae was their teacher for homeroom and English and they passed from class to class, just like in high school, rather than staying in one room. Her father was their math teacher. Most of the kids didn't like having him because he gave a lot of homework and very hard tests. Jenny wanted to hide when the kids got mad at him and said bad things.

One day Tommy said, "Who does he think he is? God? No one can do this much work. What a dumb jerk!" Then he noticed Jenny. Blushing, he said, "Sorry, Jen. He's just not fair."

By now, Jenny knew that Tommy was special to her, so she didn't want to disagree with him about her father or act as if it mattered to her. "That's okay, Tommy. My mother says that a lot of things aren't fair. I know my dad isn't always fair. I have to go now. See ya tomorrow."

Jenny went home by herself that day and walked kitty-corner across the wheat field. She needed to be alone. More and more, it seemed to her, there were opposite things in her life that she couldn't figure out. She loved her father and wanted everyone to like him, but sometimes when he was mean, she didn't like him, either.

When she got home, her mother was at the sewing machine. Her mother made all their clothes except for Jenny's father's. Jenny knew she was very lucky. No one in her class had clothes nicer than hers. Most of the girls were like Lois; they had to wear hand-me-downs that didn't fit. There was one girl in her class, Irma, whose mother made her clothes, too. They were awful, but Jenny's weren't. Jenny's mother didn't like hand-me-downs. When someone gave her old clothes, she would take them all apart and wash the material. Jenny would help her press the pieces and pin patterns on the fresh bright cloth. Jenny could look in magazines, find any dress she wanted, and her mother could make it. Everyone at school envied her, and she liked that. It made her feel better than other girls at school. She never admitted this to anyone, but she knew it was true.

A great feeling of love came over Jenny as she entered her parents' room. She wanted her mother to hold her as she had done when Jenny was little. She sat on the bed and told her mother about school things. She didn't know how to say, "I'm so confused and I need you to help me." She couldn't ask for help because she didn't know she needed help. She just felt lonely and confused.

She stretched out on her mother's bed and looked at the small framed picture on the wall above the bed. No matter where they lived, her mother always hung this faded photograph over her bed. Jenny knew the story made her mother sad, but she asked again anyway, "How old was I when my brother died?"

"You were five months old, just a tiny baby," her mother replied.

"Why did he die?" Jenny asked.

"He got sick one night. I called the doctor, but he didn't come because he didn't think the baby was that sick. After a while, I took you to the neighbors and took him to the hospital. He died in my arms. But you know all this, Jenny. Why are you asking me again?"

"I dunno. I just forgot, I guess."

Jenny felt close to her mother when they talked about things that used to be. She liked talking about when she was little and all the things she used to do to get in trouble. Jenny's mother would say, "I could never keep track of you; you always had a mind of your own." Or she'd tell about their friends, the time the McCays's barn burned, or the time they moved the whole town to build the dam.

I wonder if my mother knows how confused I am? I want to ask her questions, but I don't know what the questions are. The only ones I know to ask are about when we lived in Idaho. Maybe mothers are just hard to talk to. Lucille's mother screams at her all the time. At least my mother is soft and gentle.

41

"Can I go visit Lois?" Jenny asked.

"Yes. Just be home in an hour."

As Jenny walked across town, she decided she shouldn't bother her mother with all these thoughts in her head. In fact, she was starting to be afraid to talk with her mother. Sometimes her mother knew things about her, and Jenny had no idea how she knew. What if her mother asked her questions about her father and what he did at night? That would be awful!

Her father always said, "This is our secret. Don't tell your mother." If her mother asked, it would be hard to lie to her about something she knew was important. So she should just not talk to her mother. That would be the best thing. *Just don't think about talking about these confusions. Don't talk about them. Don't think about them.*

She wouldn't even tell her mother that when Tommy's mom took them to the movie last Saturday and gave him money for a Coke at the drug store, he had paid for Jenny's soda. It was very exciting. In the movie they had held hands in the scary part, and Jenny liked how it felt. Perhaps when they were in high school, they would go to dances and stuff, and Tommy would be her boyfriend. Jenny didn't know what this had to do with her father. She just knew they were both secrets.

Seventh grade was starting to be more fun than ever before. At Christmas, they were going to have a dance at school. Jenny's mother had made her a beautiful dress out of soft flowing pink material. She wished her father wouldn't attend the dance, but he was a chaperon. Nobody else's father would be there, and she was beginning to not like the way he looked at her.

Lucille had been playing records and teaching Lois and Jenny how to dance. Jenny finally told them that Tommy was her boyfriend, and Lucille asked if he'd "done anything." Jenny then told something she had kept a secret for a long time. At the church party and at her birthday party, when they played Spin-the-Bottle and afterwards, Tommy had kissed her on the mouth. Not just once but several times! She thought she must really love him, because she had gotten a big lump in her throat and butterflies in her tummy. The last time he kissed her, he had put his arms around her and held her close to his body. Jenny had put her arms around him too. It was just like in the magazines! Lucille and Lois were impressed. She made them promise they would never, ever tell anyone.

The night of the Christmas dance was like a dream come true. It was wonderful to grow up, to be a girl, and to feel beautiful. Miss Snyder had talked Jenny's mother into letting her curl Jenny's hair into a "marcel" wave just like Miss Snyder's. Jenny's hair was naturally straight, and it was fun to put in all the little finger waves.

Everyone in junior high was there except Irma, whose parents didn't believe in dancing. Jenny's father was so busy talking to other teachers that he didn't even watch her. Tommy's father came to drive them all home, and she sat in the front between Tommy and his dad. Mr. Thompson smelled nice, and he didn't tease her as most fathers did. He just asked if they had a good time and if the music was good. Jenny waved good-bye from the front porch and ran inside out of the cold. Her mother was listening to the radio while knitting a sweater for Adam.

"Oh, Mother, I had the very best time of my whole life, and I had the prettiest dress of anyone!" Jenny bubbled. "Everyone said I did. Can I wear it to church on Sunday?"

"Yes, I suppose so. Be sure to hang it up, though." Her mother was warm and pleasant. They kissed good night, and Jenny went to bed with laughter in her toes and stars in her eyes. As she crawled between the cool flannel sheets, she didn't even bother to pray to the mask to scare away bad things, and she didn't wonder if her father would come tonight. She was completely filled with being twelve years old and liking it.

Chapter 7

A special thing happened that winter. Jenny decided to be an actress. There was a theater in town, next to the Post Office. Sometimes movies came there, but it was mostly traveling road shows. They came in winter, and everyone in town went.

The show that came that winter was the Glen and Dora Players. They sent a notice ahead to say they needed six children to be in the play for a school scene. Jenny's English teacher decided to have an Essay Contest to choose the six students.

Tommy and Jenny were the best speakers in the class, so Tommy was mad they hadn't just been picked. Jenny told him it wouldn't really be fair, and they could win, anyhow, if they wrote good essays.

The essay was entitled, "Why I Want To Be in the Community House Play." Jenny wrote and wrote until she knew she had a good essay. She looked up all the words, too, so she wouldn't spell anything wrong. By the time she had finished, she thought she would die if she didn't get chosen. But she did, and so did Tommy.

When they tried out for the play, they had to read lines. The director said Jenny's voice carried the best, so she had the most lines. Tommy had lines, too, and the boy he played got in trouble for pulling a girl's curls. It was great fun. The play ran three nights in a row. On the last night, there was a big party, and all the parents brought food.

Jenny had decided she would even quit school to be in a road show. Her father told her that when he was in high school, the same thing had happened to him. A road show had come to town and needed a leading man who would have to learn a lot of lines fast. The Principal had told them that her father could do it, and that summer, her father traveled with the road show! In the fall, though, he had gone back to school. Jenny thought how wonderful it would be if her father were in the road show now. They could travel from town to town and never have a house or have to go to school: just be in plays, have hundreds of people watch them and clap for them, and take bows.

Before long it was May Day, and the first tiny rock daisies came into bloom with their little grey leaves. Jenny had been making paper baskets for days, one for every one of her friends and one for Bernice's grandmother, who was too sick to even get out of her chair any more. She put flowers in all the baskets and took Jimmy in the wagon to deliver them. He loved knocking on the door with her, then scurrying to hide, and watching to see the people's surprise and the way they looked around to see who had left them the flowers. May Day was great fun. It announced that the long winter was over and spring was really here.

Occasionally Jenny thought about her father's nightly visits, but mostly she didn't. One night after he had stayed in her room an extra long time, she had realized how much better it was not to try and figure it out. It was easier just to forget. And forgetting took away the confusion. She quit begging her father not to touch her, and she relaxed the way he told her to. He would talk to her softly, and tell her how much he loved her, and how she was his special girl. When he kissed her on the mouth, Jenny thought, *I just won't smell him and he won't be my father, just nobody doing this.* When she did that, she found that his kiss wasn't that bad. He kissed her all over and touched her all over, and in the morning, Jenny didn't remember.

47

She was never late to breakfast any more. It helped never to cause any kind of trouble, because it upset her mother when things didn't run smoothly. Jenny felt she would be safe as long as her mother didn't find out. Forgetting meant that nothing had happened. Forgetting was good.

Chapter 8

Summer was coming. Much to Jenny's surprise, she was starting to like growing up. The State Music Meet was coming up, and the school band was going to perform. They had been practicing and practicing, and their mothers had made them all new satin capes. The capes were black on the outside, orange underneath, and fastened at the neck with a braided button. Her mother said it was called a "frog," which didn't make sense, but it made the capes look very fancy.

Jenny's father was the band director. She played the clarinet, and Adam played the cornet. He was the youngest in the band, and Jenny knew he must be very good or he wouldn't be allowed to play. When they marched, sometimes he would fall behind and skip some steps to catch up, but that was okay. As Jenny grew up, she felt more and more love and understanding for her young brother. He was sensitive and gentle, and he very clearly loved her No one else had a little brother as smart or as talented. She was very proud of him.

It was the most wonderful trip. Jenny had her own money for lunch, and she and her friends went to Woolworth's. She had never been in a restaurant without her parents. Tommy sat next to her, and they split a chocolate soda. In the afternoon, they competed and played their very best. They won first place for a band their size.

Jenny's father always wanted to win. Being second was not good enough for him, and Jenny was good at coming in second. He would say, "That was great, Jenny, you were just great . . . and you should have paused more after

. . ." or, "You did the last paragraph without enough emotion. You should have won. Next time remember what I tell you."

Jenny tried hard, but most of time she was second. Thank goodness the band won first place! Now he would be in a good mood for a long time.

All the parents were happy. On the way home, they all stopped and ate again in a restaurant. That made two special things, since Jenny had never eaten in a restaurant twice in one day.

Yes, growing up is going to be great, she thought, *and next year I will be in the eighth grade, getting ready for high school. I can hardly wait!* Jenny savored the joys of this exciting day.

That night, Rachel spent the night, and they promised to be friends forever and ever. Jenny was still sure that she would be an actress or a movie star. She had been to see Sonja Henie and Dick Powell at the movies, and she felt it would be wonderful to be a movie star. She couldn't skate, but she could sing, and she would learn to dance.

Rachel decided she would come to Hollywood with Jenny and sing in a night club. She had a beautiful voice, better than Jenny's. She sang "Going Home" at the Music Meet and got a Blue Ribbon. Sometimes Rachel sang at church with her sister.

They dreamed their dreams aloud, and drifted off to sleep, thinking of long flowing evening gowns, spotlights, and handsome men who looked like Prince Charming.

On the last day of school, the entire town drove over to the river for a big picnic. There were sack races, three-legged races, and relay races for every age. Mr. Larson from The Mercantile gave candy prizes to everyone, and the bank gave everyone a new pencil.

In the middle of the baseball game, lightning and thunder struck, and everyone ducked for cover. Jenny ran with Lois and ended up in Rachel's car with the McKracken kids. They all piled in the back seat. Jenny landed right on top of John Lewis McKracken. He was in the eighth grade but he was 15 years old already and really big. Jenny didn't like him because he was dirty and smelled bad. Her mother had said we should never judge people, so she was ashamed of her feelings, especially since the McKrackens were poor.

John Lewis reached over and grabbed Jenny onto his lap with one hand. With his other hand, he squeezed her breast.

Oh, no! Jenny thought, and pushed his hand away. "Stop it!" she said, and hit him. Everyone suddenly stopped squealing and laughing and looked at her. She knew she was beet red. "J-J-John Lewis p-p-pinched me," she said.

"Well, you didn't have to hit me," John Lewis said, and everyone laughed.

John Lewis' sister, who was Jenny's age, said, "Here, Jenny, sit by me. You keep your hands to yourself, John Lewis, or I'll tell Mom," she admonished her brother. Jenny thought she would die, and figured everyone knew what he did. Maybe John Lewis even knew about her father? *Can people actually tell what I've done?* she wondered.

"Look, look! A rainbow! The rain has stopped." As quickly as they had piled in, they piled out, and went running through the wet grass. Jenny looked around for her mother and saw her sitting with a group of ladies on a big tarp. She walked over and sat down by her mother.

"Are you okay, Jenny? I told you not to eat two hot dogs," her mother said.

"Oh, yes, I'm fine. I just thought maybe Jimmy wanted to go for a walk. I'll play with him for a while."

"Why, how sweet, Jenny. He's with your father over there. Keep a close watch."

"I will," she said, and crossed the picnic grounds.

Jimmy spotted her and came running into her arms. "C'mon, Jimmy, let's go for a long walk. Maybe we'll see a meadowlark or a butterfly, and we'll pick some pussy willows to take home."

Jenny didn't rejoin her friends. She rode home in silence, pretending she had a stomach ache. She had been having a lot of stomach aches lately, so no one questioned her.

Maybe there is something wrong with me. Everyone seems to be looking at me.

Jimmy cuddled closer and slept all the way home.

After church on Sunday, they had fried chicken, and it wasn't even any-one's birthday. Her mother had made a chocolate cake, Jenny's favorite. When dessert was served, Mrs. Bennett said, "Jenny, your father has some-thing very important to say, so please stop chattering and listen."

"Yes, Mother." *This doesn't sound good. I haven't done anything bad that I know of. I hope Mother isn't sick again.*

Her father said, "After our camping trip this summer, we're not coming back to Spring Creek. We're moving."

"Oh, no!" Jenny cried. She was surprised that she had the audacity to protest so loudly. "We can't move! These are my very best friends. I won't go! I want to stay here."

"See, John," Jenny's mother said, turning to her husband. "I told you she would be upset."

"That's enough, Jenny. We're moving and you will have to like it. We'll go camping for a month, and then we'll be here for two weeks. You'll have plenty of time to tell everyone good-bye."

53

"But Daddy," Jenny implored, "what about my friends in the country? What about next year in school? I don't want to move. I like it here. Why can't we stay here? Mommy, tell him no." But Jenny saw by her father's face that this was not negotiable. He was getting angry. She felt as though she would die. "What will my friends say?" And she pushed back her chair, ran to her room, and slammed the door behind her. As she heard her father follow her, she grabbed the pillow, covered her head, and lay face down on the bed.

"Young lady, you come here and shut this door quietly. When you can behave yourself, you can finish your dessert." Her father's voice boomed in the small room. Jenny did not want him to come any closer, so she slid off the edge of the bed and went straight to the door and shut it quietly. "I'm sorry," she whispered, "I'm sorry. Can I have my cake now?"

Chapter 9

Jenny's new room was bigger than her old one and had two big windows. Her clothes were in the closet; her bed was made. As soon as she put her mask and her map of the world on the wall, the room would truly be hers. When she opened the yellow trunk, her heart skipped a beat and tears welled up as Jenny remembered the big party at the church when they left Spring Creek. Perhaps everyone in town hadn't been there, but it had seemed that way. It was another of those times Jenny never understood: how could she have such opposite feelings at the same time?

I was happy because my best friends came to tell me good-bye, but I felt sad because I had to leave. On top in the trunk was her special box with letters and cards in it. Tommy had given her a card and a diary with a lock; Dorothy and Rachel had given her her very own copy of A Secret Garden. She had read it three times already. She kept the card from Tommy inside the book so no one would find it. They had promised to write each other. Jenny had kissed him all on her own and told him she would love him forever.

She had opposing feelings about being in this town, too. In all directions there were mountains. It seemed smaller than Spring Creek, but perhaps it was just more spread out. The highway ran right through the middle of town, and all the stores except the hardware store were on the same side of the highway.

Most of the houses were up the hill in back of town. Once again they had a big house with an upstairs, and that was exciting. Across the highway were the railroad tracks and the creek. The streets were lined with trees. Jenny liked the mountains better than the miles of flat land, but she didn't like not knowing anyone. She wondered how long they would live in Custer.

School would start soon. Jenny felt more grown-up and ready for the eighth grade. During the summer, her mother had let her grow her hair long and fixed it in shiny black curls. They already came past her shoulders. She was definitely no longer a girl, but a young woman. Her father had forbidden her to go without a shirt. He said he'd take her bicycle away if he caught her one more time riding naked from the waist up.

Part of growing up was having her mother keep track of her periods on the calendar. Jenny was not allowed to swim or ride horseback when she was having a period. She still hated menstruating. It was one part of growing up that made her want to be a boy. The man who owned the grocery store, Mr. Wylie, was also chairman of the school board and he had three horses that Jenny could ride. This was the closest Jenny had come to having her own horse, and it seemed stupid not to go riding just because of a period. Apparently, it was a rule that her mother really meant. Jenny had tried lying about it a couple of times, but her mother kept a very close track.

By the time school started, Jenny had managed to meet most of the girls her age who lived in town: Becky Wylie, Sarah Brown, and Michelle Knox. Michelle's parents were divorced, and she lived alone with her mother and little brother, Steven. Jenny learned from Becky that Michelle's father had run off with some woman and no one knew where he was for a long time. Then one day, he had written a letter from Great Falls and sent some money. Michelle's mother did ironing and sewing, but they were still very poor.

Jenny had become very aware of money and the part it played in people's lives. Because she had taken care of Jimmy so much, she was an excellent baby-sitter, and the principal and the History teacher had already had her sit for them. If she did a good job, she knew there would be steady jobs and she could count on a certain amount of money. She was going to take sewing in school, and with her baby-sitting money, she could buy her own material. And her father said the eighth grade had a basketball team; she

57

thought for sure she could get on it. Summer had, surprisingly, taken away the pain of leaving Little Creek, and she was excited to begin a new adventure.

On the first day of school, Jenny took Adam to his class and showed him the door to her class, right across the hall. Jenny noticed how little he was compared to most of the other boys and wondered if that was why he was timid and shy. *Maybe he will grow soon, like I did this summer*, she thought as she turned to walk toward her new classroom.

Mr. Black was her teacher. She had already met him at the Teachers' Party that Mr. Wylie had given last week. Becky took her hand, saying, "C'mon, Jenny, stand with me and maybe we can be seatmates. He might make one of us move, but I don't think so if we're quiet."

The bell rang and everyone in the central hall scurried to get in line. First, second, and third graders were downstairs in the big, square, white building. Upstairs, the fourth, fifth, and sixth grades were in one room. The seventh and eighth grades were in the other. The high school, which was a new brick building, was built to extend out back. Jenny had visited her father's classrooms downstairs in the high school. He had brand new drafting tables and shop equipment: saws, drills and lathes. She understood now that her father had changed jobs so they could have more money. After sitting on one of the high stools by a beautiful new drafting table, she thought maybe she would be an architect and design houses. That would be a great job and would probably pay a lot of money.

Mr. Black did not make her sit with someone else. She and Becky shared a desk. Jenny had not seen desks like these before, one top and one seat, wide enough for two people. After books were handed out and Mr. Black had talked about schedules and homework, school was underway.

From behind her brand new U.S. history book, Jenny examined the three rows of double seats that made up the eighth grade. Most of the kids came to school on big yellow buses. According to her father, their parents were cattle ranchers. Some of the boys were really big. A boy named Stan sat across from her. He had said, "Hi," when they first sat down. She had met him at church. Becky wrote on her note pad: "Isn't he cute?" Jenny blushed, embarrassed to be caught looking at the boys. In no time, the lunch bell rang.

Jenny's family always ate lunch together, except in the middle of winter. If her father had study hall or kept someone in his classroom, Jenny or her mother would take his lunch to him. It was always hot soup or stew, so it was hard to carry the heavy tray, and Jenny didn't like to do that job. She'd offer to feed Adam and Jimmy to get out of it.

Lately her father had taken to saying things to her about what they did at night. He'd say, "I'll see you tonight, Sweetheart." These comments made her feel sick. She wished he wouldn't remind her of what she was trying to forget. Today, though, lunch was fine, full of chatter about school. Jenny felt happy again.

When she returned to school, everyone was lined up outside waiting for the doors to be opened. Jenny felt a sudden yank on one of her prized new curls. Surprised and puzzled, she turned to face the blond girl directly in back of her. "Stop that," she said in a loud whisper. The stocky girl just grinned and said, "Why? Are you going to make me?"

This behavior seemed unusual to Jenny, especially from a girl. She looked around for Mr. Black, but he was still in his room. There was another hard jerk. "Where did you get the pretty curls? Does you mother still fix your curly locks?" the taunting voice sneered.

The bell saved Jenny from total shame and humiliation. Everyone, absolutely everyone, was staring and listening. At their desk, Becky slipped her a very strange note. It read: "Don't mess with Mary Lou. She's the toughest girl in school and can whip most of the boys."

Jenny read this note over and over. She could not, for the life of her, imagine a girl fighting anyone, except maybe her brothers. *And what did she mean: don't mess with her? I haven't done anything. I was just standing there.*

She didn't like this Mary Lou at all. She was mad at her, but what could she do? If she caused any trouble at school, she'd be in much bigger trouble at home. Her parents would be ashamed of her, and all their friends would know. Perhaps she should just ignore Mary Lou and act as if she didn't care.

That's what I'll do, I'll just ignore Mary Lou, she decided, putting her racing mind to rest.

When class was dismissed, Jenny fooled around at her desk, straightening things, hoping to stall until Mary Lou was in the bus. But Mr. Black questioned her. "Are you okay, Jenny?"

"Oh, yes, sir . . . I-I-I'm just looking for my spelling words. Good-bye," she stammered through her fear and embarrassment. Jenny hated it when she didn't know what to do.

Out in the hall the coast looked clear, and she headed straight for the double door. But right outside on the top step stood Mary Lou. Before Jenny could jerk free, Mary Lou had a tight hold on a massive bunch of curls. Jenny grabbed at her hair to stop the hurting. There they were on the top steps for everyone to see: Jenny holding fast to the hair close to her scalp, and Mary Lou jerking and laughing. What she said seemed very strange to Jenny. "Just get this, Curly Locks. Just 'cause your old man is a teacher here, don't think you're anybody in this school. I run things in the eighth grade, and don't you forget it."

Someone hollered, "Old Beak Face is comin'!" and before the words were finished, Mary Lou let go. Jenny wanted to bolt, but Adam's teacher was already on the step saying, "No loitering on the steps, girls. Either get on the bus or go home."

In an instant, everyone was down the steps and walking the cement walk toward the bus. Jenny had never felt so humiliated. As she headed toward home, she turned to Mary Lou and said as casually as possible, "You're safe here at school, but don't you ever lay a hand on me away from here." Jenny bolted off without waiting for a reaction from anyone.

That was on Monday. By Thursday, Jenny felt pretty relaxed about Mary Lou. Nothing was said all week, and when they were fitted for band uniforms, she and Mary Lou talked about how long they had been playing instruments. Mary Lou was very good at the trumpet. Jenny thought to herself, *Well, maybe she's not so bad.*

Becky told her that Mary Lou's mother had died when Mary Lou was eight or nine years old, and she lived all alone on a big ranch with her dad. People in town said someone should make him get a woman to clean and care for Mary Lou, because she just ran wild at the ranch. One thing Jenny knew for sure was that everyone in school was afraid of her.

The next couple of weeks were filled with the beginning of school new books, new routines, new friends. So many things were new and exciting, like the new band uniforms, white skirts with blue and white capes. Science class was held in the brand new laboratory at the adjacent high school, and gym class was in the new gymnasium. Jenny had never been in gym before.

She loved the uniform rompers and white tennis shoes. She knew if she tried very hard, she could be on the high school basketball team next year. Mary Lou was stronger than she was, but no faster.

Jenny discovered something new about herself: she wanted to be a winner. She thought of the Declamatory Contests back in Little Creek, and how she and Tommy had always seemed to be competing. She had wanted to win them, but it hadn't mattered if she didn't. Winning had always had something to do with her father, with wanting to make him happy. She had wanted him to like her and to know she was doing the best she could, but she had never particularly cared if she was first or second.

Now, Jenny wanted to be first. She wanted to win. She wasn't sure if it was just part of growing up or if it had to do with the new town and the new school. Maybe it had to do with the challenge Mary Lou had given her.

She had taken to playing football after school in the lot next to her house. She loved the rough-and-tumble feel of her body smashing into someone else's, falling on the soft earth and hanging onto the ball when she got it. One day her father stopped after school and watched them. He commented to her mother at the dinner table, "I'm not sure Jenny should be playing football. She's too old for that kind of play —basketball and baseball, maybe, but not football."

Jenny's breath stopped as she envisioned her father interfering with yet another part of her life. Everyone played ball after school. Jenny was fast and strong, and she wanted to play. There were only four girls who played football after school. Mary Lou had to take the bus home. Jenny liked it when she didn't have to deal with Mary Lou. To her surprise, her mother answered matter-of-factly, "She needs to get to know the kids here and she's close to home. It's not too rough. She'll be okay."

Her father said, "This town is very different than any place we have been before. At the teachers' meeting last week, they set up the first boxing match of the season for ages all the way down to the first grade. Maybe, if Adam put on a pair of gloves, he'd learn how to stand up for himself." He looked directly at Adam.

Jenny hated it when her father treated Adam that way. She knew how it felt. It seemed sometimes that nothing about her was okay with her father, and maybe he didn't like Adam, either. Jenny started feeling confused again. She excused herself and went to her room to read.

Jenny had always loved to read, but this year, a whole new world had opened up to her. She discovered Alexander Dumas, and was lost and in love with the Count of Monte Cristo. As she lay on her bed, she studied the map of the world on her bedroom wall and wondered about all the places on it. There were so many places she had never been! There were so many times in history she had never lived in: Jerusalem and the Crusades, Russia and the Cossacks, Africa and slave trading, or Mexico and the Aztecs!

When I grow up, I'll travel around the world. Then I'll go on a river boat to New Orleans. I'll see Independence Hall in Philadelphia. Maybe I'll go to California and see the Golden Gate Bridge.

By now the dashing, daring Count of Monte Cristo was forgotten. She decided to mark the places on her map where she wanted to travel . It was great fun, and the map was covered with X's marking her favorite places.

Something special happened that night before she drifted off to sleep. Jenny began to glimpse the full meaning of growing up. She would not always live at home with her parents. She knew she would miss Adam and Jimmy, but she would leave some day. She had the whole wide world to live in; all she had to do was choose a place. That night she dreamed she had read all the books in the library so she would know about every place in the world.

When the doorknob turned in the middle of the night, Jenny wasn't afraid. She pretended she wasn't there in bed. She held the sheet up to her chin and kept her eyes closed.

She was speeding across the hills of Southern France in a horse-drawn carriage. It was the dark of night, and she had a message that must be delivered by dawn. She stopped at an inn to rest her horses and told the boy in the stable to rub them down and give them water. They were beautiful animals and served her well. Once inside, she joined the inn keeper and asked him for food and drink, saying to his inquiry about a room, "No, I can only rest for a while. I must reach Paris by morning." She left the stable and took the reins for the remainder of her ride.

The door shut. Her father had left. She was warm and comfortable after her fantasy. It didn't matter about her father. When she grew up, she would leave, forever and ever. Adam would never want to be away from his mother, so he would have to stay at home. Jimmy would miss his sister, though, so she would have to take him with her. They would go away forever to the ends of the earth maybe even to the moon.

Jenny smiled at her dream and slept.

Chapter 10

Today was the first football game of the year. They were playing their arch rival, Silver Park, and everyone wanted to win. The band would march and play before the game and at half time. Jenny had a hard time concentrating on her school work. The day seemed to last forever. Finally the bell rang, and she went straight to the band room for her uniform. Her mother had pressed her new white pleated skirt. It was spotlessly beautiful.

The football field was in back and to the side of the gym, so it couldn't be seen from the band room, but she could see cars and buses coming, and people from town walking to the ball game. Mary Lou told her that the buses stayed until the game was over. Except for boxing, football was the most important thing that happened in town.

They left the band room together and watched by the corner of the gym for Mr. Clark, the director. The band would march to the field and then play "The Star Spangled Banner." Jenny was so excited she could hardly stand it. She kept fingering the notes on her instrument. If she made a mistake or her clarinet squeaked, she thought she would just die. There was nothing worse, except maybe starting too soon.

The band lined up, and marched out on the field. They played the national anthem, and Jenny didn't make any mistakes. They filed off the field, the director's whistle blew, and the first game of the season started.

Jenny glanced toward her mother sitting in the stand with Jimmy. She smiled and waved to Jenny. It made Jenny happy when her mother was happy, although she didn't understand why her mother's happiness was so important to her.

At half-time, the score was 7 to 0 in favor of Silver Park. The band director gave them a big pep talk. "Step high, listen to the music, and give our Custer team a real boost like you mean it!" In the middle of the field, they marched to form a big "C," and everyone stood up and cheered. When they had finished playing, they marched off the field and took their instruments back to the band room. Then they hurried back for the beginning of the second half.

From behind her, Jenny felt a quick pull on her hair; Mary Lou had taken a hold of a handful of curls. "Stop it, I told you," Jenny said tersely, jerking away. Mary Lou laughed and ran on ahead of Jenny.

Jenny turned to Becky, puzzled. "What's the matter with her anyhow? Is she going to start that again?"

Becky shook her head and repeated her previous admonishment. "Just don't mess with her, Jenny. It's not worth it."

"Well, she better not do that again or else!" Jenny declared, surprised at her intense feelings of anger.

The game was underway and Mary Lou was forgotten when Jenny felt another sharp tug on her scalp. Without a thought, Jenny turned and grabbed two handfuls of blond hair. Mary Lou lost her balance and fell to her knees. Jenny followed her to the ground, hitting and shoving at her tormentor.

"I told you to keep your hands off me, and I meant it! And keep your hands off my hair!" Jenny screamed, as she pulled Mary Lou's grasping hands free from her tangled tresses.

Her band hat went flying, and so did her full pleated skirt. In the dust and dirt, she kept Mary Lou down and straddled her squirming body. Mary Lou was bigger than Jenny and her years of ranch work showed in her strong body. But Jenny was so furious that nothing seemed to stop her. She slammed Mary Lou's arms into the soft dirt and repeated, "I told you not to pull my hair, and I mean it!"

Kicking, pulling, and screaming, the two girls rolled and turned on the soft earth. Blood trickled from Jenny's nose, and Mary Lou brushed her bleeding lower lip with the back of her hand. By now, the football game had lost a large portion of the audience as a circle of shouting students surrounded the fighting girls. A surge of power coursed through Jenny's body right through the top of her skull. She slammed Mary Lou down for a final time. Just as she straddled her again, she felt her father's iron grip on her shoulder. In a cold, angry voice, he said,

"You go directly home and clean this filth off yourself and stay in your room until your mother and I come home. Now!"

Jenny ran from the field without looking at anyone and didn't stop until she got home. Panting and crying, she assessed the damage she had suffered and spent the next hour cleaning herself and washing blood from her white skirt and blouse.

She got into bed. As she lay between the cool sheets, her fear of her parents' anger subsided. She felt a deep satisfaction. *I whipped her, I really did. I was scared, but I was mad. I have never been so mad in my whole life. I bet she leaves me alone after this! She may run the whole school and everyone may be afraid of her, but she doesn't run me and I'm not afraid of her.*

Another thought came to Jenny, and she doubled her fists.

No one runs me; I do! I'm in charge of me. No matter who they are or who they think they are, they do not run me. I DO!

She fell asleep and was awakened by the sounds of supper being prepared and her brothers playing in the front room. Maybe I won't get to eat, she thought to herself. Father is very mad. I wonder what he'll do to me?

Her mother opened the door and without smiling or even looking at her, told her to come and eat. At the table, everyone acted as if nothing had happened. They talked about the football game. Custer had won, and the Wylies were coming over to play cards. They had asked if Jenny could baby-sit, but her father had said no.

Jenny didn't know if she should finish eating and excuse herself, or whether she should stay at the table, so she just kept fooling with her food. Soon enough her father said, "When you finish doing the dishes, your mother and I want to talk to you about this afternoon. We'll be in the front room. And the Wylies will be here at 7:30, so don't waste your time. And don't leave any pots, or you'll just have to do them in the morning."

Jenny hated washing pots and pans. She usually left at least one pan if she could, but it never worked. She had to wash it in the morning, anyhow. She hurried through the washing, but she wasn't as scared as she thought she would be. It was a bad thing to do, getting in a fight, but Mary Lou had asked for it, and Jenny had warned her. No one had the right to be such a bully. She would do it again if Mary Lou gave her any more trouble. It had to do with who was in charge of who. Jenny's fists were doubled up again as she walked into the front room and sat down on the couch across from her mother's sewing chair.

Her father was at his desk. He turned in his chair, cleared his throat, and said, "Young lady, do you have any idea how humiliated and embarrassed your mother was today by your behavior? I can't believe you would deliberately hurt her in such a way. Exactly what do you have to say for yourself?"

Jenny was caught off guard. She had expected anger and punishment, but it hadn't occurred to her that she had shamed them. She flushed and peeked over at her mother, whose eyes were also downcast, focusing on her knitting needles. Tears came to Jenny's eyes. In a barely audible whisper, she managed, "I'm sorry, Mother."

"I think you can do better than that! There was your mother, sitting in the bleachers, trying to watch the ball game. Well, Margaret, you tell her how ashamed you are."

Her mother put her knitting in her lap. She sighed that awful kind of sigh, as if she couldn't stand the sight of Jenny. "I have never, ever in my entire life been so humiliated and so shocked! I didn't think I would ever live to see the day that my daughter . . . my daughter would make such a fool of me in front of the entire town. When I heard the scuffling and fighting and saw the crowd turning from the football field to watch the fight, I thought, how will I ever be able to protect my children from the toughness of this town? And then, through the crowd, I see my daughter; dirty, filthy, wallowing in the dirt in her white skirt. I couldn't believe my eyes! To my dying day I'll never forget my shame. If we hadn't already invited the Wylies over, I don't think I'd be able to look them in the face. Everyone knew how embarrassed I was. Betty said, 'Well, someone should see that the child gets some mothering. She starts trouble like this all the time. Her father treats her like a ranch hand. You're lucky, Margaret, that Jenny didn't get hurt real bad.' But I know she just said that to make me feel less humiliated. I just can't believe you did it, Jenny."

Jenny felt totally worthless. She hadn't thought of her mother at all. She knew if she made trouble at school, her father wouldn't tolerate it, but she had never thought about it having anything to do with her mother. Maybe no one would want her to baby-sit after this.

"I washed my uniform," she said feebly, blinking back the tears.

"It's a good thing. If those stains had stayed overnight, they'd never come out. And you're certainly not getting a new one," her mother said.

"Jenny," her father commanded, "you tell your mother you're sorry as if you mean it. Then go to bed, and I don't want to come in and find you've had the light on all night."

Tears rolled down Jenny's cheeks, but she bit her lip so as not to sob. Without looking up, she said as clearly as she could, "I'm sorry, Mother."

"Look at your mother when you say that," her father demanded.

Clenching her fists, Jenny blinked, looked at her mother, and said clearly, "I'm sorry, Mother. May I go to bed now?"

"Yes, and I don't ever want to see such a thing again," her mother responded. "Good night."

"Good night, Mother. Good night, Daddy," Jenny perfunctorily replied. She walked to her room, and quietly shut the door behind her.

I'm ashamed, but I'm angry too. They didn't even ask me what Mary Lou did! And besides that, are they going to punish me? One thing I'm sure of. Mary Lou better not mess with me again, or I'll get her where no one will know about it. Or else, who knows what would happen to my mother?

Jenny punched her pillow with her fist. *Sometimes I hate being a girl. Boys can do anything and it seems to be okay. They don't have to wear shirts. They can swim all the time, play football, ride their bikes clear out of town, go to the railroad tracks, and fight when someone picks on them. It's definitely better to be a boy. You can grow up to be a count, an explorer, a pirate, anything you want.*

But even as she dreamt of being a boy, Jenny thought too about how hard she would work to help her mother tomorrow to show her that she really, truly was sorry for making her mother ashamed of her in public. She would get up early and clean her room very quietly and then make bran muffins for breakfast. If she was very quiet building the fire, they wouldn't even hear her, and it would be a surprise. Then when she had the whole house cleaned, she'd take Jimmy out to play and read him a story for his nap time. Maybe she would have time to chop some kindling wood and stack it on the back porch. Jenny's mother was always pleased when Jenny worked hard. She told her friends what a good helper Jenny was.

That night, when Jenny's father sat down on the edge of the bed, Jenny didn't pretend he wasn't there. She put her arms around his neck and told him how sorry she was that she had been bad, and he held her very close and told her that he loved her very much and that she was very special to him. While he touched her all over, he kept telling her that he knew she didn't mean to be bad. She had parts of her that were very bad, he said, like the parts of her that he touched. That was why he touched her, because he was her father, and because he didn't want her to ever do any bad things with boys.

Jenny thought her father must know what was best for her, so she lay very still while he touched her inside and out. After a while, when she didn't like it anymore, she pretended she was asleep. He kissed her good night and reminded her that she must never tell her mother about what she was doing with him. Her mother would not understand, he said, and she would die of shame.

71

After he left, Jenny thought about that. She didn't see how anyone could truly die of shame, but her mother had been very upset that night. Maybe she would just cry forever or something, or go crazy. It didn't matter. Jenny knew she would never tell her mother. She didn't even think of it. Why on earth would she tell her mother she did a terrible thing like that? She never again thought of telling or not telling her mother.

On Sunday, after church, Becky and Stan and Jenny walked to Stan's house together. "That was a great fight with Mary Lou," Stan told Jenny. "No one has ever whipped her. There's some guys that could but they'd get in such trouble, they just avoid her. You were great! What did your dad do?"

"Oh, not much," Jenny said, feeling embarrassed that she hadn't gotten in more trouble at home. "I had to stay in my room. My mom was real mad, though. She said she'd die if I did that again, so I don't know what I'll do if . . ."

"Oh, never fear," Becky interrupted. "Mary Lou will never touch you again.

You know Wendall Curtis? He has a whole bunch of sisters and his folks don't care if he hits girls. Last year, he beat the tar out of Mary Lou and she hasn't pushed or hit any guys since then. She's just a big bluff sometimes."

Stan's Aunt Ethel was home from church by the time they got there and she asked them in for cookies and milk. Stan lived with his aunt and uncle; his older brother lived with their father in California. Their mother had died when they were little, and since then they had gone back and forth from his aunt's house to California. At Christmas, his brother was coming to Aunt Ethel's again.

Becky and Stan agreed to meet Jenny after Sunday dinner and ride their bikes up the hill in back of town. It was a great day, and everything at home seemed to have returned to normal. When suppertime came, they sat down to bowls of steaming rice with pats of melted butter, sugar, and cinnamon. It was one of Jenny's favorite Sunday suppers. Once again, all seemed well in her world.

When she got to school the next morning, the buses were just pulling away, and there stood Mary Lou. Jenny had forgotten about her, and the sudden reminder caught her off guard.

"Hi, Jen. Take a look at my lip. It's still swollen," Mary Lou called across the school yard. "You're some fighter for someone as skinny as you. You caught me by surprise or I'd have smashed you. If I'd really meant it, you wouldn't have stood a chance."

"Well, I told you to leave me alone," Jenny said testily. "I don't like anyone fooling with my hair."

"Well, hey! Do you wanna do a geography project with me? Mr. Black said we could work with someone and I haven't chosen anyone yet."

"I sort of said, 'Yes,' to Becky. Maybe we can all three do something if we ask," Jenny replied. She wasn't sure if she should trust Mary Lou, but she didn't want any more trouble.

The bell rang. When they entered the big front hall, it seemed to Jenny that everyone went quiet and moved to make a path for them to walk through. Maybe not, but they were first in line. Stan poked her with his elbow, shook his head, and grinned. Jenny now "belonged" to the eighth grade in Custer and it felt great.

Chapter 11

One thing Jenny soon discovered about the eighth grade was that she was very busy. She had band, basketball, her new sewing class, and the effort to get good grades. School had always been pretty easy for Jenny, and she liked it, but she didn't care much about grades. They seemed to matter mostly to her father. "Your father is not going to like this B minus," her mother would say, or, "Think how your father will feel if you don't do better."

And she was right. Jenny's father would get angry and say things that made Jenny feel bad and stupid. She tried, but somehow it was never quite enough.

Now, though, since she had decided she was in charge of herself, she planned to get all A's. Spelling and mathematics were the hardest, but she knew she could get A's in those subjects too. Mary Lou had always been the best in everything: best grades, best ballplayer, and best speaker. Everyone took it for granted that if there was an award, Mary Lou would win it. In the past, Jenny wouldn't have minded. Now she wanted to be Number One.

She thought about it when she studied and when she was going back and forth to school. She figured she could read one book a week if her mother didn't catch her with the light on. It became an obsession. She read one book at the table, one in the car, and another one while walking to the store. Wherever Jenny was, she read. Some of the characters in her books became real people to her. She thought about them even when she wasn't reading. She wrote stories about them for English class. She proudly announced to her family, "I'm going to read more books than anyone in the entire school, and I'm going to do a book report on each one."

Jenny's project became so important to her that one day, Mr. Black kept her after school. Returning three book reports to her, he said gently, "Jenny, these are wonderful reports. I'm pleased with how much you're enjoying your reading, but you must make your reports shorter. I don't need to know about each character in the book. Just write a few paragraphs telling what the book was about and why you liked it. A book report should only be one or two pages, not ten or twelve. Perhaps one day," he added, "you'll write your own book."

Jenny had mixed feelings about what Mr. Black said. She didn't like feeling scolded, but she liked him and wanted to please him. As she walked home, however, she straightened it out by determining that yes, indeed, she would write her own book or perhaps she would be a newspaper woman and be an editor of a big newspaper. She had already written several stories for the school paper, and there were those interviews she had done of her teachers. Yes, that would be a good thing to do!

Days were getting shorter, and it was beginning to get cold. The end of October came around and it was Halloween again. Jenny talked her mother into having a party. She started out by saying, "No," but when Jenny suggested that Adam and his friends be included, she agreed. Adam did not seem happy in this new town, and he missed his old friends. A party would be good for him.

Halloween was on Friday, so there wouldn't be any school the next day. On Thursday, Jenny hurried home. She made gingerbread and cleaned up the kitchen, extra clean. They would bob for apples and eat those, and make popcorn on the warm kitchen stove. Her mother would make spiced apple cider Friday morning. After school, Jenny would decorate the house and cut out Jack O'Lanterns with her brothers. By six o'clock, it would be dark and they could light the candles to reveal their pumpkin faces. Jenny liked being organized and ready for things ahead of time.

Friday at noon, she and Becky were deep in confidential conversation about their costumes when two high school boys sat down next to them. One of them said, "Hey, Jenny, what are you doing for Halloween?"

Jenny didn't know his name. She thought he was Emily's oldest brother.

She felt suspicious and a little apprehensive, since it was Halloween. "I'm having a party at my house," she said. "Everyone is already invited."

He raised his eyebrows, winked, and said, "Well, I'm Larry, Emily's brother. She told me about your party. I thought you might wanna come with us and have some real fun."

"I can't, I'm having a party with my brother, Adam. We've planned it all week," Jenny replied uncomfortably.

"That's too bad. We really wanted you to come out with us. We've got some great fun planned: soaping store windows and pushing over some leftover outhouses. I don't suppose your old man lets you out much though, does he?" Larry queried.

"No. But I guess if I had known sooner, I could have gone," Jenny said defiantly.

"That's okay, Jen. Maybe you can help us. You know that trailer your dad has in his garage? We figure it would be a real trick to haul it out of town and really shake him up. Nothing bad, you know, just a joke. But we looked, and he's got a lock on the garage. Why don't you unlock it for us? How about it, Jen? Just for fun."

"Oh, no. I couldn't. He'd kill me if he found out! I couldn't do that."

Larry put his arm around Jenny's shoulder and winked again. "Oh, Jen, he'll never know you had anything to do with it, and it will be such fun Monday morning to hear how mad he is. He'll never suspect you. Come on."

"I-I-I dunno how," Jenny stammered.

"Sure you do," Larry encouraged. "Just take the key, unlock it, and make it look locked. We'll do the rest, nothing bad, just roll it out of town a little ways." He gave another squeeze to her shoulder. "Everyone will be surprised and impressed that you helped. We always trick the teachers, and your dad's so strict. We just wanna play a joke. Say you'll do it. Be a good scout and do it, okay?"

"How soon do I have to unlock it?" Jenny asked.

"Oh, not before ten o'clock. We'll do your place last, okay?"

"You're sure you won't break our trailer? He'd kill me."

"No, no, Jen. Just a trick . . . a Halloween trick. No harm done, okay?"

"Okay, Larry, but nobody better ever tell that I helped."

The lunch bell rang. Larry jumped up and ran off, calling, "Don't forget now. You're real swell. I knew we could count on you."

As they went to class, Jenny confided in Becky. "Becky, don't you breathe a word to anyone, okay?"

"Oh, I won't tell, Jenny. Larry is the most popular boy in school. Did you see how he hugged you? Don't worry, I won't breathe a word."

That night, Jenny was nervous about how to follow through on her promise to Larry. She had never deliberately done anything against her father's wishes. He would be furious, and she knew it. It was exciting. She didn't quite understand why the thought of her father in a rage was so exhilarating, but it was. She imagined what it would be like when he found out, which she was sure would be first thing in the morning.

The timing was important, to make sure that no one missed her when she was outside. Her chance came midway through the party.

Thank goodness, I included Adam, she thought. His friends are so wild bobbing for apples, they won't miss me. She grabbed the key from its hook on the back porch, unlocked the padlock, and dashed back in the house.

It was a great Halloween party. After everything was cleaned up and the family had gone to bed, Jenny wondered if she dared sneak out and see if the plotted-for deed had been accomplished. She had just about worked up the courage when she heard her father's footsteps approaching. Shivering, she pulled the covers up to her chin.

Oh, no! Not tonight, of all nights. Why does he have to come here tonight? He makes me so angry. I hate this.

Jenny had an angry impulse to scream at her father and tell him, "I hate you. Get out of my room. Don't touch me!" Instead, she closed her eyes. By the time the doorknob turned, she wasn't there anymore. She was becoming an expert at disappearing into her mind.

In the morning, she was still mad at him, but she was also scared. She didn't know if the trailer was gone or not, but she didn't have to wait long to find out. There he came, straight from the garage. She knew the trailer was gone. He looked very mad.

"Some of those damned fool kids took my trailer!" he stormed. "I don't know how the hell they got in. They didn't even break the lock! But I'll tell you for sure, I'll find out who did it, and they'll be sorry."

Jenny's heart was in her throat. At least she thought it must be, because she couldn't swallow. Suddenly he turned on her. "You probably knew about this all the time!" Grabbing her by the shoulder, he continued to shout. "Just who in this blasted town took my trailer, and where is it?"

He let go of her arm. Jenny's feet felt frozen to the kitchen floor. *I'm glad they took your dumb old trailer, and I don't care if you ever find it! Everyone, especially the boys, will be glad to see you so mad.*

He left the house, slamming the door behind him. When he came home at lunch without his trailer, he was smoldering. He talked all through lunch about how rough and undisciplined this town was and how disrespectful people were of other people's property. Jenny had to work on her sewing project, so she excused herself. She spent the rest of the day wondering where the trailer was and what would happen to Larry and his friends when her dad found out. She was sure he would kill her if he ever discovered that she had unlocked the door. He was so preoccupied with his anger, he hadn't even asked how the door got unlocked!

Jenny felt strange about her father's anger. She was scared, but she felt pleased too. As if he deserved it or something. It was like the feelings she had when kids at school said how mean her father was. She wanted to defend him and say he wasn't a bad person, and she also wanted to agree that he was mean.

Sometimes Jenny loved her father and thought she would do anything in the world for him, even at night. Other times she hated him and wished he would go away forever. But then what would they do without him? How would they eat, and who would buy their clothes? Becky didn't have a father, and look how poor the family was. Jenny didn't want to be poor, she was sure of that.

Jenny helped her mother with dinner. Afterward, she put Jimmy to bed and played a game with Adam. All the while, her father talked about the way he'd gone around town telling everyone to look for his trailer. Other people had had things carted off, and some outhouses had been tipped over. So the indictment of Halloween and disrespectful kids overshadowed the issue of his trailer. Jenny couldn't wait for school on Monday. She hoped that Larry would tell her what they'd done with the trailer, but she didn't want her father to see them together. If her father had lunch duty, she wouldn't be able to talk to Larry at all.

Jenny had left Alexander Dumas for Jack London, and the Pacific Northwest was calling her. In her books, Jenny left the day-to-day world she lived in and traveled wherever the pages carried her. She knew the characters in her books as well as or better than she knew her friends, and found their lives much more exciting. She could imagine herself as a character in any story she chose. At church, in school, she imagined herself into stories. She did it when her father came into her room, too, but she pretended to herself that it was different at night. More and more Jenny realized that she had to forget the night.

That must be how they make movies. People have pictures in their heads of what the words and feelings look like, and they make a movie. Perhaps she'd be a movie star after all. It would be very glamorous.

Monday proved to be as tense as Jenny expected. The seventh and eighth grades had to march into the high school auditorium, where Mr. Wylie admonished everyone for the unwarranted pranks in town on Halloween. Then Mr. Kincaid, from the hardware store, announced that none of the merchants in town would allow any students past seventh grade in their stores until a committee was formed to wash the soap off everyone's windows. To make it fair, Mr. Wylie said that whoever volunteered for the job would earn extra credits. Enough kids put their hands up that it was settled.

Then Jenny's father got up and did a terrible thing. Since he taught shop and mechanical drawing, almost all the boys in school were in his classes, and he said they would all get graded Incomplete until his trailer was returned. A buzz went around the room then. Mr. Wylie stood up and dismissed the assembly.

Now everyone will hate my father. Oh, how awful! Jenny's thoughts were interrupted by Larry grabbing her elbow.

"Hey, Jen, do you think he means it?" he whispered.

"Oh, I think so," she said. "Once he gave me a D and I didn't think he ever would. If he said he would, he will. He doesn't go back on his word." They had reached her door and she was glad for classes to be underway.

But she couldn't concentrate on the plight of "Evangeline" or the conquest of Mexico by the Spaniards. Her mind was a kaleidoscope of images and thoughts moving, moving, moving, never stopping long enough for her to make any sense of them. Mixed in with the thoughts was a fireworks display of emotions: fear, guilt, shame, more fear.

Why? Why did I ever do such a stupid thing to my father? What possessed me? What will we do without his trailer?

She remembered going with her father to look at the trailer for the first time. She must have been only ten, and they were going to move to Middle Creek.

Jenny didn't remember moving from Idaho to Montana. It had happened in stages. First her father had moved, and then she had gone to live with him while he went to school. Months later, her mother and Adam had joined them. Jimmy hadn't been born yet.

Jenny let her mind drift back through the years. There had been a happiness then that seemed to be gone now. *Perhaps it was just because I was younger, but maybe . . . just maybe, it might be because of my father.*

She and her father had lived together by themselves. He had gone to school and Jenny had helped him. She had no idea why she was there with her father in a tiny apartment while her mother and brother remained in Idaho. Even though she missed her mother sometimes, she felt very important. She went everywhere with her father. She cooked for him and cleaned the house for him. On Saturdays, he filled the washer, and she washed their clothes. The lady who lived on the other side of the clotheslines would invite her for tea and they would visit. Jenny pretended the lady was a gypsy or a fortuneteller because she wore bright silk clothes and smelled sweet and exotic.

Even when they were back together as a family, Jenny had gone with her father whenever she had a chance. It had been a beautiful, warm spring day when they drove out to Miss Hand's parents' house in the country to look at the trailer. Miss Hand had been her teacher, and Jenny had stayed at her house when she had the chicken pox. Mr.

Hand scooped Jenny up with a big hug and laughingly said, "My, aren't you getting to be the big girl! Who's going to be my girl if you go moving away?"

Jenny didn't answer. She knew that grown-ups just say things like that and don't expect an answer. She took her father's hand as they walked out toward the barn where the big trailer was. He walked all around it, looked at the tires and the axle underneath, then picked up the hitch to see if it was in good shape. Jenny followed him as though she knew all about trailers. He turned to her and said, "Well Jenny, what do you think? Shall we get it?"

That was another one of those no-need-to-answer questions, so Jenny didn't respond, but asked, "May I go in the house and say hello to Mrs. Hand?"

"Sure, run along. I'll call you when I'm ready to leave."

When they were well on their way home, Jenny asked, "Are we going to get Mr. Hand's trailer?"

"Yes, I think so," her father said. "I have to see how much it costs to put a hitch on the car first. It has to be welded on."

83

The very next week, Jenny and her father had gone back to Mr. Hand's place and bought the trailer. They had a lot of fun pulling it through town and parking it in the alley. Jenny helped. When it came time to move to Middle Creek, they had room in the trailer for everything they owned. On the back of it, they stored things for picnics and camping. It took three days to drive all the way north to their new town. It was a grand adventure; picnics every day and sleeping out of doors.

Being all together is the best way for a family to be, Jenny thought.

Suddenly she was jerked back to the present by Mr. Black's touch on her shoulder and his voice saying, "Jenny it's time for spelling. Take your nose out of that history book."

Wendall laughed under his breath, which reminded Jenny that she didn't like him and wished he didn't sit across from her. He always looked at her, paying more attention to her than to his school work.

It's no wonder he keeps flunking, she thought.

Between the spelling words "experience" and "expectation," Jenny's mind left her school work again. She wished school would end for the day. She was feeling near panic. If she told her father what she had done, he would want to know who put her up to it, and she'd have to tell. If she did that, she would never, ever have another friend. But if they didn't get their trailer back, what would they do without it? Every summer, they took their tent and camping equipment to the woods and used the trailer to haul wood home for the long, cold winter.

She couldn't understand now how she could have done such a thing to her family. She thought of telling her mother how bad she had been, but that wouldn't solve anything. Her mother would make her tell her father anyhow. Tears welled up as she realized how she had betrayed her family.

By the time Jenny reached home, she had a terrible headache and felt sick to her stomach. She called, "Hi, I'm home," to her mother, threw her body across the bed, and cried herself to sleep.

She must have been asleep about an hour when she woke with the worst pain she had ever experienced. She reached up and held her head. It felt as if it might burst if she didn't do something. It hurt too much to move, and she felt she would vomit all over if she had to. Suddenly, the decision was no longer hers. She managed to roll her upper torso off the bed as an awful green liquid spewed from her throat. As she gagged, her mother appeared in the doorway.

"Jenny, Jenny, what's wrong? Why didn't you say something?" Her mother lifted Jenny back onto the bed.

Jenny threw herself in her mother's arms as her body was racked with sobs. "Oh, Mommy, my head hurts so bad I can't stand it! Help me! Please help me!"

"You must stop crying, Jenny. That just makes it worse. Here, put your nightie on. I'll get you some aspirin," her mother said calmly, and left the room.

Jenny felt better after throwing up, but she still couldn't seem to stop crying. The pain was so bad she didn't remember what happened in the next couple of hours. Her mother put cold packs on her forehead and the back of her neck and gently rubbed her back, all the while saying, "Jenny, Jenny, I know it hurts, but you must stop crying. That only makes it worse."

Some time after dark, she finally stopped crying and drank some warm tea. Her mother gathered Jenny in her arms, held her hand, stroked her arms gently, and whispered to her just to relax and go to sleep.

Two remaining tears rolled down Jenny's cheeks as sleep finally came to her. *If your mother knew what a terrible thing you had done to the family and how bad you really are, she wouldn't love you anymore. No, you must keep this secret forever. You are such a bad person.*

Jenny didn't know if the voice was inside her or outside. It didn't really matter. What the voice said was true.

Jenny's mother said she could stay home the next day if she still felt sick. She had a hard time deciding which would be worse: to stay home and worry all day, or go to school and worry all day. She opted for going to school. She didn't feel good, but she wanted to know what had happened about the trailer. She wondered how many people knew that she had unlocked the garage door. If her father carried through with his threat of giving incompletes, that, too, would be her fault. Everyone would hate her and her father. No one mentioned the trailer all day, which made the day seem longer and longer.

Just before supper, there was a knock on the door. Her father opened it, and there stood three of his students, one of whom was Larry. He spoke first. "Mr. Bennett, we're responsible for taking your trailer and we don't want everyone to get in trouble."

"Come on in, all three of you, and shut the door," her father said sternly.

Jenny looked up from her place at the table and met Larry's glance. Just as quickly, she lowered her eyes in embarrassment.

"Do you have anything else to say for yourselves?" her father asked.

One of the other boys spoke up. "We're very sorry, sir. We only meant it as a joke, and I guess we just didn't think. The trailer is okay. We set it by the garage."

"What I haven't figured out is how you got it out without breaking the lock," her father said. "I'm sure I had that lock shut." Jenny caught her breath.

Larry said, "Well, no, sir, you must have left it open, 'cause we checked it earlier in the day when we first got the idea. It was open all day, so it was easy."

"No excuse for you boys to pull a damned fool stunt like that, though. I figured someone would make sure I got it back. If there's anyone else in on this, you better let me know. There will be extra assignments for you when you report for class tomorrow. Now get out of here, we were just sitting down to supper," her father said, dismissing them.

Jenny prayed to herself that no one in her family would ever find out that she had opened the padlock. She couldn't make herself believe that Larry would go on lying for her; she was sure he would tell, since he was being so honest as to bring the trailer back.

At school the next day, Larry met Jenny by the band room and apologized. He said they had taken the trailer out to the edge of town where her dad could have found it very easily the next morning, but some other guys took it much farther out and no one would say where it was.

"You were a great sport, Jen, to open the lock. No wonder you were scared. Man, alive! I had no idea he would be so mad. He was swell today, though. We just have to turn in one extra drawing," Larry said.

The lump in Jenny's throat prevented her from expressing her gratitude for the lie. Instead she just muttered, "That's okay . . . uh, I have to go," and turned from the hallway to the music room. She could feel her heart beating from Larry standing so close to her. She thought he must be the nicest smelling person she had ever smelled. His hair was long, straight, and light brown like his sister's, and he put something on it to keep it back that smelled wonderful.

Mary Lou bumped Jenny's elbow as she opened her clarinet case. "Hey, Jen, what you doin' talking to Larry in the hall?" she asked with a twinkle in her eye.

"Oh, nothing. We were just talking about things," Jenny answered. She was ashamed of what she had done, but she was also glad that Larry had lied to keep from getting her in trouble. It must mean he liked her.

On the way home from school that day, Jenny asked Becky, "Have you ever been kissed by a boy . . . you know, really kissed?"

"What do you mean, really kissed? You mean long like in the movies?" Becky asked.

"Yeah. You know, not like spin the bottle or just kid stuff, but really, truly kissed."

"No, I guess not. Have you?"

"Oh no, never, but I think about it."

"Who do you wanna kiss, anyone special?"

"Nope, I was just wondering, I guess. Nobody special. Are you going to work on your sewing?"

"Yes, my mother's working at the store. Do you wanna come over?"

"Yes. I have to baste the top of my dress together. I'll see you in twenty minutes." The two girls parted for their separate homes.

Chapter 12

Later at Becky's house, they made cocoa and cinnamon toast, to take into Becky's room. While Becky tidied up the kitchen, an idea formed in Jenny's mind.

Becky is truly, truly my very best friend, and she would never break a secret. Maybe, just maybe . . . well, I'll ask her, Jenny decided. The girls got on the bed, took their shoes off, and put their needlework in front of them. Jenny began, "Becky, we're the very best of friends, aren't we?"

"Oh, yes, Jenny. I've never had such a close friend as you. We'll be friends forever."

"I've been thinking that we're such good friends, we could practice with each other," Jenny said.

"Practice what, Jenny?"

"Practice . . . you know, kissing. How will we know what to do if a boy does kiss us?"

"Oh, Jenny. How could we do that? We're both girls! Girls don't kiss each other like that."

"Well, I could, because I could just pretend I was a boy. Boys have more fun, anyhow. I'd like to be a boy."

"You would? I dunno, Jenny. It would be good to know how it feels and know what to do."

"Do you wanna kiss me first, or shall I kiss you?"

"Oh, it's your idea, so why don't you go first."

The two girls reached awkwardly across the bed toward each other and very hesitantly touched lips. Jenny was nervous, but she was determined. If Larry ever kissed her, she didn't want him to find out she didn't know how. They touched again, and Jenny suddenly felt very excited inside.

"Let's lie down on the bed and put our arms around each other as if we were really, truly kissing," Jenny said. They had a long embrace, holding each other close so that their whole bodies touched.

"Gosh, Jenny," Becky whispered, "it's not hard at all, like I thought it would be. You kiss very good, like you actually know how."

"Oh, I guess some things just come natural. I rode a bike the first time I got on. Some people take forever."

For the next few weeks, Jenny and Becky met after school at Becky's and practiced touching and holding each other. One day, Jenny got so excited that she slid her tongue through Becky's open lips. She wondered what it would be like to touch Becky "down there." She didn't say anything about it to Becky, but she knew Becky must be thinking the same thing by the way she pushed her body against Jenny's. Finally, close to Christmas time, Jenny asked her.

"Becky, why don't we touch each other down there and we'll know how that feels, too. I mean, not really . . . since I'm not really a boy, but we could pretend."

"You mean take our panties off? In the middle of the day? Here, at my house?"

"Sure, what difference does it make? Nobody will know. If it feels good to be kissing, that must feel good, too, don't you think?"

Jenny didn't want to let on, but she had been touching herself for a long time, and it did feel good. Sometimes she felt guilty, but mostly she just didn't think about it. And she would never tell a single soul that she did it, not even her very best friend.

"Let's do it, huh? I'll do it first, and you say if you like it. If you don't, I'll stop," Jenny assured Becky.

As the late afternoon sun filtered through the warm window shades, Jenny and Becky took the step that became a pattern for the rest of the year. Sometimes, they would put Jenny's mother's sewing machine in Jimmy's wagon and take it to Becky's house and work on their sewing first. They also did their school work and baked cookies or gingerbread.

While Jenny was away from Becky, she thought more and more about how it would feel to be that close with a boy. She remembered Rachel's cousin and how his bare leg had felt against hers and how it had felt when Tommy hugged her in their secret hiding places. Sometimes when she and Becky were passionately caressing the whole afternoon away, Jenny would pretend that Becky was Larry.

One day, the most amazing thing happened in her body. She thought perhaps she had felt it before, but she wasn't sure. Her heart beat faster and faster. She felt warm all over. Suddenly her whole body quivered. Inside, it felt like a sky rocket had gone off. She touched her lips to Becky's extended nipple. They collapsed in each other's arms. After a little while, Becky whispered in her ear, "Oh, Jenny, I love you so much. I want us to love each other forever and ever, and never love anyone else."

Jenny stroked Becky's short brown curls, and didn't say anything. She didn't know if she loved Becky, and she sure didn't know about this "forever and ever"; but she didn't want to hurt Becky's feelings.

After that, Jenny began going home after school. Her mother had been complaining that she was gone too much, and she didn't want her to suspect anything. There was another thing that bothered Jenny, too, and that was the way Becky hung around her all the time. At first it was nice to have someone special, but even Mary Lou said one day in the lunch line, "Hey, can't you ever get rid of her?"

Jenny shrugged her shoulders and said, "She's okay. She just doesn't want us to talk about boys. Maybe it has something to do with her father."

Stan had been complaining, too, that Jenny was always with Becky, and he had a two-handed bridge game she liked a lot. Both she and Adam had learned to play. Sometimes she did the right thing and her father was pleased with her. She was terrified when she made a mistake, but it was worth it when she did it right. Becky didn't like games, but Jenny did.

Besides, Stan's brother, Bob, was coming from California for Easter. When he had been there at Christmas, they sort of fooled around together, necking and kissing, but she wasn't allowed to take boys in her bedroom, so they had to stay in the front room all the time. They went tobogganing several times, and he always sat in back of her. A couple of times, when they were going really fast, he rubbed his mittened hands across her breasts. They pretended it was an accident, but they both knew it wasn't. It was exciting.

Jenny wanted to talk about it to Becky. She wanted to share how it felt to be petting with Bob. It was sort of the same as with Becky, but Jenny liked it better with Bob. She certainly couldn't tell Becky that! Bob said that Jenny was a good kisser and Jenny wanted to tell Becky that too, but she didn't want to hurt her friend's feelings. Becky was very sensitive, even about Mary Lou. It was almost Valentine's Day, and Jenny decided to make Becky an extra special Valentine so she'd know she was her best friend.

Jenny was in the kitchen one evening, helping with supper, when her mother reminded her about her doctor's appointment on Saturday in Middle Fork. They had shopping to do, too, and her mother said if they finished soon enough, they could go to a movie.

"Can Becky come?" Jenny asked.

"No, not this time, what with going to the doctor. I'm very concerned about these headaches you're having. You've been having them every three to four weeks since last fall, and that's not good."

"Is Jimmy coming?"

"No, your father will keep the boys. We must have all the time we need. I don't know what they might find."

Jenny was worried. What could they do? Look in her head? And, more and more, she disliked being alone with her mother. She asked too many questions, and she hardly ever liked Jenny's answers. She'd say things such as, "You shouldn't feel that," or "You mustn't think that." Jenny was learning that it was better to just be quiet around her mother, or try to find something else to talk about, like her home economics teacher. Jenny's mother didn't like her because she didn't agree with the things she taught.

At dinner, her father talked to her about her headaches and said he was worried, too. He said it wasn't right for her to get so sick. The headaches always made her sick to her stomach.

Later on, when her father came to her room, he said if she would be more relaxed and let him do what he wanted, it would help the headaches. Jenny was reading Uncle Tom's Cabin, and she didn't want him to talk at all. It made it harder to stay with the story. He wanted her to touch him the way he touched her, and she hated it. When she had to touch him, she found she couldn't pretend it wasn't him. A few times, she had been able to imagine that he was the handsome son of a plantation owner who had stolen into her room and slipped into her bed. But the pretending didn't work tonight. She didn't want to touch her father, but he kept putting her hand there and telling her to rub it.

Jenny concentrated as hard as she could, and pretty soon she didn't feel anything. Even the story was gone. There was nothing but darkness. Sometimes she would be surprised to find that he had gone, and she hadn't even heard the door. That frightened her, because it meant he could come in and she wouldn't hear that, either. It seemed important to know when he came in, so she listened for the doorknob every night. Going to sleep got harder and harder as she lay awake, listening. Some nights, it felt like she didn't sleep at all. Darkness came over her like a blanket and covered her. It was frightening to never remember what had happened in the darkness. But forgetting was also a friend. The more demands her father put on her and the more things he wanted her to do, the harder forgetting was. When he wasn't around, it was easier.

Chapter 13

Earlier than usual, Jimmy came crawling into bed with Jenny with his favorite story book, Raggedy Andy. She wondered how many times she had read him that book, but then she laughed at herself, remembering how many times she had read her favorite book, The Secret Garden. After one reading, they played hide-and-seek under the sheets for a while until Jenny had an idea. "Jimmy, why don't you and I make French toast for breakfast? It's my favorite."

"Mine, too," he answered, even though Jenny wasn't sure he knew what that word meant.

She dressed quickly and scooped Jimmy up in her arms as they headed for the kitchen. Jimmy handed her the small kindling wood for the fire as Jenny explained: "See these small pieces of paper, Jimmy? You have to wad them in small pieces tight, but not too tight, then put the kindling in. After the kindling, you need to put in at least two nice pieces of wood, three is better; they should have split sides, not bark, it catches faster. It's important to know how to make a good fire. I can make a campfire just as good as any boy. Learning how to make a good fire is the first thing you have to know to be a good cook. Did you know that?"

"Uh huh," he nodded.

"No you didn't, you silly. I just told you," Jenny said, touching his blond head. "Let's get the milk and eggs. Besides, you're only three and that's not old enough to build fires."

Jenny loved it when her parents were happy with her, as they were with the beautiful breakfast she and Jimmy served. There were bright blue and white checkered napkins at everyone's place. Each person's plate had three perfectly thin orange slices beside the French toast.

Her father praised her and gave her a hug. "You're getting to be almost as good a cook as your mother," he grinned. Jenny was pleased. He always said that, except when she made mistakes. Then he'd tease her and say, "You expect me to eat this? What is it?" Like her first batch of baking powder biscuits. They were so hard, everyone was glad her mother made good gravy.

Her mother said, "Good cooking takes practice. Don't tease her." Jenny dreamed that one day she would make bread and cinnamon rolls as delicious as her mother's.

"Come on and eat, Jenny, you're daydreaming again. We have to be on our way so as not to be late," her mother prompted. "Dress warmly. I want to get home early, but we might have a cold snap by late afternoon." Her father expressed some concern about the two of them driving in the wintertime, but her mother paid him little attention as she cleared the table.

"I'll do those," her dad volunteered.

As Jenny went to her room to get ready, a warm glow filled her heart, and she felt very thankful for her parents and her family. In their family, all the work was equal; everyone did everything. Her mother called it "working together." Her father did dishes and helped with the laundry; her mother chopped wood and dug up the garden. Adam was learning to dry the dishes standing on his green stool.

Her mother also said, "When we all co-operate, we have more time to play." So a lot of times on Saturday afternoons, while Jimmy was asleep, they made popcorn or cookies and played cards together. As she sat on her bed putting on her long, warm cotton socks, Jenny contemplated the "X's" on her map of the world. She would visit her family often, she decided, as she traveled around from country to country.

As she climbed into the car, Jenny was still in a reflective mood. She hoped her mother would concentrate on her driving and not ask a lot of questions. As they drove, Jenny watched her mother and wondered about her. Her mother was the most important person in her life, but it was not the way it used to be between them. Nothing had been the same since Jimmy was born or perhaps even before then. Jenny wanted to be the best daughter in the world and make her mother happy, but she couldn't help wishing that her mother would be happy without Jenny having to work so hard at it.

"What are you dreaming about now, Jenny?"

"Oh, nothing, just thinking."

"Thinking about what?"

"Oh, I dunno."

"Jenny, why don't you talk to me any more? I worry about you. A mother and daughter should talk, but you get more withdrawn all the time. What's the matter with you?"

"Nothing's the matter with me. I dunno what you wanna talk about."

"Sometimes when I talk to you, I don't think you're listening. You seem to be off somewhere else. If something is bothering you, you know you can tell me. That's why I'm here."

"Nothing's bothering me, Mom; I'm fine. There's nothing to worry about. If I need to talk, I'll talk to you."

"Jenny, you aren't fooling around with boys, are you? You remember all the things I told you about boys and men and what they think of you if you're loose with them. You do want to be a decent, respectable girl, and now that you're menstruating, you could get in trouble, you know. I trust you're not doing any foolish things like that."

"Why would I do anything like that? I know better than that. That's disgusting. I don't wanna talk about it."

"All right, dear, but don't forget the things I've told you. And please talk to me if you need to. That's what mothers are for. I just don't want anything bad to ever happen to you."

"Nothing is going to happen to me. Do we have to talk anymore? I need to read my history book; we have a test next week."

Her mother sighed the awful sigh that Jenny hated. Jenny clenched her fists and wondered, as she frequently did, *Why am I angry so much lately, and why am I so angry at my mother? All she does is ask me these dumb questions and worry about me. But then again, she helps me all the time. She makes me beautiful clothes, better than anybody else's mother, and she lets me do whatever I want in my room. And as long as my work is done, I get to visit my friends and go places as much as I like.*

I just wish she wouldn't ask me these questions. They make me so uncomfortable. I want her to leave me alone. She already told me the doctor will ask me a lot of questions. It seems that all grown-ups know how to do is ask questions. I'm not sure why that makes me so angry, but it does.

If we knew why I had these terrible headaches or what to do about them, we wouldn't be going to the doctor in the first place. If I knew what to say to Mother, I'd say it just to make her happy, but I don't know what to tell her. I don't know what she wants, and then she worries because I can't answer her. One thing for sure, I'm not going to get in any trouble with boys, so we won't have to talk about that.

Her mother was right about the doctor. He did ask a lot of questions, mostly about her period. Jenny hated talking about her period. It seemed to be such a big deal. No, she didn't have cramps. Yes, she was regular. No, it wasn't too much and no, it wasn't too little. Sometimes the headaches came at the same time and sometimes they didn't. No, her mother didn't have these kind of headaches and no, she didn't eat anything that might cause them. On and on. It took forever, and in the end, he told her mother to keep doing what she'd been doing. Jenny would probably outgrow the headaches.

Outside, Jenny exclaimed to her mother, "What good did that do? He didn't even give me any medicine. What does he mean, I'll outgrow them?"

Jenny was aware that she was angry again, and her mother's admonishment didn't help. "Now don't be upset, Jenny. He did the best he could. I didn't think there was much he could do, but your father insisted we come and ask. Come on, relax. We'll go to Penney's and choose material for a couple of spring dresses; they have a sale. I think when we get your new shoes, we can buy stockings to match the material we get. Let's have a good time together."

"Okay, Mom. I'm sorry I was angry, but I hate the headaches. They make me so sick, I just want to die."

"Well now, Jenny, they're not that bad. You must learn to relax and you'll outgrow them, like he said."

Jenny kept her thoughts to herself. *She'd think differently if it was her being sick. Maybe I will die, or maybe I'll go crazy. How can she say they're not that bad? She doesn't know.*

Besides, I'm sick of being told to relax. How do I do that? Maybe something really terrible is wrong with me. What am I supposed to do to relax? My father says, 'Relax.' My mother says, 'Relax.'

Jenny looked up "relax" in the dictionary. It had to do with being loose, less strict or severe. Jenny's parents were very strict, her friends all agreed. How could she relax when she always had something to do? Relaxing was a puzzle. Jenny decided it must be one of those words that means different things to different people. Maybe it had something to do with the headaches, and maybe it didn't. She wished the doctor had given her some medicine to make them go away. It felt to Jenny like the headaches were somehow her fault. Everyone seemed to agree, now, that if she would just relax, they would go away. But she didn't know how to do that. Jenny felt doomed and wished they had never seen the doctor.

When Jenny and her mother reached Woolworth's, they had grilled cheese sandwiches, and Jenny had a root beer float, which she loved. By mid-afternoon, when they headed home with their purchases, the visit to the doctor's office was far behind her.

Chapter 14

Jenny didn't mention the doctor to Becky or to anyone else. Becky and Jenny had a great adventure to plan. Mr. Black was going to take Miss Haley to West Yellowstone to meet his mother during Easter vacation. Everyone knew they were sweet on each other, although at school they acted as if they weren't. They asked Jenny's parents if she could go with them. When her parents agreed, she was allowed to choose any friend she wanted to go along.

Jenny did think of other friends, but she knew Becky hardly ever got to do anything special, so she invited her. They had to plan what they would take, and they had all kinds of secret ideas about how to catch Mr. Black and Miss Haley holding hands or kissing. Jenny's mother told her that she and Becky were going along so that the townspeople wouldn't talk.

"Do you think they'll sleep together and maybe they'll bribe us to never tell? How much do you think it would be worth?" Jenny queried.

"Well, I think the trip itself is a bribe!" Becky said. "I've never been to Yellowstone Park. I won't breathe a word."

They went to Yellowstone and there were enough kisses, hugs, and secret looks to satisfy both girls' need for romantic fantasy. When they reached Mr. Black's mother's house, Miss Haley slept in the spare room with the girls. They guessed Mr. Black slept on the couch. It didn't matter, anyway.

They had fun dipping their handkerchiefs in every pool of steaming sulfur water they passed. It was Jenny's idea, so when they arrived home, they would have something from every place they had been. It seemed almost sacred to Jenny as she folded the yellowed cloth for the one hundredth time.

On the way home, she confided in Becky, "When I leave home, I'm going to travel all over the world: Africa, India, and Australia. I think I'll save this handkerchief to dip in all of the famous seas and rivers I come to. Wouldn't that be a great idea?"

Becky, always admiring of Jenny's mind, replied with some awe, "Gee, Jenny, you have the most exciting life! That'll be wonderful. I wish I could do that."

Once settled at home, Jenny hurried to Stan's house to see if his brother, Bob, would be spending the summer. She was a little embarrassed about her feelings, but even more excited. As she opened the gate to Aunt Ethel's yard, she thought about Stan and Bob.

How strange to have your parents divorced.

She remembered living alone with her father and how important she had felt. She had been the only person in her father's life, and she had liked being so important to him. It was very lonely at times, though, without Adam and her mother. Once she had gone on the train to visit her mother. As she brought her thoughts back to Stan and Bob, she figured that was what it must be like to have your parents divorced: special and different, but lonely.

Stan answered her knock on the screen door, and they walked off toward the river. She told him about her trip to Yellowstone and her plans for building her own shelter in the woods this summer. Bob was not coming to visit after all, and oddly enough, Stan was glad.

They decided to wade across the icy river, even though it was still too cold. By the Fourth of July, the freezing glacier water would be warm enough for a swim. Waiting for the river to warm was like waiting for the first strawberries. Just as the anticipation made them sweeter and juicier, it made the river warmer.

As they stepped around the big boulders and shied away from patches of snow, Jenny felt the strength of her young body against the water. She stood still and felt the water rushing past her legs. She looked ahead to the rolling ranch hills that led to the mountains in the near distance. Jenny loved the mountains more than any other place. She always felt safe there, and the tall pine trees were like sentinels on guard, protecting her.

Stan's voice interrupted her dream of the mountains. "Jenny, what's wrong? You look strange. You're not mad, are you?"

"No. I'm just thinking, I guess. Thinking how much I love the mountains and how I can't wait for our camping trip. I wish you could come with us. We could build a shelter together, like the clubhouse, only out of pine branches instead of old boards."

"Wow, could I?" Stan's excitement filled the quietness as they reached the other side and sat down in the warm sun.

"Oh, no. My mother would never let me bring a boy camping. It's a lot that I get to bring Emily for a week."

Jenny had been out to Emily's for several weekends. Her family had a big ranch. Once she had gone when they were branding cattle. Everyone had helped, and Larry had let her ride his horse. Now Emily was coming with her for a week. They were going to pick her up at the ranch on the way to the mountains.

"I can't take a boy," she continued. "My mom always thinks I'm doing bad things with boys . . . you know."

"Well, you did do stuff with Bob when he was here. He told me, but I knew it anyhow."

"No you didn't. You're just making that up. Besides we didn't do anything . . . and Bob promised not to tell."

Jenny was suddenly very angry. She jumped up from the rock and ran upstream to the old fallen log that crossed the narrow part of the river.

If he follows me, I'll push him in. Boys are stupid!

"I'm sorry, Jen; I shouldn't have said that. I just wish you liked me as much as you do Bob." Stan tripped a little on his words, but with his hands in his pockets, he resolutely followed Jenny. "I really like you."

Jenny had reached the center of the log. She turned to look at Stan. He was really serious, she realized. "Well, I like you, too. You're my friend, one of my very best friends."

Stan stood balanced awkwardly beside Jenny and they watched the sparkling water rushing underneath them.

This is crazy. Stan is my friend. How could this be? What if he kisses me like his brother did? I'll fall off the log!

Jenny wondered what he thought she did with Bob. They had just necked a lot, and he asked her if she wanted to see his you-know-what, and see how big it was. She told him no.

What did he tell his brother? Oh, this is awful! Why did he break his promise not to tell?

Jenny said aloud "Well, I better get home," and turned to finish their journey across the river.

"Hey, Jen, don't be mad," Stan pleaded. "I just thought maybe . . . well, maybe you would go to the Prom with me. The high school voted that eighth graders could go, you know, with parental permission. Aunt Ethel said I could go."

"I dunno if my parents will let me go. Besides, I don't have a dress. Do you know how to dance?"

"Well, we could practice. Ask them, Jenny. Ask them, will you?"

"I'll think about it," Jenny responded, but her thoughts were already rushing a million miles an hour. *Maybe if I go to the Prom, Larry will dance with me. That would be the most wonderful thing in my whole life. I know Larry likes me, even if I'm only an eighth grader. Maybe I'll tell Stan yes, if it's okay with my mother.*

"I'll think about it," she repeated to Stan, as they headed back to town. They stopped at the grocery store on the way home, and Stan bought a licorice stick. Stan's father sent him a regular allowance, so he always seemed to have money for a treat.

That night at the supper table did not seem the right time to mention the

Prom. Jenny's father wasn't in a very good mood. He spent most of dinner talking about how boys in his class didn't take school as seriously as they used to. "Things come too easy," he said. Jenny wondered what he meant by that, since she felt as if school got harder and harder. She was glad she didn't have to have her father for a teacher again.

Jimmy spilled his milk and Jenny jumped up fast to wipe it up. After supper she bathed him and cleaned the milk off. She read him a story, which gave her time to think out her plan of asking permission to go to the Prom. Before she did the dishes, when her father wasn't around, she would ask her mother about the Prom. If she was on Jenny's side, it would be easier. They'd have to figure out how to get a dress, though. But something would happen, it always did, if you wished hard enough.

As she started to dry the dishes, her father came in, took the dish towel from her, and picked up a plate. "You're sure quiet tonight, young lady. Something bothering you?" he asked as he took another plate.

"No, Daddy, I just have a lot of homework. I have a big history test tomorrow, and I'm practicing all the dates and places we have to remember. I'm fine." She wished he wouldn't help her. It wasn't a good sign, but she cleaned off the table and tried not to think about anything. She put away the pans and hung the towel up to dry.

"Good night, Daddy. Thanks for helping me."

"Fine, Sweetie. Be sure to kiss your mother good night. She's especially tired."

Jenny slipped past her father quickly to avoid kissing him. She had learned that when he did special favors for her, she could expect him to come to her room that night.

Sitting on her bed, saying dates over and over, she had a great idea. As soon as she heard her parents switch off the lights and go to bed, she put her idea into action. Quietly and methodically, she slid each dresser drawer out and placed it on her bed. With the drawers empty, she was sure she could lift the dresser and put it in front of the door, and she did exactly that. The drawers back in place and the dresser solidly against the door, she slid between the sheets and waited for the doorknob to turn. She knew he would come, and he did. Her heart was racing, and she felt her hands clench the top of the sheet; he couldn't get in!

Why didn't I think of this before? How great! He can't come in.

There was a long silence on the other side of the door and then she heard his footsteps recede across the front room floor.

What a great idea! He can never get in again! She curled up in absolute satisfaction with herself and went to sleep.

Jenny woke early. She moved the dresser back the same way, one drawer at a time, and was in the kitchen before her mother. She built a fire and put water on for oatmeal. She'd have plenty of time to go by Becky's and practice one last time for the history test. It was the happiest day she had had for a long time.

I'll get to tell Stan 'Yes' today if my parents let me go to the Prom. Maybe I'll ask at breakfast.

When they sat down, her father cleared his throat and everyone hushed; he was going to say something important. He looked right at Jenny, and she knew at once she had better not ask about the dance this morning.

"Well, young lady, I checked to see if you turned off your light before I went to sleep last night, and you had your door blocked. Just exactly what was that all about? You have something to hide in there?"

Jenny was stunned. Her mind raced. *What will I say? What can I say?*

"Uh . . . uh . . . oh, nothing . . . nothing. I just got the idea that if robbers or kidnappers came, I could block the door with my dresser and they couldn't get in my room. I was trying it out."

Her mother's startled face wore a frown. In her most worried voice, which Jenny hated, she scolded, "Jenny, what a stupid idea. You read too many books. What a silly idea. We have nothing to rob and certainly no one would come here to kidnap you. Those kind of people want money and we don't have any."

Jenny breathed a silent sigh. *At least she didn't know why I moved the dresser there.*

"What on earth could you be thinking of, Jenny? What if the house caught on fire? We wouldn't be able to get in your room. Don't ever do that again."

Jenny didn't look up. She murmured, "I'm sorry. I just didn't think, I guess."

Her father cleared his throat again. "Your mother is right. It was very dangerous."

"I'm sorry. I didn't mean anything," Jenny hurriedly whispered, as she slid her chair from the table. "Excuse me, I'm meeting Becky to go over the test questions, okay?" And she was gone.

She let the screen door slam behind her and started running. If someone called her back, she'd be out of earshot. She was ashamed about what had happened at the breakfast table, but as she kicked a stray rock down the road, she knew she was also very angry.

Sometimes I just hate him. Sometimes I just want to kick him or something. She kicked another rock. As it sailed down the road, she imagined it was her father sailing off into space, calling to her, "Jenny, Jenny, I'm sorry. Please don't kick me."

112

By the time she reached Becky's, her shoes were dirty from kicking rocks, but she had forgotten she was kicking them. Jenny knew Stan would be waiting for her, and she didn't want to see him, so she stayed close to Becky and kept chattering about the test and going camping. She started to tell Becky about Stan and the Prom, but then stopped. Probably no one would ask Becky, and it might make her feel bad.

They had talked about it when the high school Prom Committee announced that eighth graders could come. The eighth grade was bigger than the ninth or tenth, and a lot of the eighth grade girls got asked by the ninth and tenth grade boys. If you were invited by a high schooler and it was okay with your parents, you could go. So the committee had decided that eighth grade boys could go, too.

Jenny had hoped Allen would ask her. He was a ninth grader, but he had already asked Emily. She had hoped someone would ask her, but she hadn't even considered Stan. He was her friend. Besides, she hadn't asked her parents yet. And if her father was mad at her because of the dresser, he might say no. She resolved to ask her mother as soon as she got home from school, and get her on her side. That would be best.

She didn't stop at Becky's, but went straight home. As she walked up the front steps, she could hear Adam crying loudly as if he were hurt. She ran through the front door to the kitchen, and there he was, sitting on the kitchen table covered with blood. In response to her startled look, her mother said, "It's just a bloody nose, but his sweater is ruined."

"You mean his new sweater from Aunt Claudia in England?"

"Yes. I might be able to fix it, I don't know. You wash Adam up and put some bandages on those bad places. I'll see what I can do to wash this sweater."

Jenny saw that he'd suffered more than a bloody nose as she gently washed her brother's scrapes and bruises. "What on earth happened to you?" she queried.

Through his diminishing sniffles, Adam told of the fight he had had with Butch McClain.

"A fight with Butch McClain!" Jenny exclaimed. "How could you have a fight with him? He's twice as big as you! How did that happen?"

"I dunno," Adam answered sheepishly. "He just told me at school he was going to get me, and on the way home, he did. I didn't do anything. He said I was a baby . . . and I'm not a baby."

Jenny didn't know any more than Adam why boys picked on him, but they did. It made Jenny mad when he didn't stand up for himself. But Butch! Butch had no right to pick on someone half his size. He was nothing but a bully.

"You just stay out of his way, Adam. I'll take care of Butch McClain. His whole family thinks they're so tough. Let's go to the store. I have five cents, okay?" And off they went.

The next day, Jenny waited at lunch for Butch McClain. He was a seventh grader, and nobody really liked him. His father drank a lot, and they were very poor and very dirty. As she saw Butch swagger into the lunch room door, she watched, fell in beside him, and matched his stride, saying: "How come you picked on my little brother? He never did anything to you."

Jenny's mother said that sometimes people can't help being poor, but there are no excuses for being dirty. Jenny agreed with her. She couldn't stand

133

the whole McClain family. One time she had had Sissy McClain for a social studies partner, and she found out the McClains weren't very smart either.

"What's it to you, anyhow?" Butch said. "He's just a big baby. Besides, he pushed my kid brother in the lunch line, and nobody pushes a McClain around."

"Oh, yeah?" Jenny retorted. "We'll see about that. You lay your hands on my brother again, and you'll be sorry."

Butch laughed as he walked away to join his friends. "Ha! Look who's talking. Better watch your mouth or your nice pretty clothes will be ripped to shreds, too."

Jenny heard Becky's frightened voice. "Jenny, what are you doing picking a fight with Butch McClain? All the McClains are mean. You're in for real trouble."

"No, I'm not," Jenny replied. "I'm really strong, especially if I'm mad. If I was a boy, I'd be the strongest person in this whole school!"

"Jenny, that's crazy! How do you know that?"

"I don't know how I know it, I just know it, okay? He better leave Adam alone."

On the way home Jenny wondered about what Becky had said. After all, Becky is my best friend. *Maybe I am crazy. Sometimes I feel crazy, what with trying to get good grades, being a good friend, being a good person in my family, and making sure my mother doesn't find out what I've been doing with my father.*

Something was strange with her mother, too. Lately she seemed especially tired, and she was always asking Jenny questions. Not big ones, but things like "Are you okay, Jenny? Are you sure?" as if Jenny wasn't sure about her own self. She'd ask about her friends at school and her teachers, and if she was troubled about anything.

Jenny made up lies sometimes, just to satisfy her mother, little lies that she figured she wouldn't get caught in, like, "I have a book report due Friday, and I haven't finished my book yet." When Jenny said things like that, her mother would encourage her and remind her that she always did well on book reports. She would also give her extra time in her room to study.

Jenny loved her room. She was glad that she didn't have to share it with anyone. On the wall was her map of the world from the National Geographic. On either side, she had pasted pictures of the places she was going to go. One of her favorites was the Swiss Alps. If the Swiss mountains were more glorious than Montana mountains, they must truly be magnificent.

On the wall next to her bed, Jenny had tacked up a map of the United States. She knew every capitol and every state flower. She could also identify the flag of each state. She had chosen this theme for her 4-H Club project this year, and was appliqueing a map of the United States on her bedspread. It was almost finished, and it should be, if it was to be entered in the State Fair.

So far Jenny had only been to Idaho and Wyoming, and once to Canada. Often when she was in her room, Jenny thought about running away, but she didn't know how. She also knew it would be painful for her mother and brothers if she were not there. Her mother often said, "Jenny, I don't know what I'd do without you." But some day she would leave. She knew that, just as she knew she could whip Butch McClain.

Jenny was startled from daydreaming by her mother's knock. "Jenny, it's 5 o'clock. Were you going to fix supper? If you need to study, I will."

"No, I'm coming. I want to make that recipe with mashed potatoes on top."

"Okay, dear. I'll take the laundry off the line. The fire is built."

As Jenny gathered up her books, which she hadn't looked at, she wished her father would follow her mother's rules. Her mother said no one should enter the privacy of someone's bedroom without knocking and being invited in, and she never did. It made Jenny's room really, really safe, except at night.

The new casserole was good, with the golden brown mashed potatoes on top. Jenny had become an excellent cook. It was something she and her mother could share, and besides she got lots of praise from her family.

Midway through supper, Adam announced that Butch McClain had pushed him down on the playground, but Miss London saw him and told Butch to behave himself. More than that, Adam proudly revealed, Butch had said, "Listen, you twerp, you better tell your sister to mind her own business, or she'll be sorry."

"What's this nonsense?" her father asked.

"Oh, nothing really," Jenny answered. She kicked Adam under the table. *Butch was right. Adam is a twerp. Why didn't he keep his mouth shut?*

"I don't want you messing with any of those McClains, do you hear me? Not for any reason. They're a bad lot. I won't tolerate any more fighting from you, young lady. Do you understand me?" Jenny's father admonished.

"Now, John. Jenny felt really bad about Adam getting hurt so badly by Butch. I'm sure she didn't mean anything. There's so much fighting in this town, I just don't understand it," her mother said.

"Just don't let me hear of you doing anything with those McClain kids. Not even Sissy. Do you understand? Answer me!"

116 "I don't even like Sissy McClain!" Jenny said. "She's dumb. Besides, Butch is bigger than me. Why would I mess with him? I don't like him, either."

Later, when Adam was drying the dishes, he told Jenny he was sorry; he hadn't meant to get her in trouble. Jenny gave him a hug and told him it was okay. It was no big deal, anyway. However, she would beat up on Butch, and Adam better not say a word or she'd beat up on him, too.

Once Jenny had been worried and nervous when she told lies. Now, though, lies didn't matter. Lying was the only smart way to get by and stay out of trouble. It was more important to stay out of trouble than to not tell a lie. Adam didn't seem to know that yet, but then there were a lot of things he didn't know.

Butch's words were a challenge; she had to follow through. How she was going to get him, she hadn't figured out yet, but she would. Before she went to sleep, Jenny decided to deal with Butch on Friday. That way she wouldn't have to see him the next day. She would be safe on Saturday. She had agreed to clean the house that day and watch Jimmy so her mother could finish her pink satin prom dress. Jenny was surprised by how quickly her parents had said "Yes" about the dance.

She had watched more fights in the last year than she had seen in her whole life. One time at supper, when her mother was fretting about it, her father had said, "It's because all the folks here are ranchers or cattlemen, and we are used to living with farmers. They have different ways of surviving."

He must be right, Jenny thought, because to survive in Custer you had to know how to fight.

By the time Friday came, Jenny had made a plan. She left band practice early to carry it out. She had picked the perfect spot, an old empty garage next to the Hardware and Feed store. Across the tracks was the only way to the McClains', and Butch usually went home that way. She could count on him being alone because no one else lived over there. Jenny knew she had to surprise him. Otherwise, she didn't stand a chance.

Her heart pounding, her mouth dry, Jenny stood plastered against the side of the building, waiting. It seemed like forever, but finally she heard Butch say good-bye to Wendall Smith, who was going to his job at the grocery store. Just how many steps it would be after he crossed the highway, Jenny wasn't sure, but the gravel on the side of the road would help her hear him coming. She had to be fast. One step past the side of the building and she would jump him from behind.

It worked. Butch went plummeting to the wooden walkway with Jenny astride him like a horse, hanging onto his mop of dirty brown hair and smashing his face against the boards. "I told you to leave my brother alone, didn't I?" she said between clenched teeth.

Butch got to his knees and threw Jenny over into the gravel road bed, where she landed with a thud. Anger pulsed through her body, and just as he rose to nail her down, she kicked with all her might. Her aim was good, right in the crotch, and he fell with an agonized cry. Jenny bent over him, planting her knees in his biceps where she knew the bones really hurt. Her fists flew, hitting him over and over while he moaned and groaned in pain. Butch's mouth was bleeding, as well as his nose, but Jenny couldn't seem to stop. She just kept beating the blue blazes out of him.

Suddenly a hand grabbed the back of her blouse, and a voice from a million miles away said, "Hey you two, what's going on here? Trying to kill somebody? If you're this mad, we better get you into the ring." Pulled to her feet, Jenny looked up into the face of Mr. Kincaid from the hardware store.

"Save my soul, if girls aren't getting meaner all the time! You okay, Butch?"
"Yes sir, I'm not hurt," Butch said, as he looked toward Jenny. "Mary Lou
told me not to mess with you if you were mad. Guess she was right. I could
have whipped you easy, if you hadn't been a girl."

Jenny thought it best not to say anything. She was relieved when Mr.
Kincaid said to run on home before they got into any more trouble.

She and Butch went their separate ways, Jenny hoping that her father did-
n't have any business at the hardware store. She was pretty sure Butch
wouldn't say anything, unless he lied and said he had beat her up. Probably
he wouldn't. It was too risky, considering he wasn't well liked, and it would-
n't do to have it around school that a girl had whipped him.

As she walked up the hill to her house, Jenny wondered why there were so
many rules about being a girl or a boy. When she was younger, she wanted
to be a boy all the time, but lately, she felt different about it. She loved the
feel of the pink satin against her body, and when she imagined being a
grown-up, she never wanted to be a man.

118 On Saturday, the pink satin dress was finished. As Jenny stood before the
mirror while her mother pinned the hem, she wondered why she had ever
wanted to be a boy. She liked what she saw in the mirror, and she appreci-
ated her mother for being such a good seamstress.

"Mother," Jenny asked shyly, "do you think I am pretty?"

"No, Jenny, you mustn't think thoughts like that about yourself. You have
nice hair and pretty eyes, but beauty is inside of people. You mustn't admire
yourself; that is vain."

"Oh, well, I just wondered. The dress is beautiful, and I love it . . . and I
thought it looked beautiful on me." Why it is so bad to feel good about
yourself? If the dress is pretty, why can't I be pretty?

"Yes, dear, the dress turned out very nice. Now take it off so I can do the
hem. Why don't you make that lemon dessert for supper? There'll be
enough left over for the Wylies. They're coming over to play bridge."

That night when Jenny went to bed, she thought about Beth in Little
Women and Longfellow's "Evangeline" and wondered about being a
woman. She had never thought about herself as a woman before. She knew

she was a girl and that was okay, but being a woman was different. Thinking about being a woman seemed important now, and that had never occurred to her before. She touched her body with her finger tips and felt an excitement that reminded her of being with Becky. They weren't doing that any more. It didn't seem right, what with Becky following her around all the time. It was better just to be friends. They never talked about it either.

Jenny let her hands rest on her flat abdomen and let herself imagine that she could have a baby growing inside of her. She remembered when Jimmy was born, how tiny and exquisite he was. She had been in awe at the miracle of him growing inside her mother. It would be nice to have your very own baby, but Jenny winced. She knew how the baby got there, and she was never, ever going to do that. Never, ever! She knew if she was totally determined, she could be strong enough not to do that.

She had to be strong if what was inside of her was so bad that she would do bad things with boys. She thought maybe when she grew up, she would be a prostitute or a whore. She was afraid she wouldn't be able to stop herself. There was a part of Jenny that didn't believe her father when he told her he had to do these things to her so she wouldn't be bad. He said he wouldn't even think of doing such a thing, except he loved her and he wanted only to protect her from the badness in her. None of this made much sense to Jenny. It was too confusing.

Sometimes she could pretend she was asleep. He would touch her gently and kiss her body, and it felt kind of good if she didn't think about it being him. She also knew that she could make up her mind to anything. Hadn't she got straight A's in spelling, which she hated? And hadn't she beat up Butch McClain? She pulled the covers up to her chin and dozed off, resolved to never, ever make a baby with anyone certainly not with her father. She would fight him forever, and then she would leave home.

At Sunday school, everyone knew about the fight. "How on earth did you ever whip him, Jen?" Stan asked. "Mr. Kincaid told Aunt Ethel that Butch McClain looked like he'd been in a meat grinder."

Jenny didn't want to talk about it. "It wasn't that hard really. I surprised him, and I hit him where it hurts the most. Anyone could do it if they just made up their mind. I don't like people that bully other people. I never have."

"What did your folks say?" Becky questioned.

"Nothing. I guess they don't know. My dress is finished for the dance next week, wanna come and see it?" Her friends understood that the subject was closed.

While her parents stayed for church, Jenny walked on home with Adam and Jimmy and started Sunday dinner. She was sure, all the time she mixed the meat loaf, that she would have to deal with the fight when they got home. At least she'd say he started it, and she wouldn't tell where she kicked him. Sure enough, in the middle of dinner, her father cleared his throat "Well, young lady, I have to go to church to find out you had a brawl with that young McClain kid. What do you have to say for yourself?"

"Daddy, I'm sorry, but he started it, and I didn't know what to do but protect myself. Then he pulled my hair and made me real mad. I told him to leave me alone." Jenny hoped she was convincing.

Her father continued, as though she had not spoken. "You know how humiliating these episodes are to your mother. It would seem that you could give her some consideration before the whole town starts talking. Do you ever think of her?"

120   Jenny felt trapped, but she thought she had better go on. "Actually, no, I didn't. I'm very sorry, Mother, but he had no right to pick on Adam the way he did. He bullies everyone littler than he is. I just wanted Adam to know I would protect him, no matter what. I didn't mean to get so mad, and I didn't mean for Mr. Kincaid to tell everyone."

Her father knew she was getting upset. Jenny felt as if he enjoyed it. Why did he always have to talk about things when they were eating?

"It doesn't seem to me that a young woman who fights in the streets ought to go to a formal dance. You'll probably step on everyone on the dance floor. What do you think, Margaret?"

"You know that's up to you, John, but she was defending Adam. I don't understand how she gets herself into these things. It's so embarrassing to try to explain to everyone. But I know how upset she was at the way he picked on Adam. And she's been looking forward to this dance for so long. And there is the dress. Perhaps if she acts like a lady now and then, she won't have to be such a tomboy."

Jenny's parents always talked to each other as though she wasn't there, but her father always seemed to mellow some when her mother spoke, so Jenny just prayed he'd listen to her now.

"I've got no use for those McClain kids," he said, "but if you get into any more scraps like this, you come to me and let me settle them, you understand? Now finish your dinner." And he ended the conversation.

Jenny said, "Thanks, Dad." She forced herself to swallow every last bit of meat loaf and potatoes on her plate. She glared at Adam so he would know to keep his mouth shut. To her mother she said, "Can Adam and I make peanut butter cookies when the dishes are done?"

It was her mother's intervention that had kept her father from doing something really mean. Jenny wondered if her father was mad at her in the daytime for fighting with him at night, but that didn't make any sense. In Jenny's mind, the two experiences were not related.

Things were different between Jenny and her father. She was always on the alert with him and always expecting something bad to happen, but she wasn't afraid any more. Sometimes, she didn't even care what he thought or what he wanted. That seemed disrespectful to her, but it was the truth about how she felt.

She didn't remember having these thoughts before she had the fight with Mary Lou. In fact, she hadn't had these thoughts before she moved to Custer. It must be the fighting that made her different.

No one, not even her father, could be completely in charge of her! It was important to keep telling herself that. When he came in her room at night, she fought with him and told him to stop. She would push on his arms and clench her fists, and when he tried to kiss her on the mouth, she would bite her lips, closed tight. She had also discovered a way to lock her legs together and keep them locked. Her father would plead and beg; then he would get mad. He never got madder than Jenny, though. Sometimes the blackness would come, and Jenny wouldn't remember what happened. But most of the time, she just stayed mad.

If he wasn't so big, I'd just whip him. That was silly because he was big, and she could never overpower him physically. However, it felt good to think about it.

The dance was even better than Jenny had dreamed. She danced every dance. Even some juniors and seniors asked her to dance and showed her the steps.

It was awkward at first with Stan's Aunt Ethel bringing him over to get her. He had on his church suit, and he brought her a pink and white Carnation corsage. When he saw her in her pink satin dress, he blushed and said, "You look really pretty, Jen. That's a great dress."

Jenny liked him saying it, but it felt strange; he was her friend, after all. After the dance, her father drove them home since he had had to chaperon the dance. Jenny didn't like being alone in the car with him after they took Stan home. She sat way in the corner and kept chattering about the music and the dancing. When they stopped in front of their house, her father gave her a hug and said, "You looked very pretty tonight, Jennifer. You are going to be a beautiful woman someday."

Jenny felt so happy! She turned and gave him a big hug and thanked him for bringing them home.

Her mother was waiting up to hear all about the dance. She asked her all kinds of questions, and Jenny was happy to answer. "Did everyone like your dress? Who did you dance with? Were the decorations gorgeous? Did they have enough punch and cookies?"

Her mother made cocoa and told Jenny about her own first dance. She also talked about going off to Normal School and bobbing her hair. It was one of Jenny's favorite stories, and her mother had a picture, too. Her father dozed off in his chair. Her mother came upstairs with Jenny, unzipped her dress, and put it on a hanger. She even tucked Jenny in bed and gave her a kiss, like when she was little.

"Thank you, Mom. I had the most beautiful dress at the dance. Everyone said so and couldn't believe you made it, even though they knew you did." Jenny hugged her. "I love you, Mom."

"Yes, dear, I know. Now go to sleep." Her mother smiled and shut the door behind her.

That was the happiest day Jenny had for a long time.

Chapter 15

The next few weeks were a flurry of activity at home and at school. They were going camping as soon as school was out, so everything had to be packed and ready. They didn't usually go so early, but the man with the wood-cutting saw had something else to do in August. They needed wood to burn in winter, so her parents and their friends got wood together.

In the summer, Jenny didn't have to worry about her father. He was like a real father. She would follow him for miles, carrying his fishing basket, until he had his limit. That summer, she and Adam had an All-Summer's Contest about who could eat the most fish. It was Jenny's favorite meal: fresh-fried, rainbow trout and boiled potatoes with butter, salt and pepper.

All the logs were snaked[1] down the mountain trail so all that was left was the sawing and chopping. One reason Jenny was so strong was that she had snaked logs for three years. She could haul them down a dirt trail or in the river. Her mother and father argued every year about girls doing such hard work, but her father always won. Jenny had her own rope and a good strong pole to keep from being bumped by a log.

Not far from their campsite was an old log cabin. Jenny wondered how many logs it would take to build a house. At night her mother would make a pan of warm water for Jenny to wash up with, and after she ate, she would go right to sleep. She liked not having to sleep in the tent with her parents and little brothers. She had her own place made out of pine boughs[2]. She didn't have to do the dishes, either. No wonder she liked summer so much!

Just before the Fourth of July, Jenny and her father went to town to buy groceries and fireworks. On the way back, they went by the Newsome Ranch and picked up Emily, just as they had planned. On the Fourth, the Fire Ranger came by and said he'd be over that evening to help her father with the fireworks. All day long, Jenny, Emily, and Adam shot off firecrackers. They tied some together, shot cans into the sky, and even blew up some houses they had made out of sticks.

All too soon, summer was over. They were moving out of the big house on the hill to one closer to town. Jenny never knew why they moved so much, but her parents always seemed to have a reason. The new house had its own generator on the porch for electricity instead of the generator that the town owned. All the houses on one end of town were on the town's generator, and it was always breaking down. She guessed that was a good reason to move, especially since they had an electric washing machine and an electric sewing machine.

Jenny asked her mother if she could have the front bedroom and she said, "Fine." It had two windows, one in the front and one on the side. Her father also gave her a small desk and told her that being in high school made studying all the more important. He had given Jenny a silver dollar for having all A's on her final report card. Becky was visiting at her father's house, and Stan was in California. They would both be home by the time school started.

Jenny also had a new book, Gone With the Wind. Her mother forbade her to read it, so she hid it under the bed. There didn't seem to be any reason not to read it; it was a wonderful story. Her history teacher, Mr. Carson, had more books than anyone she knew, and he let her borrow any book she wanted. It must have been exciting to live in the South. As Jenny read about the giant plantations, about being rich and having special people to take care of you, to feed you and iron your clothes, it occurred to her that that sort of life wouldn't be so bad. But no one should ever be a slave to another person. People should not be bought and sold like cattle and pigs. No person should have to work for another person unless he wanted to. Everyone should have equal rights. She wondered, Why did they have to have a war? Why can't people agree about important things? The civil war was a puzzle to her.

Jenny's parents were both Southerners, but they didn't talk about it much. Last year when she had been studying U.S. History, Mr. Black had said that the U.S. treated Negroes and Indians badly. When Jenny mentioned it at the dinner table, she was shocked at how angry her father got. He pounded the table with his fist and said, "Teachers shouldn't put things like that in kids' heads. Niggers and Indians got what they deserved."

Jenny started to argue with him, but soon realized this was no political discussion. She never mentioned it again, but she still thought Mr. Black was right. Her father was the same way about Catholics. He said if he ever caught her hanging out with one, he'd tan her hide. There weren't many Catholics in town, so it didn't matter, anyway. People were Methodists, Lutherans, or nothing at all, not like in Willow Creek, where everyone had gone to church.

High school wasn't that much different from the eighth grade, except for Study Hall. Everyone was together for assembly in the morning. The freshman class was the biggest: nineteen students. There were only twelve seniors. Lots of kids didn't finish high school. In the eighth grade, the science and history teachers had come to Jenny's classroom, but in high school, the students went to different rooms, depending on the subject. Jenny didn't like science much, even if they did have a laboratory. She hated the idea of cutting up dead animals.

In a day or two, summer was all but forgotten. The only news was that Sissy McClain was in the hospital. She had nearly died from a gunshot wound in her hand. No one seemed to know how she had gotten shot. Her brother Butch said, "How would I know? I'm not her keeper. It wasn't me." Some people thought maybe Butch had shot her, but it was probably just an accident.

Summer had been so wonderful and so carefree, Jenny had forgotten all about her father. One night, shortly after school started, he came in her room again, sat on the edge of the bed, and rubbed her body with his hand. Jenny pretended she was asleep, hoping the darkness would come or the stories would start in her head. She acted as if she didn't hear him trying to persuade her to not fight with him anymore. She didn't want to fight him. She just wanted him to go away.

"I have to do this, Jenny. It's for your own good. It's because I love you so much. You make me have these feelings. I won't hurt you, Jenny, I promise."

Jenny lay very still as he kissed her all over, and when he took her arms and put them around his neck, she left them there. She tried very hard to imagine that she was running through Charleston, searching for Rhett, but it didn't work any more. The man next to her smelled like her father; he felt like her father. When he moved his hot body on top of her, it was her father. Jenny clamped her legs together. "No, Daddy. Please."

"Just try, Jenny. I know you can," he whispered.

Jenny heard the edge in his voice. "I tried, Daddy, but I can't. I can't! You hurt me!"

"You fight me, Jenny."

"I'm going to be sick. Stop! Please!"

He put his big hand over her mouth, and for a minute she thought she'd choke. Then he suddenly got up and left.

Jenny didn't think other fathers did things like this. She had read everything she could get her hands on, and nowhere in all the books about growing up or having babies or getting diseases did it say anything about having sex with your father. The next time they went to Bozeman, she'd look in the university library. The only topics she knew to look up were Sex and Pregnancy, but it was a hopeful enough idea that she was able to go to sleep.

On the following Wednesday, her father was home when she walked in the door; he had a stack of books in front of him. "Your mother's at the church, Jenny, and I want to talk to you. You know I have been patient and generous with you, but you're going to have to stop fighting me every night."

129

Jenny felt sick all over. He had never mentioned it in broad daylight before. During the day, they acted as if it never happened, and Jenny liked it that way. She didn't want to talk about it.

"Sit down here, beside me. I want to show you something." There were markers in the books, and he opened one. It had pictures of people with sores all over them. One picture was of a man's privates. They were in color and truly horrifying. Jenny didn't say a word as he opened another book with a picture of a woman huddled in the corner of a room. Underneath it said, "Hopelessly Insane."

"See this?" her father asked, pointing to the pictures. "This is what I'm trying to protect you from. That's what's wrong with that McClain woman so that not one of her kids are all right. Do you want that? Answer me!"

Jenny shook her head. "No, I guess not," she whispered.
"A loving father tries to protect his daughter from this sort of thing. Now, you think about it. Who knows who else in this town is afflicted? I see the

boys watching you. You better pay attention to your dad. He knows what's best. You must trust me."

In her mind, Jenny just wanted to escape. She wasn't the least bit worried about getting any of those awful diseases because she knew she would never do anything to get one. And she wasn't going to let her father do it either.

Something is really wrong about all this. Otherwise, why would it kill my mother if she found out? It's just wrong. I know it is. This doesn't make any sense.

"I have a lot of homework. May I go now?" Jenny asked.

"Sure, Sweetie. Just don't forget what I told you. Think about it."

Jenny thought about it, but not for long. She had already made up her mind. The pictures her father showed her had nothing to do with her. She had better things to do with her life. She had decided to be a journalist. She had written a story for the school paper and was doing a cartoon strip about things around school. Being a journalist would help her leave home and travel around the world.

130

1 A method of dragging or pulling logs with a rope or chain down a prescribed trail to a waterway or lumber camp.

2 Branches cut from the trees, loosely woven in a mat on the earth to form a soft bed. Beds of pine boughs were believed to be very good for treatment of hay fever and summer allergies.

Chapter 16

One great thing about school starting was that Halloween wasn't far away. Mickey, whose parents owned the grocery store, was having a Halloween party, including a scavenger hunt, which Jenny was helping to plan. She had knocked on doors and asked different people in town if they would participate, and now she was working on the clues. They had to be tricky enough to be hard, but easy enough so people didn't get discouraged.

On Saturday, her mother was taking Becky and Jenny to see "Gone With the Wind." It cost a whole two dollars for the Saturday matinee. Mary Lou had already seen it and said it was fabulous. Jenny had saved enough money for a poster with Clark Gable's picture on it. He was so handsome and so much more interesting than the dumb boys at school. They hardly mattered anymore. They seemed so immature, except for Stan, of course. They were still friends, but it was different now. Sometimes they held hands or walked by the river with their arms around each other, but he never tried to kiss her or touch her. Jenny liked that.

The party was a great success; everyone came and the scavenger hunt was super. Jenny was extra nice to Allen, hoping he would invite her to the Prom in the spring. He liked Mary Lou, but Mary Lou wasn't too keen on him.

Jenny and Mickey made sure that Jenny was Allen's partner for a couple of games, and they arranged for him to be on Jenny's team, so they spent practically the whole party together. Since Allen lived next door to Jenny, they walked home together afterwards. They agreed it was one of the best Halloweens ever. Before saying good night, they made a plan to study their science together early in the morning, then pick up Stan and Becky for a bike ride. There weren't many days left before frozen roads and snow.

As fall moved into winter, school got more and more difficult for Jenny. In fact, life in general got more and more difficult. All she could think about, night and day, was how to stop her father from doing what he was doing to her. He seemed relentless and determined, as night after night, he came to her bed and pressed his hot body close to hers. All her nightmares seemed to be coming true: she couldn't stop him.

"Please, Daddy, you're too heavy! Please, Daddy, don't hurt me! Why are you doing this to me? No, no, no! I will not help you. You hurt me!"

As many nights as she could, she stayed with friends or asked her friends to stay over, until her mother complained about it. Jenny had figured out that if all the housework was done, her mother was more likely to say yes, so she worked very hard at cooking and cleaning, and helping in every way she could.

Mary Lou was a big help to Jenny, even though she didn't know it. There were so many things that happened after school and on Fridays that Mary Lou often stayed in town instead of taking the bus home. Most of the time, her dad came to town on Saturday and picked her up, but sometimes she stayed all weekend. Sometimes Emily stayed, but Emily's big brothers drove back and forth from town in the pick-up, and Emily usually went with them.

Jenny thought about running away, but she had no idea where to go. Yellowstone Park was the furthest she had ever been, and she knew she had to have money. So far, she had saved $12.40. Every time she added a dime or a quarter, she counted it again and wrote the amount on a piece of paper. This summer she would be fourteen, and perhaps she could get a job out in the country and live with someone else. Maybe, if she was very, very determined, she could get away from her father. Nothing else seemed to matter.

Jenny's birthday and Christmas came, but things didn't change. Even her anger didn't stop him. She thought of biting him, but she was too scared. One day, when she was baby-sitting for Mr. and Mrs. Little, Mr. Little put his arm around her and scared Jenny half to death. She thought he had done that once before, but couldn't remember. She hated forgetting things, but she knew she did. She felt crazy some days. She became consumed with making sure she was never alone with Mr. Little or any other man she baby sat for. She was glad she wasn't in the eighth grade any more, where she might have to stay after school with Mr. Black. Who knows what might happen to her?

They must all know about the part of me that makes my father do this.

Every Sunday, Jenny prayed in church that she would be very strong and keep her father from hurting her and that her mother would never find out what she was doing. She used to pray that God would make him stop, but that hadn't worked, so her faith in God had wavered some. If she could only make it to summer.

One day in Sunday school, she asked her teacher, "What about prayers that you pray and pray and still nothing changes?"

The teacher's reply caused Jenny to wonder more about God, whom she had never questioned before. Mrs. Lucas assured her, "God knows what is best for us; therefore, He must choose how and when to answer our prayers."

Jenny knew what she wanted, but she wanted it now. She decided to keep praying just in case He changed his mind. In her heart of hearts, she knew how bad she was, and begged God to understand that she was doing the best she could. But nothing changed.

One night, after she had had a particularly long talk with God, the doorknob turned again. Jenny hid under the covers and locked her legs together. The battle began. His voice, his smell, his touch seemed to be all over Jenny as she began her plaintive, whispered supplications.

"No. No, Daddy. Please don't hurt me. Please, please, please! Oh, no, Daddy, you're hurting me . . . hurting me, hurting me. NO, DADDY! NO!"

The sound in her throat was no longer silent, no longer a forbidden secret, her scream entered the room. It was as though someone separate was crying out for her. Like a vise, his huge hand clamped on her open mouth, and she choked on the silent scream. Her mind, her heart, and her body were consumed by the scream, the scream no one could hear. She felt her fingernails cut through the skin of her palms. Through her bloodstream surged months of pent-up rage.

Nightmare figures surrounded her as she fought the two-hundred-pound mass of determined flesh. Familiar darkness consumed her. Demons and fire raged in her young body. Jenny unlocked her legs to kick him, but his vise-like grip burned like fire, grabbing her, clutching her. Screams swelled in her mind as her whole being spiraled. Night after night, running and running, with horror fast behind her, Satan's darkness swimming around her, twisting and turning, twisting and turning. Even in the terror and horror, Jenny could hear her own voice,

No one is in charge of me, not even you . . . not even you! Vomit rose in her throat. Jenny choked. The voice inside her raged, *Stop! Stop! Stop!*

Suddenly she felt the sharpness of a dagger. A hot, piercing, thrusting dagger attached to her father ripped her entire body in two. She was split from her crotch all the way to her shattered mind. Throbbing, pulsating movement was all about her and inside her. Jenny's darkness turned to death. As she swam in a dark, velvet pool, death caught and held her.

No sound. No breath. No Jenny.

Dead forever. Gone in the darkness.

Chapter 17

Sometime later, Jenny opened her eyes to the darkness and heard the muffled voices of her mother and father. They sounded angry, but she couldn't distinguish the words. They never fought. Why was her mother screaming at her father? She slowly turned her head, and for a fleeting moment, thought of escape. Escape to where? Besides, she couldn't move. She felt stuck to the bed. She touched her face to see if she was still alive and rubbed her fingers in the warm trickle that ran across her leg. The voice in her head silently sobbed,

He hurt me . . . he hurt me . . . I can't move.

Jenny pulled the covers over her head to protect herself and prayed as the sound of her parents voices joined her unconscious. *Please. Please, Daddy, don't tell her. Don't tell her. I'll do anything you want, but don't tell her.*

Unconscious again, Jenny did not stir until dawn. She heard the familiar sounds of her father making a fire in the kitchen. She was like two people: one talked, the other listened.

Jenny, open your eyes.

I can't.

You must, it's morning.

Her body felt unattached to the voices, as though they were above her, having a conversation about her. Before, when she had heard voices, they were inside her head. These were not. They were outside her.

She took a deep breath, opened her eyes a little, pulled the sheet off her face, and was startled to see that her hand was covered with blood. Her legs felt frozen. Perhaps they weren't there at all. She reached down to see if her legs were still alive.

The voices over her talked some more:

Jenny, you have to get up. Get up!

I can't, I'm hurt. I can't move.

You have to. You can't just lie there. You have to go to school. Move your legs!

Her legs began to move. Jenny looked under the sheet. She couldn't feel her legs, but they were still there and moving. There was blood all over her nightie, her sheets, her legs and tummy. Everywhere. The sight of the blood gave her sudden energy. She knew she was badly hurt, but she also knew that nobody must ever, ever know. Although her whole body felt as paralyzed as her legs, if she just closed her eyes and forgot it hard enough, she could get up. And she did.

It felt for a moment as if the darkness would cover her again, or worse yet, as if she would vomit. But she didn't. As she pulled at the bloody sheets, the tiny fingernail cuts on her hands smarted and oozed drops of blood, which she quickly wiped on the sheets. Moving carefully, she dressed herself. Then she quietly opened the bedroom door and headed for the kitchen. If she could just get through to the laundry room without getting caught . . .

But at the kitchen door, she was confronted by her mother. "Jenny, what are you doing?"

"Uh . . . oh, I started my period. I have to wash my sheets.

"Well, soak them in cold water while you eat your breakfast. There's plenty of hot water to wash them later. We'll put some towels in with them."

The words followed her into the laundry room. "You're late for breakfast," her mother added.

As Jenny finished with the sheets, she noticed the bathroom door was open. She crossed the kitchen quickly and shut the bathroom door. There she washed up as fast as she could. She wondered how she could possibly take her seat at the table across from her father. She stood at her chair only briefly, however, and without raising her eyes, sat down and swallowed spoonfuls of hot oatmeal. To her surprise, it tasted good. The voice in her head sighed and said to her, *Thank God he didn't tell her.*

By nine o'clock, Jenny was at her desk, studying for her history test and wondering if her mother would let her go to Mary Lou's for the weekend. They were going to be branding calves, which was always an exciting event for Jenny. For the moment, she had forgotten last night, and by some miracle, she had also forgotten the painful hurt in her body. On the walk to school, she had thought of hiding in the hayloft all day or going to the river, but the voices over her head saved her again. One voice said, *I can't go to school. I can't move. I hurt. It's too hard.*

And the quick and confident answer was, *Yes, you can. You have to. No one must find out what you did. You have to go to school. Just keep walking. You'll get there. Just keep walking.*

Jenny wasn't sure where the voices were coming from, but she was grateful and did as she was told. They seemed to help her. One voice was so confident, it must be her friend.

At lunch, Mary Lou said it was fine with her dad if Jenny came over for the branding. Emily's dad and brothers were coming to help. The next weekend they were all going to Emily's house to brand. Maybe she could go then, too. Saturday they would still be rounding up strays, and she could ride horseback all day.

For a long time, Jenny had wanted her own horse. Perhaps some day she would have one, coal black stallion or maybe a golden Arabian with a white mane and tail. Horses cost a lot of money, but perhaps someone would give her one. After all, hadn't Mrs. Brady's sister given her the beautiful opal pendant just because she liked her? Jenny's mother said it was very expensive. Maybe some day, someone would give her a horse just because they liked her.

"Jenny? You okay?" Mary Lou asked. "You look like you just went to China or somewhere."

"Oh, I was just daydreaming, I guess . . . wishing I lived on a ranch like you and had my very own horse. You're really lucky, Mary Lou."

"Oh, sure, I suppose so, but living on a ranch is more hard work than fun. Besides, who would I stay with if you didn't live in town? One of us would have to be here, otherwise, we'd never have any fun like picnics and ball games and dances, right?"

Mary Lou seemed to sense Jenny's preoccupation. As they moved from lunch to science class, she put her arm around her friend. "It's hard to believe that we got off to such a bad start. I didn't think I'd even like you, and here we are best friends."

"Just shows what you know," Jenny replied, and they moved easily into the rest of the day. But as the school day drew to a close, Jenny had a hard time not thinking about going home. She wished she didn't have to, but she hadn't come up with any new thoughts about how to do anything differently. Eventually, she would have to go home. She would have to make her bed. If she was lucky, her mother wouldn't ask a bunch of dumb questions. She could read and perhaps fall asleep. She was very tired.

As she neared home, which was only a few blocks from school, Jenny saw her mother in the backyard, taking down the wash and folding it into the basket on the ground.

"Hi, Mom," she called and walked into the yard in time to pick up the basket.

"Are you okay, Jenny? You look kind of pale," her mother said.

"Sure, I'm fine. I'm just tired. I had a terrible nightmare last night and I couldn't get back to sleep." Confident that her secret was safe, Jenny ascended the porch stairs. In the house, she scooped up her own sheets and headed for her bedroom. As she walked across the front room, the voice over her head startled her. *You're doing great, Jenny. Just forget last night. You can do it. No one will ever know.*

Once inside her room, Jenny lay down, exhausted, and stared at the ceiling. She was looking for the voice that had come in the night. Seeing nothing,

143

she decided to see if it would talk to her.

"Who are you and how do you know what I can do?" she whispered fearfully.

I'm part of you, Jenny. I'm here to help you. With me to help you, you can do anything you want, and you don't need anybody else.

"Are you my conscience?"

No, not exactly. But I'll be there when you need me, and I'll help you with the hard things. Just listen. I'll be there.

"How did you help me get to school this morning? I didn't think I could move, but I did."

I can do all kinds of things for you, Jenny. I can help you remember things you've forgotten and I can also help you forget things you don't want to remember. I'll only be there when you need me the most.

Suddenly the voice was gone. *But she must be a friend, because I sure couldn't move this morning, and I don't feel anything now. Maybe I'm going crazy. But I did have to get up, and I did have to go to school. Maybe she can help me make my father stop what he's been doing, forever.*

Jenny slipped into a sound sleep and didn't awaken until her mother called her for supper. Everyone seemed happy and relaxed at the table, and Jenny chattered about school and going to the branding at Mary Lou's. As Jenny cleared the dishes, she decided that having a Voice for a friend must be part of a dream.

For the next few nights, Jenny lay under the covers waiting like a big stiff board for the doorknob to turn. But nothing happened. After a couple of weeks, she started falling asleep without watching the door. And when the nightmares came, it was her mother's gentle voice that soothed her and rubbed her back so she could fall back to sleep.

Sometimes her father sat too close when he helped her with her homework, and sometimes he helped her with the dishes and kissed her good night on the mouth, which she hated. But he never came to her room again. He never said anything more about the bad part of her or what he had to do.

Jenny began to pretend it had never happened. It was better that way. She could forget.

Chapter 18

The school year ended, but Jenny would not be spending any more exciting days at the ranches around Custer. Nor would she go camping on her beloved mountain. They were moving again.

Part of Jenny felt bad, but another part didn't care that much. She was used to it, and there would be new people where she was going. The only strange part was that she didn't know where she was going to go to school next year. All her parents had told her was that her father had a painting job for the summer, and that when fall came he'd have work in another town.

There wasn't a big party this time when they left, but there were lots of little ones and lots of tears. Becky, Mary Lou, and Jenny promised to be friends forever and to write often. Stan said that perhaps they would see each other at the university. Jenny didn't say anything for fear of hurting his feelings, but she and Mary Lou were planning on going to school back East. Mary Lou had already sent for catalogues to Northwestern in Chicago and Stevens College in Missouri. They were going to live together and take journalism. Jenny still wanted to take drama and be an actress, but she knew Mary Lou would laugh at that.

As she took her treasured maps off the walls of her bedroom, she thought that as a journalist, she could keep her promise to herself and travel to all the places marked on her maps. No, she didn't mind moving so much this time. New places were exciting, even if they weren't out of the state.

When they arrived in Milltown with their trailer and all their worldly possessions, Jenny's family drove to the hotel where they were going to be staying. Years ago in Idaho, they had lived in an old hotel while her father painted the schoolhouse. This hotel was not as fancy, but it had a restaurant and soda fountain, which made it more interesting.

Jenny and Adam were to share a room. Jimmy would be in with their parents. The surprising news was that her mother was going to cook in the restaurant kitchen and Jenny would be her helper. It was a real job because she got paid for the hours she worked. Sometimes when it was busy, she helped wait on tables in the dining room.

Just off the dining room was the soda fountain, and Jenny soon knew that was where she wanted to be. The girls in there had so much fun, what with all the boys from the CCC[1] coming in every evening and weekend. Her mother didn't want her hanging out there very much, but in the afternoon when everything was finished in the kitchen, she'd sneak over and hang out behind the counter. She became friends with Irene, the girl who worked afternoons; she would be a Senior next year.

One afternoon, Irene asked Jenny if she could go to the movies with her on Saturday night. Jenny was surprised when her mother said, "I don't see why not. Irene seems like a very nice girl. I just don't want you hanging around with any of those CCC boys. Heaven only knows what kind of backgrounds they have."

Jenny knew that Danny, the cute one, would be at the movies because he had told her so the day before. He had asked how old she was, and when she said she was fourteen, he snickered. "Don't suppose your mom would let you go to the show with me?"

Jenny had blushed and told him, "No, I'm not allowed to go with boys." She didn't want to tell him she couldn't go with boys in the CCC or older boys. Anyway, her parents hadn't exactly said that. She just knew it.

When the girls reached the movies, Danny and his buddy were hanging around the ticket booth. Danny stepped into line with them, and with a grin, said to Jenny, "Hey, how great! Can we sit with you girls?"

Jenny felt nervous and uncomfortable, but she watched for Irene's lead. Irene just smiled and said, "Sure, why not? It's a public theater."

Jenny felt pretty stupid that she hadn't thought of that to say, but she filed it away for future use. They bought some popcorn and found four seats together. A few moments into the movie, Danny took Jenny's hand. She didn't know if she should leave it there or take it away, but she liked it, so she left it there.

He leaned over closer, put his arm around her, and Jenny felt a kind of slow blush tingle all over her skin. She looked up at him and thought, *So, this is flirting . . . Flirting with someone I don't even know! I like it!*

All through the movie Danny had his arm around her and held her hand. When the movie was over, Danny's buddy suggested they go get a soda.

149

Before his sentence was finished, Jenny said in a panic, "Oh, I don't dare go there with you. My mother would know, and I'd get in trouble." She wasn't sure how she knew that, but she did. It was bad enough to meet boys at the movie!

"There's not much else to do in this hick town," Danny retorted. "Let's walk down by the river. I saw a path there last week, and there's a lot of light from the moon." With that idea, they were off.

Irene and the other boy (Jenny never did get his name) walked way ahead, and pretty soon, Jenny couldn't see them anymore. It felt okay, though. Jenny was more comfortable with Danny by herself. He stopped walking suddenly, and began holding her very close and kissing her. Jenny felt her head get light and dizzy. There was a familiar knot in her stomach. It felt natural to bend her knees and sit on the patch of grass under the tree. Before long, they were lying down, necking, petting, and holding each other. Jenny's stomach was full of butterflies, and she hoped they wouldn't make her throw up. Sometimes they did.

This is what Becky and I used to dream about, and now I'm doing it! This feels
like absolutely the most amazing experience I've ever had. Better than the first swim in the spring when the water was so cold that I felt totally alive all over when I dived in. More exciting than the first time I jumped a hurdle with Mary Lou's horse! It's as if I'm flying, only I know I won't fall. This is like Scarlet and Rhett.

Suddenly she shivered. Danny had put his hand underneath her panties.

Oh, God! What will I do now? I shouldn't be doing this; it's not going to stop! Danny was slipping her panties down around her knees. Jenny felt completely out of control. She was still kissing him, but she didn't want him to do that part.

A voice in the tree above her said, *Just tell him to stop. Tell him no.*

Jenny snapped out of her passion and pushed him away from her. "No, Danny, no! Don't do that to me. "

Although Danny heard her, he pretended he didn't and kept pushing himself against her.

Lock your legs, Jenny! Lock your legs!

"You can't do that. Stop! Stop!" Jenny said, and burst into tears.

In astonishment, Danny released Jenny, He touched her tears with his fingertips and said gently, "Jenny, it's okay, I'm not going to hurt you. What's wrong? You've put out before . . . c'mon."

"No, no, no!" Jenny retrieved her dangling panties. "I have to go now. Where's Irene?"

"Oh, they're okay. But c'mon, Jenny. I won't get you pregnant or anything. Please? I really like you. I've been waiting and waiting for a chance to be close with you. I won't hurt you, you'll see."

Hard as she tried to hold them back, more tears spilled over her eyelids and down her cheeks. "No, no, no! I never have! I never have! I want to go!" Jenny jumped up and brushed off her light cotton skirt.

Undaunted, Danny reached for an embrace, and Jenny found herself once again in his arms. This time, she managed to stay in control of all the mixed-up feelings that his kisses provoked. She reached down, removed his hand from her backside, and started walking the path back towards town. *151*

They didn't talk, but they held hands, and at the hotel, Danny kissed her briefly. Holding both her hands he said, "It's okay, Jenny. I haven't had a girl all summer since I left California, and you're so pretty, I just forgot myself. Maybe we can go to the movies next Saturday."

Jenny said, "I have to go," and hurried up the stairs to her room where Adam was sleeping. As quietly she could, she let her clothes drop to the floor and reached under the pillow for her pajamas. Just as she slipped under the covers, the door opened and her mother entered the room. Jenny kept her eyes closed, hoping her mother would think she was already asleep, but of course, that didn't work.

"Jenny, where on earth have you been? I have been out of my mind with worry. The movie was over hours ago, and your father walked all over looking for you. Where have you been?"

"Nowhere," Jenny replied.

"Nowhere! Don't lie to me, Jenny, that will only make matters worse. Where have you been?"

Jenny searched in her mind for a way out. Finding none, she decided to tell the truth. "We went for a walk by the river and then I realized how late it was. I'm very sorry you were worried."

"What do you mean, 'we'? You went with some of those CCC boys, didn't you?"

"Well, we didn't go with them. They were just sort of there." Suddenly an idea germinated in Jenny's mind. "This guy asked Irene to go for a walk and she said 'yes' and they just walked off. I didn't know what to do. I thought I should stay with her, so Danny, this guy I know from the soda fountain, helped me follow her." Jenny relaxed. That sounded good to her.

"Did you do anything with him?" her mother asked in an accusing voice.

"Do what? What do you mean?"

"You know good and well what I mean. Did you do anything?"

"No, I wouldn't do anything like that. It just got later than I thought. I lost Irene. I don't even know where she is. Danny was nice enough to walk me home."

152

"I'll bet he was. Don't expect to do anything else this summer, young lady. Wait till your father finds out about this." Her mother left the room, none too quietly.

Oh, well, Jenny thought. I knew she'd be mad, so it wasn't too bad. But what will I tell Danny? I know I'll never get to go to another movie. I hope she doesn't say anything to Irene. I didn't want to get her in trouble, but that's what happened. Jenny felt more comfortable. Her eyes closed, and she was asleep.

The second time her mother opened the door that night was in response to Jenny's nightmare screams. She grabbed her daughter's shoulders and shook her awake. "Jenny . . . Jenny, wake up . . . you're dreaming."

Jenny clung to her mother, half awake and half asleep, and her body jerked with sobs.

"It's just a dream," her mother soothed. She loosened Jenny's clinging arms and laid her head back down on the pillow. "Shhhh, shhhh. It's just a dream. Go back to sleep now. Relax and go back to sleep."

Jenny's body stopped shaking, and her sobbing ceased to control her. She rolled her head from side to side, half hearing her mother's voice, and reached to hold her mother's hand. As her mother gently stroked her forehead, Jenny fell back to sleep.

In the morning, despite a headache and an upset stomach, Jenny went to the restaurant kitchen. She cooked eggs and potatoes for a lunch time potato salad and drained the dishes left from late diners. Her mother was busy with breakfast. They had acknowledged each other, but hadn't really spoken.

She was surprised, as she reached for the big salad bowl, to hear her mother say, "Jenny, you don't look well. Are you?"

"No, I have a headache. I think I had a terrible nightmare last night."

"Yes, you did. I couldn't wake you. I don't know why you get those things. Perhaps it's your eyes. Where did you sit in the movie?"

"I sat in the middle like you told me, and I didn't eat any junk, either. They just happen, I guess. Can I have an aspirin?"

"Yes, dear. Go on my dresser and get two. Then sit down and eat breakfast with Adam and Jimmy. You have plenty of time before lunch to make the salad."

Jenny didn't go to any more movies or on any more walks that summer. Danny didn't ask her, and in a couple of weeks, all the CCCs left town. They worked for the Forestry Department and moved around all over the country. Irene said some new boys would replace those who had left, but Jenny's intuition told her it was best to forget boys for the summer.

She became preoccupied with her growing savings. There wasn't that much to spend money on, so she let it accumulate in an envelope buried in her dresser drawer. One day, a man came in the soda fountain selling radios and watches and other things. Jenny bought a radio with twenty dollars of the money she had saved. She signed a contract to pay the man ten dollars a month for two more months; and he gave her a little book with the envelopes for her to mail her money in each month.

It was exciting to have her own radio and listen to whatever she wanted. She had no idea why her parents got so angry at the salesman. After all, he had helped her. She didn't have the whole forty dollars to give him. Her

father ranted and raved and said, "Exactly where are you planning on getting the rest of the money? School starts in two weeks and we're moving!"

Jenny knew it was another one of those questions that didn't require an
answer, so she didn't say anything.

"Damn fool thing is only worth twenty dollars anyhow," he declared. Jenny
was glad that he had not been home much this summer. Sometimes he was
gone for several days at a time. And he was wrong about her radio. It was
worth even more than forty dollars. The man had told her so, and he had
liked her and wanted her to have it.

Jenny had a new awareness: she didn't care what her family thought anymore. She knew what she thought, she knew how she felt, and that was all
that mattered. What puzzled her was she didn't feel the need to argue about
it anymore. They could do what they did, and she would do what she did.

As she finished the dishes and hung the towel to dry, she smiled to herself
and thought, I guess this is what it means to grow up. Pretty soon, I'll be
able to leave if I want to.

Later that night, as sleep was about to overtake her, she turned the knob on
her new radio to "Off." She felt a calm inside that she hadn't felt for a long
time. Her last waking thought was, I'll take my radio with me wherever I
go.

1 Civilian Conservation Corps. A New Deal Program providing employment for young adults.

Chapter 19

In two weeks they moved to Missoula. Her parents told Jenny that Missoula was a university town, and living there would make it easier for her to go to the university. All Jenny thought of was Mary Lou and their promise to go back East to school together. But she was learning not to say her thoughts out loud to anyone. If she needed to talk, she'd talk to herself. To herself she said that she was not going to the university in Missoula, and that was that.

Jenny had a strange feeling that her life would never be the same as it had been in the little towns of her past. All that had gone on before, all the years up until now, were in what was called "the past." It had something to do with the feeling of "growing up." She wasn't a little girl anymore. Sometimes that was exciting. Sometimes it seemed lonely and difficult.

Jenny also knew that she didn't want to be a boy anymore. She didn't know why; she just knew she didn't. She bought white shorts with some of her summer savings, and shaved her legs. Her mother had a fit about that, but Jenny didn't care. Her mother didn't seem to like her very much any more, and it didn't matter the way it used to.

Things were also different with her father. He never came to her room any more, although Jenny still watched and waited for fear he would. He did, however, give her hugs she didn't like and rubbed his big heavy hand against her breasts. Sometimes he would reach for her, and she could see in his eyes that he was going to kiss her on the mouth. She hated that and tried very hard not to breathe so she wouldn't smell him. The smell reminded her of the awful part of him she hated, and she would be afraid again that he was going to come to her room. But the Voice came and encouraged her to forget it, and eventually she did.

The Voice was like a good friend or a guardian angel, and even though Jenny thought it was strange and continued to wonder if she might be a little crazy, she paid attention when it advised her. It always helped, so eventually it became a part of her. Sometimes she would find she had to tell a lie to stay out of trouble, and the Voice would say, *That's okay, that's what you have to do. Don't pay any attention to what other people think and do. You know what you want and need. You have to protect yourself.*

Sometimes when Jenny needed the Voice, it wasn't there, but not often. Once at church Youth Group, she thought she might ask if other people had a Voice, but decided it wouldn't be worth it if she found out it was something bad. You could never count on the church. They had a lot of contradictory rules and ideas.

The first few weeks in Missoula were days of inner thoughtfulness as well as exploration for Jenny. Blocks and blocks of beautiful trees lined the streets, and there were big white houses with green lawns. Town was across the river, and there were so many wonderful stores: JC Penney, Montgomery Ward, Woolworths and the big Mercantile. Jenny's mother had always made most of her clothes, so it was new and fun for Jenny to walk into a dress shop, try on skirts and sweaters, and act as if she was going to buy something. There was a music store with new black ebony clarinets in the window, and a flower shop with green plants growing all over inside and a glass case with vases of carnations and roses.

School hadn't started yet so she didn't know anyone, but that was okay with her. It was almost as if she was in a movie visiting in a strange new land where no one knew her. She was in a mystery. She felt as though she was visiting a strange family, too. They had two children instead of three, and she would live with them until she finished high school and travel about the earth and become a writer. By the time summer was over, Jenny felt very grown up and separate from her family. She still loved them, but she was different and she knew it, even if they didn't.

Just before school started, her parents came home to the small house they had been temporarily living in, and her father said, "Come on, everybody, we have a surprise! We found a new house, and we have to move in right away."

Adam was already in the car with her parents, so Jenny boosted Jimmy into the back seat and off they went. Missoula had paved streets and sidewalks almost everywhere. Leaves were turning red and yellow, scattering here and there across lawns that were still green.

As they drove from one street to the next, her mother began to talk to them, but Jenny sensed it was mostly to her. She said, "We are going to stay in this place and live here for a long time. We have bought a beautiful big house, and if we all work very hard, it will be the best thing that ever happened to us."

Jenny felt her mother's excitement, especially in light of the fact that her mother never even talked about their many moves. "There! There's the street, John. It's the third house. Do you have the key? See, Jenny? The big white one that's empty. There are four bedrooms upstairs and one downstairs, and a real dining room. Adam! Don't touch the car door handle until your father has completely stopped," her mother admonished.

In a moment, they all piled out and crossed the short span of grass to the front stairs. As her father unlocked the door, Jenny peered in the etched glass window and couldn't believe her eyes, "A real staircase . . . I could get married here," she thought, and up the stairs she ran.

Just to the right was the front bedroom with two huge windows that looked onto the street. The floors were a beautiful golden brown and shiny, perfect for dancing. Down the hall were two more spacious rooms with lots of light. At the end of the hall, there was a smaller room with a tiny dormer-shaped window.

Jenny flew downstairs and interrupted everyone to inquire, "May I have the front bedroom? Please, please? It's incredibly grand, I love it. Please?"

Her mother's face clouded, and she put her arm around Jenny's shoulders. "We'll talk about all that later. We have to go back home now and fix supper. Tomorrow will be a very busy day."

There must be a secret here, Jenny thought. *How come Mother didn't really answer me?* Jenny hated half-answers, but had learned over the years to keep her own counsel.

She definitely did not like the downstairs bedroom, which had big bushes outside that covered the windows and kept out the light. Why couldn't she have the room she wanted? There were certainly enough rooms, more than enough. Her mother usually saw to it that Jenny got the room she wanted. She would say, "Every girl should have her own room," and most of the time, Jenny did. So she wondered why her mother hadn't answered her.

At the supper table, the mystery was revealed. They were going to share the big white house with boarders from the university. There would be three boarders: two in the front bedroom and one in one of the other big rooms upstairs. They would eat breakfast and supper with the family, and that would help pay for the house.

It seemed a strange idea to Jenny, but it was okay. She wasn't sure her mother liked the idea, but perhaps it was because of the extra work. So far, her father didn't have a new job, and that was strange, too. They usually moved because of a new job.

Oh, well, thought Jenny, *I'll get one of the big bedrooms upstairs, and school starts in a week.*

By Monday morning, they had moved into the new white house. *This house is like the town,* Jenny mused, *bigger than any place I've ever lived. And I'm bigger, too, inside.*

She and Adam walked to the junior high school together and awkwardly said, "So long," to each other. They had always been together, and although neither of them wanted to admit it, these schools seemed big and strange to them. Down the street from the junior high was the big two-story high school. It took up most of the block, and there was a huge dome-shaped gymnasium across the street. Jenny had never been to such a big school with so many students. She was nervous, but excited, a familiar feeling for her.

She had registered last week and been assigned a Big Sister to help her the first few weeks. Her name was Joyce, and she seemed nice. As Jenny walked through the big double doors and headed toward the library where they were to meet, she was glad to have Joyce, even though it had felt awkward to be a newcomer and have a stranger show her around like a little kid. Joyce showed Jenny her first-period class and agreed to meet her at the cafeteria for lunch. By the end of the first day, Jenny felt she belonged there. Names, faces, rooms and assignments all blurred together as she walked home, but she liked it okay.

The school library was huge and she could go there every day during study hall. In biology, there was a genuine laboratory with dissection kits and microscopes. She wasn't sure she wanted to do the dissecting, but the equipment was fascinating. As she passed by the windows of the corner grocery store, her reflection looked back at her and she liked what she saw. She was definitely a new person. She wasn't sure who this new person was, but she would get to know her day by day.

Jenny was fascinated with her new-found knowledge. *Amazing!* she thought to herself. *I can be whoever I want to be. I just have to keep deciding every time something new comes along, who I am; then I'll know what to do. I'll just ask myself, and I'll know inside. If I'm not sure, I can ask the Voice, and it will help me.*

Her footsteps on the back stairs had a new lightness, and as she opened the door, she called to her mother and dashed upstairs. At the top of the stairs, she ran smack dab into the last of the new boarders.

"Oh, Floyd!" she breathlessly exclaimed, "I'm sorry. I didn't see you."

Floyd's open hand caught her around the waist. "Whoa, there. You in a race or something? Almost sent you tumbling back down the stairs." He grinned as he set her free.

As she walked the short distance to her room, Jenny enjoyed the warm tingle just under her skin, and she let the first blush fill her body as her heart beat quickened. She didn't dare think Floyd liked her. He was a college student and he was soooo handsome! He always looked right at her when he spoke, and his eyes always had a smile, too. They were a deep green color, with specks of brown.

The other two boarders were nice, but they seemed very busy. One of them ignored Jenny, the way her parents did sometimes, when they talked about her as if she wasn't there. It was extra work, cleaning their rooms and cooking extra food, but it was like having company all the time. Jenny liked it. Perhaps it wouldn't be so bad to stay home and go to the state university after all.

By the end of the second week, Jenny had joined the debate team, tried out for the pep band, and been invited to a party after the first football game. Her mother said, "No," but Jenny knew she'd find some way to go. She wasn't going to refuse an important person like Allen, a football player and a class officer.

By the night of the game, she still hadn't figured out what to do, but she intended to go to the party anyway. It didn't matter that the last words she'd heard her mother say were still ringing in her ears when the game ended: "Jenny, remember you are to go to no one's house. I don't know these people. You may go to the soda fountain, but be home by eleven o'clock."

She didn't breathe a word of this to any of her friends. After all, wasn't she grown up? And didn't she have the right to decide where she would go?

In the car, Allen offered her a bottle of rum and some cokes. Jenny said, "No, I don't drink," but when he handed her the bottle, she took a sip so as not to seem dumb. She had never tasted alcohol before, and she didn't like it very well.

They were in the back seat, and she didn't know who was driving. They had lost the ball game, so no one wanted to talk about it. Allen said the pep band was great, and they'd win the next game. He had his arm around Jenny, and suddenly he leaned over and gave her a long, hot kiss. Jenny's stomach fluttered, and her whole body leaned toward his. As the car swerved around the corner, his tongue slid into her mouth. Jenny gasped, let herself respond, and wondered how far away the party was. The tires squealed, the car stopped suddenly, and they were there.

At first, the party was fun. Everyone danced, and Jenny met some kids from her classes. Most of the party-goers were juniors or seniors, which made Jenny feel important since she was only a sophomore. After a while, it got so jammed that she couldn't really dance, but before long, she noticed a lot of kids were leaving.

She went to look for Allen. She was anxious to leave, since she had no idea what would happen when she got home. Allen was nowhere. Jenny opened every door in the big, unfamiliar house. Every room was filled with adolescent lovers in various stages of undress. She didn't look long enough to see if any of them was Allen. She ran to the front door and stepped into the chilling autumn night.

Then she realized she had no idea in which direction her house was. With tears stinging her eyelids, she re-entered the empty front room and sat down at the piano bench, near the door. She swallowed her tears and played some random chords.

Allen must be somewhere. He'll come soon and take me home. He was probably just upset because I wouldn't drink anything after the one sip in the car. But I've decided that I won't drink and I won't smoke. I don't like the way either one tastes. I'll just wait, and he'll take me home. He wouldn't bring me and not take me home.

She soon ran out of chords. Just as awkwardness consumed her, a slight boy slid onto the bench beside her.

"Oh, hi, Gordon. Do you play?" Jenny asked.

"Oh, about like you do. We could play together," he replied, so they did for a while.

Jenny already liked Gordon, who was in the debate club. He had had polio when he was little, and his legs were never okay after that. They didn't grow much, so he was short and used crutches to help him walk. He was a genuinely nice person and began to ask friendly questions about Jenny's previous homes and her family. Jenny realized she and Gordon were just sitting there being polite, but she didn't know what else to do but keep talking.

Suddenly, Gordon reached over and took her hand saying, "Hey, Jenny, you want me to walk you home? No telling where that jerk Allen is."

Jenny was so thankful she just blurted, "Oh, but I don't know where I live! Well, I know my address, but I don't know how to get there from here."

Gordon laughed. "Don't worry, I've lived here my whole life."

It was one of the nicest times Jenny had had since coming to this new town. The walk made her think of her friend, Stan, and how she missed him. She and Gordon didn't talk as personally as she and Stan had, but it was nice. Gordon seemed to be so comfortable with himself. Wilkie was running against Roosevelt for President, and Gordon had made a bet with Allen that if Roosevelt won, Allen would push him all the way to the train station in a wheel barrow waving a sign on his back saying, "I Voted for Wendall Wilkie."

Gordon was smart. He wanted to be a lawyer. Jenny shared her dreams of being a journalist. He said he thought she would be very good at it. They talked about politics and religion. Gordon was Jewish, her first Jewish friend, which was a new experience for Jenny. She liked him and was grateful for his friendship.

Jenny had no idea what time she arrived home. The walk had gone slowly with Gordon, but she didn't think it would be polite to try to hurry him. He said he lived only a few blocks from her house, not too far from school. He squeezed her hand before he turned toward his house. "Don't be too hard on Allen. He's a great guy, he just drinks too much and forgets what he's doing. He'll be sorry on Monday."

He may be neat all right, Jenny thought, *but he's not taking me to any more parties and then ditching out on me!*

The light was on in her mother's room, and as soon as Jenny opened the door, her mother's voice pierced her ears. "Jenny! You come here this instant!" And Jenny did just that. She stopped in the doorway and noticed that her father was not there.

"Where's Daddy?" she asked. Anything to prevent the inevitable.

"He drove to Helena for a meeting. He won't be back until Wednesday. Where have you been? I've been sick out of my head with worry. I distinctly told you that you could not go to a party at someone's house that I don't know. And shut the door! I don't want our boarders to know how you behaved."

165

Jenny took her time shutting the door, and stepped inside just enough to lean on the dresser. *This calls for a lie,* she thought, *but she'd have to make it up as she went along.*

"I got lost was the main thing that happened," she said, letting a few tears fall. "I didn't mean for you to worry, honest I didn't. After the ball game we were supposed to go to the malt shop, and after a while, I knew we weren't headed toward town. I told Allen I couldn't go to the party. He said he'd just take the other people there; then we'd go get a soda and he'd take me home. I really believed him, but by the time we got to Carol's house, everyone was drinking.

"I knew you'd be worried, so I just left on my own. After a while, I didn't know where I was and got lost. I thought I knew where our street was, but it was so dark . . . So I found my way back to the party. There was a boy there that's in the debate club. You know Gordon? I told you about him, the guy with the braces? He walked me home, and it took a long time."

Jenny kept her eyes on her mother, always to see how her story was registering. At the end, she breathed a silent sigh and waited.

"See what I told you?" her mother said. "You don't know anything about these people. I just knew there wouldn't be any supervision. Jenny, you just have to quit trusting everyone. You could have been in big trouble. I was so worried. This boy must be very nice to bring you home. What was he doing at such an awful party?"

"Well, he was sort of in the car, too, and we didn't know what to do. It will never happen again."

"You're lucky your father isn't here. He would never put up with this, you worrying me like this. Give me a good-night kiss and get to bed. And don't ever let this happen again!"

In the weeks that followed, school became Jenny's main focus. She didn't make any close friends, but everyone liked her and that was enough. Her father didn't come home; he went to work in Helena and stayed there. Once in a while he called home, and once in a while, he came home for the weekend. Jenny didn't know how to be with just her mother. One day, her mother would say, "Yes," and the next day she would say, "No." No matter how hard Jenny tried to do what she thought her mother wanted, her mother was always worried, hurt, or angry.

Her mother didn't seem to understand that Jenny needed friends. She couldn't just do what her mother wanted all the time. She had to do what the other kids were doing. She had to stay after school for band practice. She had to go to the malt shop. She had to study at the library if she wanted to make the debate team, and she had to make the team; otherwise, how could she make close friends? There were so many kids in this school.

But her mother continued to say, "No." Jenny decided it had something to do with her father being gone. Maybe they were going to get a divorce like Becky's parents. Maybe she'd go live with her father. He hadn't come in her room for a long time, and he couldn't possibly be as unreasonable as her mother.

In the meantime, she made up as many stories as she could about where she was and what she was doing. She even said she'd been at band practice when she'd been at the library, or at the library when she'd been at the Malt Shop. It was a kind of game she played with her mother. She didn't know exactly why she played it. Most of the time her mother didn't believe her anyway.

For the third time, Floyd had come into her room at night, and she didn't know what to do about it. The first time had been terrifying and intoxicating at the same time. He smelled wonderful, as he always did at breakfast time, and his hands were soft and gentle. He knelt on the floor by her bed and whispered in her ear about how beautiful she was. He told her he couldn't sleep from thinking about her and wanting her. His lips touched hers lightly, with just a promise of passion, and Jenny liked it. She liked the secrecy and the whispering. She liked feeling beautiful and desirable.

But last night, he had slid his leg under the covers, and Jenny's stomach had tightened up in an old familiar knot. Floyd hadn't had his pants on, and that scared her. She wished he wouldn't get so carried away.

But she didn't have to think about it in the daytime. The Voice told her how to act as if it had never happened. All she had to do was imagine it wasn't true, and it wasn't.

167

Jenny wondered what God thought of all this. She wasn't sure, any more, what the truth was, or if it mattered one way or another.

Not too long after Halloween, and before her birthday, she stayed after Youth Group at church. Everyone who hadn't gone home early went for a ride. By the time Jenny was dropped off at her house, it was much later than it should have been.

Jenny saw her mother's bedroom light on. She couldn't bear to listen to her one more time, so she sat on the back step for a long time. The night air was cold, and just sitting made her shiver. She decided to go for a walk, and ended up back at the church.

On the way, she had pretended that the minister would be there, and that she could talk to him. She wasn't sure what she would talk about, but she liked him and knew he liked her. Of course, he wasn't there, so she sat on the church steps for a while until it was too cold to sit there any more.

She had finally decided what to do. She would run away. She would go find her father.

Chapter 20

It was dark on the highway, and Jenny had to keep walking so as not to feel the cold. When cars went by, Jenny slipped into a ditch and lay flat against the side of the road. She wanted a ride, but she was far too frightened to be seen. Jenny felt frozen and lonely. A few tears brimmed up in her eyes.

Now I can never go home, she thought. My mother will never forgive me. I'll have to keep going till I find my father.

Jenny saw the big truck coming, but by now, it was all she could do to put one foot in front of the other, let alone jump down in the ditch again.

At first, the driver thought he saw the shadow of a kid along the side of the road, but just as he passed by the figure, he saw it was a girl. He slammed on his brakes and pulled over as far as he could on the shoulder of the road, just in time to see her duck down to hide. He stepped down onto the gravel and took the few strides to where she was crouched.

"C'mon, kid! It's cold out here. Get in my truck. I'll take you where you're going. It's the middle of the night!"

Jenny didn't know how to say, "No." She felt totally forlorn by this time, not sure who she was, where she was going, or why she was out here in the cold, dark night.

He seemed kind, so she followed along and climbed into the high cab. Before the rear wheels hit the pavement, Jenny was sound asleep.

Jenny had no idea how long she had been sleeping when she became conscious that the engine was no longer running. She stirred and peeked from behind her eyelids to see the driver lift his thermos cup to his lips.

"Want a sip of coffee, kid?"

"Oh, no, thank you. I don't drink coffee."

"What's your name?"

"Jenny."

"Where the hell you headed?"

"To see my father."

"And where might that be?"

"In Helena."

A grin, which began in his eyes, covered his face and he broke into a quiet, easy-going laugh.

"Then you're headed in the wrong direction, kid. I'm headed for Seattle. Know anybody there?" he asked laughingly.

"No." Jenny gulped in embarrassment. She hadn't thought about which way to go; she had just left town. She felt crazy and sick. Suddenly the Voice saved her. As clear as a bell, it said, *You can get by in Seattle, Jenny. You can get a job. We'll be okay. Just tell him to take you there.*

Her own twinkle came back as she looked across the big seat. She smiled and said in her most confident voice, "Then I guess I'll just have to go to Seattle. I'm not walking all the way back."

"Okay, kid. If you change your mind, you can stop off in Spokane. For now, you may as well enjoy the ride." And he reached across the space between them and pulled her seemingly confident self next to his body. His rough palm moved up her inner thigh. Jenny's young body stiffened as he reached his goal and slid his fingers inside her.

She was startled by the sound of his voice. "Relax, Baby. I'm not going to hurt you. Just a little fun to break up the night." Jenny heard his big belt buckle unsnap and his zipper open as he moved her body under his on the side seat. As his free hand reached to pull her panties down, she burst into tears.

"No. No. No! Please don't hurt me," she said. "Please don't hurt me."

He jerked his body away. "Jesus, kid. What's wrong with you? I'm not hurting you." He pushed her into the corner and brushed his hair back, breathing heavily. Looking sharply at her, he said, "How old are you, anyhow?"

"Fourteen," Jenny replied. "I'm sorry."

He jerked the truck door open and jumped onto the gravel below. "Shut up and just wait here. I'm getting rid of you."

After what seemed like forever, he came back. He was kind and gentle again. Jenny had thought he would be angry, but he didn't seem to be.

"I'm sorry," she said again, from her corner sanctuary.

"Hey, don't say that. I'm taking you to my sister's place. She lives up the road a piece. I wasn't going to stop there, but she'll know what to do with you. And don't you say nothin' about what just happened, you understand? It never happened. I'll be in big trouble. You don't want that do you?"

"No. I'm sorry I cried. I won't say anything."

"And don't say you're sorry, either. You should have told me sooner how old you were. Now go back to sleep."

As the big truck rolled across the state, Jenny couldn't fall asleep, but she pretended to. She could tell when they left the highway. She wondered what he would tell his sister. She had no idea what would happen next, but she figured she'd get to Seattle some way. If the Voice thought she could make it there, she probably could.

Before long, the truck driver was showing her to the door of his sister's house. It took him a while to wake his sister, but when she came to the door in her pink chenille robe, she didn't seem upset.

"Well, Hi, Hank! Didn't expect you to stop tonight, or I'd have left the screen unhooked."

"I wasn't going to stop, and I got to get going. I'm way behind. But I picked this kid up halfway out of Missoula, and she's got no idea were she's going or what she's doin'. Thinks she's on the way to Helena. Someone probably looking for her. Can you take care of it? Didn't wanna leave her out in the cold."

His sister smiled, and put her arm around Jenny's slender shoulders. "Why, of course. We'll get some sleep and take care of it in the morning. You want a cup of coffee?"

"No. I gotta get some miles behind me." He turned to Jenny. "Now listen, kid. You remember what I told you. And you got no business in Seattle. Better go home and grow up. Your mom is probably real worried about you. So long." He was gone.

"Sit down, Sweetie," his sister said in a soothing voice. "I'll make you a cup of cocoa, and then you need to get some sleep. You look exhausted. My name is Valerie. What's yours?"

"Jenny," she said as she slid behind the table and sat on one of the straight kitchen chairs. Jenny was grateful that Valerie didn't start asking a lot of questions. She just heated milk and set cups on the table while she chattered about her brother, his truck run, and how sometimes she'd catch a ride to Spokane with him. As they sat across the table from each other, drinking cocoa, a train whistle echoed through the valley. "Where do your folks live, honey?" Valerie asked.

173

"In Missoula. Well, actually, my mother is in Missoula, and my father is in Helena. That's how I got mixed up."

Jenny knew her embarrassment showed on her face, so she kept her head lowered. Valerie reached over, and patted her arm. "That's okay, Sweetie. Everybody's got problems. Don't feel bad about Hank. Did he try anything on you? You know, get fresh or anything?"

"Oh, no . . . No, he was very kind to me. Just picked me up and asked me how old I was. Then he said I couldn't go to Seattle with him, and he'd bring me here." Jenny hoped she was convincing. She was in enough trouble already.

"That's good," Valerie sighed. "He doesn't always use good judgment. His heart's good, but he's crazed about women sometimes."

"No, no. He didn't touch me. I just slept. I was so cold and tired," Jenny assured her.

"Let's see what we can find for you to sleep in . . . me rattling on like this, and you being so tired. C'mon, we've got plenty of time to call the sheriff in the morning. Sure as shooting, they're lookin' for you."

As anxious as all this talking made her, Jenny fell sound asleep. The sun was high in the sky when Jenny wakened in the strange, clean smelling room. For a few seconds, she wondered how she had come to be in this place. Then memory returned, and she closed her eyes and wished for sleep to come back.

When it didn't, she visually explored her surroundings. There were fluffy yellow curtains at the window with matching yellow roses that climbed all over the wallpaper, and there was a yellow paper rose in a vase on the dresser. It was a nice room. Jenny wondered if Valerie would let her stay. Perhaps she could get a job here and go to Seattle later.

She was startled by a knock on the door. Valerie's voice, as soothing as it had been last night, asked one of those questions that's really not a question. "Jenny, are you awake, dear? The Sheriff is here, and he needs to talk to you. We're in the kitchen."

174

Jenny knew she meant, "You have to get up now." She slipped into her rumpled clothes and opened the door to the short hall. Standing there, she couldn't remember which door went to the bathroom and which went to the kitchen. She could feel her heart pounding as she moved away from the sound of a man's voice. In the safety of the bathroom, she splashed water on her face and smoothed down her long, straight hair. She knew she had to face the Sheriff.

If I hadn't gotten so scared last night, and just did what Hank wanted, I wouldn't be here. I'd be clear out of the state! If I ever run away again, I'll plan more. I'll bring some clothes and a comb and stuff.

She opened the kitchen door, wondering if she was shaking as much on the outside as she felt on the inside.

"Hi," she said softly. Valerie came and put her arm around Jenny in a reassuring way. The man leaning against the kitchen cupboard looked huge in his tan uniform with the big silver star. Then he stood up, which made him look even bigger.

"I'm Officer McBride. You Jenny Bennett?"

"Yes, sir." Jenny spoke more towards the floor than to the officer.

Valerie nudged her over to the kitchen table and sat her down in the chair. "Here, Sweetie, have some warm tea with plenty of sugar, and I have toast in the warming oven. You must be starved. We'll fix you some eggs after you've answered some questions for this gentleman. Won't you sit down, Officer? You want a cup of coffee?"

He didn't seem so ominous sitting across the table. But Jenny's mind was whirling, wondering what he would ask her and how he knew her name.

"I been talking to your mama on the telephone," he said, "and you like to frightened her to death. She's sick from not knowing where you were. I want you to write her a letter today, and tell her how sorry you are for worrying her. Your daddy is coming from Helena, and they'll be here day after tomorrow to get you. Now I have to fill out some papers, so I'm going to ask you some questions. You just tell me the truth, and this won't take long. Valerie tells me her brother, Hank, picked you up on the highway. That right?"

"Yes."

"About what time did he pick you up?"

"I dunno."

"How far out of Missoula were you?"

"I dunno."

"Where were you headed?"

"I dunno."

"Valerie tells me you thought you were going to Helena. That true?"

"Yes."

"And what were you going to do there?"

"See my father."

175

"How old are you?"

"Fourteen. I'll be fifteen next month."

"You got no business out on the road, young lady. You're real lucky it was Hank picked you up and not some other trucker. He did you a real favor bringing you here. Valerie's a mighty fine woman, and she's agreed to keep you till your folks come. Otherwise, I'd have to put you in jail. We got no place for kids around here. Just have to keep them in jail till someone comes for them."

Jenny's stomach turned to stone when Officer McBride said jail. *Why would I have to go to jail?* she wondered. *I haven't done anything.*

Officer McBride closed his notebook, pushed his chair back on the slick linoleum floor, and unfolded his long legs.

"You stay here with Valerie. I've assigned you to her custody, so you have to stay with her. Any idea of running away, I'll pick you up right away. You understand?"

176

Jenny wasn't sure he wanted an answer, but she was sure she didn't want to go to jail. She raised her head and looked straight at him. "Yes, sir, I understand."

"She don't have to keep you, you know. It's a long ways over here, what with your dad clear across the state. You eat a good breakfast, now, and write that letter like I told you. Bye now." His big back turned, and he pulled the door shut behind him.

Jenny felt like crying, but there weren't any tears. She didn't know for sure how she felt. Just strange. While she ate the scrambled eggs Valerie fixed for her, she wondered, *What have I done that's so bad? Is making your mother worry against the law? It must be,* she decided. She heard Valerie repeat what Officer McBride had said about how lucky she was because of how much her mother loved her and how worried she was. As soon as her mother realized that Jenny wasn't home, she had called her father in case he had heard from her. Since he hadn't, they called the police and the Highway Patrol.

Valerie went on to say that after Jenny had gone to sleep last night or this morning, actually she had called the Sheriff and learned there was an all-points-bulletin out for a girl named Jenny, fitting her description. Both the Sheriff and Valerie had called Jenny's mother so she wouldn't worry. Then this morning, they had made arrangements to get Jenny home. At first, Valerie had planned to take her home on the bus. However, Jenny's father had already left Helena to come get her, so everyone thought it would be best for Jenny to stay with Valerie.

Valerie asked if she was having problems at home, but Jenny figured since they were all so concerned about her mother, she had better not admit that they weren't getting along.

She had to say something, though, so she told Valerie, "I guess I was just confused. I missed my father. I used to talk with him when things weren't right with my mother. I was late coming home again, so I just decided to go see him." Jenny also decided she had better start acting sorry, since there didn't seem to be any other way out of this mess. When the dishes were cleaned up, she and Valerie went to the store. Valerie bought some note paper for her to write to her mother.

The letter came easy, once Jenny started. By mid-afternoon, she was feeling homesick and lonely. She also felt very bad. Not just bad because she was lonely, but like a bad person. Jenny didn't actually believe she was a bad person, but it seemed like bad things were always happening to her. Bad things weren't supposed to happen if you were good. That was one piece of evidence that she had. A second piece was that she always got this sick feeling in her stomach whenever she did something she knew she wasn't supposed to do. Even telling lies sometimes made her feel sick. The third proof that she was bad was that her father had told her so.

177

She could hear her father's voice telling her that he came in her room and did things to her because he loved her, and because she was bad and only he could help her. While it was happening, Jenny hadn't really believed him, but now she couldn't think of any other reason for her behavior. She must be inherently bad. She did love her mother, passionately, and she loved her father, too. Yet she hurt them all the time. So it followed that she must have something inside of her that was truly bad to cause them so much pain.

She looked out the window at the naked autumn trees with only a few leaves left on their outstretched branches. *I feel like the tree: I have no place to hide any more. All my leaves have fallen, and everyone can see me. I am ashamed to be such a bad person.*

As she gazed out of the warm room into the cold crisp world, tears spilled out and dripped off the end of her nose onto the paper. She thought of the big brick church with its smooth wooden pews and beautiful stained glass windows; she loved to sit there and watch the sunshine dance colors through the windows onto the wood.

Jenny often cried in church, but she didn't know why. She guessed it must be because she was bad and she knew it. God confused Jenny. Just when she thought she knew who God was and what He had to do with her, something happened to confuse her.

She remembered a time she had watched a pair of beavers build a dam. One beaver, which came up really close to her, gnawed down a whole tree. She never moved and almost didn't breathe as she lay there with her tummy flat on the grass. She felt that she could have been a beaver just as well as a person. She wondered if God chose some souls to be people and some to be beavers, deer, or chipmunks, but loved all His creations equally. But if He loved her, why was life so hard and confusing? She wished she could live in the forest forever.

What happened in church, sometimes, was almost like that day with the beaver. One day, she imagined she was a ray of blue color dancing through the window. It was like magic, but she couldn't make it last very long. When she listened to the words of her teachers, she was reminded that she was a person, and more often than not, a bad one. There was hardly any way out of being bad, either, since the Bible said that even bad thoughts were held as a sin in God's eyes.

A cloud covered the sunshine, and Jenny went back to her letter. *Perhaps my mother does love me, like everyone says she does. And if she does, she must feel sad that I am so bad. I will promise her to be very, very good. And she'll know how sorry I am for being so bad. I have no idea why I kept walking until I was on the highway. Once I got started, I just couldn't stop. It seemed right at the time, but it doesn't seem that way now.*

For some time after the letter was finished and Jenny had sealed the envelope, she thought about the Voice and how it always seemed to help her out when she needed it. She thought it was good, so she usually did what it advised her to do. But what if the Voice was bad? In that case, she shouldn't pay any attention to it. The strange thing about the Voice, though, was that it seemed to have a life of its own. It wasn't usually available for conversations or arguments. In fact, if she questioned the Voice, it just left. That quality made it clear to Jenny that, indeed, the Voice was good.

Jenny, on the other hand, talked to herself all the time, with or without the Voice. She went over all the arguments she could think of before she decided anything. When it came to her, the Voice usually agreed with Jenny about the things Jenny felt most confident about. She wished that she could call on it whenever she wanted, but it didn't work that way. She never knew when it would be there and when it wouldn't. The Voice just came out of nowhere.

Jenny was startled by Valerie's voice inviting her to eat supper. She had dozed off and was surprised to see that it was dark outside. Valerie's husband was a truck driver, too, and he was due home later that night. It was easy to be with Valerie, because she talked all the time and she didn't seem to need any reply. She would ask questions, then go right on with what she thought the answer should be.

Jenny had started to feel anxious about her parents and what might happen to her, so she didn't have much to say back to Valerie. She felt thankful that Valerie had let her stay there, in spite of Jenny's being such a bad person. The thought of jail terrified her. She had never even seen the inside of a jail, but what she'd seen from the outside didn't give her any desire to find out.

She decided right then and there that she would never run away again, no matter what happened. She was so ashamed of what she had done that she wished she could make it all vanish. Right now, though, she just had to make it through the next few days.

The funny part was, when her parents arrived, they were very happy to see her. They kept thanking Valerie over and over for being so generous and kind. Every now and then her mother would say to Jenny, "I just don't understand whatever made you do such a thing. Why didn't you come and talk to me?" All Jenny could say was, "I'm sorry, Mother," and "I dunno."

Her father talked mostly to Matt, Valerie's husband, about the upcoming deer season. By the time they started home, it was as if nothing had happened.

Jenny wasn't sure if she would get punished or not. She hated it when she didn't know. She found out when she got home, however. Before she went to bed, her father called her into the front room and told her how disappointed he was that she couldn't get along with her mother. Jenny should be ashamed, he said, for putting both her mother and him through this anxiety and worry.

"Anything could have happened to you out there on the highway," he said. "You didn't use you head at all. You got some fool notion you can come live with me. Well, you can't. Your mother needs you to help her, and I don't want to make this trip again on account of you. For the next two weekends, you stay home and help your mother. She can decide if she can trust you out of her sight. Another episode like this, and you won't be able to sit down for a week. Understand me?"

"Yes," Jenny whispered, with her eyes on the floor. It was a relief to know where she stood. The weekends wouldn't be too bad only she didn't know what to tell her new friends. Maybe she could say her mother was sick. It would be terrible for anyone at school to know what she had done. Running away seemed like a shameful thing to have done, but running away in the wrong direction was just plain stupid. She was glad now that Adam didn't go to the same school. He never kept his mouth shut about anything, especially if it had something to do with her. Sometimes Jenny wondered if he would ever grow up.

She climbed the stairs to her room, wishing she had Becky or Stan to talk to. She missed having best friends. They might not understand why she did what she did, but they wouldn't care. They'd still be friends, and they'd listen to her fear and loneliness. They would also listen to her anger, and right now she was angry at her father. It reminded her of the old anger, and she wished he would go back to Helena.

Once in bed, she pulled the covers up. With her head resting on the pillow, she felt happy to be in her own bed. She was glad to be home.

Chapter 21

The days grew shorter and the nights grew colder. By Jenny's birthday, frost covered the trees and flurries of snow made a thin blanket on the brown lawns. By midday it would melt, but it would be back by the next morning.

Winter was an invitation that Jenny loved: holidays, skating parties, long evenings with her favorite books, and bowls of fragrant popcorn. School was an exciting adventure with all the extra activities to choose from. She didn't make the debate team, but underclassmen hardly ever made it, and she was a newcomer. She was an alternate, however, and she would make the team next year.

She went to some Friday night dances with Nick, whose father owned the Malt Shop. His family had come to America when he was ten years old and had lived in Chicago for two years before moving to Missoula. He said he was Greek, but there was a rumor that his family was Nazi. Someone told Jenny that they had meetings in the basement of the Malt Shop, but she never asked about it. Nick was very handsome and kind of mysterious. He was a good student and a good dancer. Jenny liked his quiet, shy ways. Though all the gossip made her mother nervous, as long as Jenny came home on time, there was no more trouble.

After school they would walk to the Malt Shop and have a coke before Nick had to go to work; then Jenny would walk home. He was like a boyfriend, but they never talked about it. Nick was intensely interested in the European war and in studying English grammar, so they studied together. Grammar was easy for Jenny, since her parents always insisted on proper usage; history was easy for Nick. This impressed her mother, so he was permitted to come to her house.

One night at dinner, Floyd teased her about having a foreigner for a boyfriend. "I understand those European men really know how to treat a woman. Is that true, Jenny?"

Jenny was embarrassed clear to her toes, considering what Floyd was still doing every other week or so. She supposed he thought that Nick did things like that with her, but he didn't. He held her hand and he kissed her, but he never touched her anywhere else. He was a gentleman. When Floyd saw Jenny blush, he knew he had her, so he went deeper.

"Oh, so I'm right, huh? Is it true they have a swastika hanging in the basement? He probably takes you downstairs at the Malt Shop. I notice you're there enough."

Jenny's anger flared. "No, I don't go downstairs at the Malt Shop, and he's not a Nazi. And besides, it's none of your business!" she blurted.

At that, her mother stopped acting as though this wasn't happening and interrupted Floyd by turning to Jenny. "Jenny, if you know any of those rumors to be true, I forbid you to see that boy again. Why, I had no idea there could be any truth to the gossip."

"There's not," Jenny almost shouted, "there's not!" She pushed her chair back abruptly, and it crashed to the floor. She bolted up the stairs, ran the few steps to her room, and slammed the door shut behind her. She stood shaking with her back flat against the wooden panel as tears stung her eyes.

"I'm not going to cry. I'm not going to cry," she said under her breath. "I hate them all. Why do they do this to me? I hate them!"

Determined to stay contained, she threw herself across the bed, holding her pillow tight over her head, as though to shut out the world. She knew her mother wouldn't let her get away with such an outburst, so she was prepared for the harsh knock on the door.

"Jenny! Jenny! Come downstairs this minute and apologize for your behavior. I'll give you five minutes while I clear the dinner plates and serve dessert. Five minutes, mind you. Floyd was only teasing and he could be right about those people. After all, nobody really knows them. They don't belong to any church or anything else and they stay to themselves all the time." With that she was gone, and Jenny felt her fist clench.

This isn't fair. I never did anything to him. Why should I apologize? I hate her, hate her, hate her!

She headed down the stairs to the dining room. Without looking at anything but her shoes, she took her place at the table and staring straight at

Floyd said, "I'm sorry for being angry. I know you were only teasing. I'm sorry, Mother," she added, turning to her mother, "for loosing my temper and knocking my chair over. May I be excused now? I have to do the dishes, and I have a Latin test tomorrow."

Floyd didn't say anything, but her mother said, "Thank you, Jenny . . . and yes, you're excused. Do a good job on the dishes. If your father were here, he'd do something about that temper. I'm sure I don't know what to do."

That night, Floyd came to her room. She knew he would. She wasn't sure how she knew, but she did. She was still angry at him and her mother. She wanted to tell him to go away, but she didn't know how. He lay right down on the bed beside her and moved his leg over her body. It was very heavy. Jenny felt trapped. She knew he was still laughing at her.

He whispered in her ear, "C'mon Jenny, don't be mad at me. I was only teasing you. I didn't expect your mother to get so involved. You don't want to spoil our little fun, now, do you?" It seemed he wanted an answer, but Jenny couldn't get any sound out of her throat. She just lay there. He went on talking, while kissing her on the neck and ear. "I guess I got to thinking of some other guy kissing you and touching you, and I have to admit, I didn't like the idea. You aren't doing anything with him, are you?

Jenny released a big sigh, and let a barely audible, "No," escape her lips. By now, Floyd had his hand under the covers, gently cupping her breasts and touching her nipples, just barely touching the way he always did. "You know, Jenny, those boys don't know anything about how to treat a girl. I'll never hurt you or make you do anything you don't want to. You just be my girl and keep our secret, okay?"

Jenny felt completely confused about her feelings. She always seemed to end up liking him touching her. And he was right; he never made her do anything she didn't want to. At the same time, she was angry at him and didn't like the way he treated her like a little kid in the daytime.

"Okay, Jenny? I'm going back to my room, now. You know you like our little secret. Get some sleep and dream of more. Good night." And he was gone.

Jenny lay awake for a long time, wondering why she had so many strange feelings. Sometimes, she wanted Floyd to do more, and she would hold him, touch his cheek, or stroke his hair, like in a movie. One night she even thought of going to his bed, but she was too afraid of getting caught. Then in the morning, she would be embarrassed and ashamed.

She remembered her father telling her that she was born with something very bad in her, and that men and boys would know. He said if she wasn't careful, she would become a whore. That was something she would never, ever do. But she did like Floyd's touching and kissing, and she didn't know how to make him stop.

Before she drifted off to sleep, she decided to read everything she could find in the library about sex, especially about whores and prostitutes. It always helped to get as much information as possible when you had a problem, and Jenny was certain by now that she had a problem. She was equally certain that she was capable of solving or overcoming any problem she had.

Chapter 22

Just thinking about Christmas in the big house was magically exciting for Jenny. She and Jimmy had been making paper chains to decorate the big front room. If they had enough red and green paper, they would decorate the stairs. Jenny could almost see the big chains in graceful swags. When they went to cut the Christmas tree, she and her mother would bring home bundles of fir branches and hang them all over the house. That fresh green aroma was the smell of Christmas for Jenny. With the pleasing addition of cinnamon and ginger, these fragrances invited the happiness and joy of Christmas into their home.

On Friday night, her father would be home, and on Saturday, they would go cut the tree. This was one of the most exciting days of the year for Jenny as they trudged through the snow to find just the right tree, the perfect tree. She didn't know for certain if Jimmy still believed in Santa, but no one was willing to take the chance that he didn't. At her house this meant that the children got at least two presents, one from Santa and one from her parents. In addition, everyone's stocking was filled with treats. Under her bed, she had a box with presents. They were all wrapped and ready to go under the tree. She still missed her old friends, but she looked forward to having the family all together again.

On the day they went to get the tree, it was so bright and sunshiny that the snow looked like a crystal lake. Jenny and her mother had packed a lunch with a thermos of hot cocoa. If they were lucky, they would find a sunny place, and her father would clear a log or stump to place the food on. If not, they would eat in the car, but not until they had chosen a tree. Up the side of the mountain, she and Adam ran and shouted, "This one! No, this one!" Jenny finally stopped still at the base of the most magnificent tree she had ever seen. She walked all the way around to see if it had any blank spaces and to her, it look like the perfect tree.

"Here, Dad, over here. This one is perfect. I've checked it out. It's perfect."

Her father arrived with Adam, her mother, and Jimmy close behind. He frowned. "Jenny, this tree is fourteen, fifteen feet tall! We'd have to cut the whole top off the tree or put a hole in the roof of the house. It's too tall!"

"Are you sure, Daddy? It doesn't look too tall. Pleeease," she begged him.

"Yes, Jenny, I'm sure. Of course it doesn't look tall out here. That tree over there is probably fifty feet, so this one looks small. Now that you have this one to go by, go find one half this size. We'd better hurry. The sun is sinking, and it will be cold and dark soon."

By now Jenny had swallowed her disappointment, and she ran to catch up with her mother. No tree would be as beautiful as that one, but soon they found one they could all agree on, and her father quickly chopped it down. She and Adam brought it across the snow to the car and helped their father tie it on top. A sudden cloud over the sun created a chill, so they were happy to hustle into the car where their mother was unwrapping hearty roast beef sandwiches and pouring steaming cups of cocoa. Jenny hugged her little brother and thought to herself, "I have the best family in the whole world."

On Christmas morning, she got the Bible she had asked for. When she opened it, there was a special page with gold scrolls in her mother's handwriting which said, "Merry Christmas to Jenny. From Mom and Dad." The day began with a special gift and ended without a fault. Two of the boarders had stayed over; Jenny was glad that Floyd had gone home. When she went to bed that night, she took her new Bible with her and turned to her favorite verse: "Faith, hope and love abide, but the greatest of these is love." Jenny was filled with the love of Christmas and wanted to stay this happy forever.

Forever did not last very long. The next day at the dinner table, her father announced that they would be moving before Christmas vacation was over. Her father's job was good, probably permanent, and at least Jenny understood the reason for moving again. Not that she liked it any better. She was just beginning to make new friends. The thing that made moving again okay was that she hated the family being separated. They didn't seem like a family when they were apart. And this time, there was a plan that included her.

Her parents were going to Helena to rent a house, taking Jimmy with them and leaving Adam with her. Just overnight, of course, and if they wanted, they could begin to pack their things. In the afternoon, she and Adam went to the movies and saw "The Blue Bird of Happiness," in which all the children were waiting in Paradise to be born. On the way home, Adam and Jenny pretended that they had been together in Paradise and had decided to be born as brother and sister.

After they had supper, she made popcorn and they played Honeymoon Bridge[1]. Although Jenny often wished she had a sister, she knew her brothers were the most important people in her life, especially since she left her friends so often. There was no one in Missoula who truly mattered to her. There were people she liked, but she wouldn't miss them. As a matter of fact, she had made some mistakes in this town, and she looked forward to starting over. She would make some rules for herself.

What would the new rules be? First, she wouldn't go to any more parties. They didn't seem to work out too well for her. And she was not going to drink. A lot of kids drank rum or beer. She had never tasted beer, but she knew it made people smell bad.

Thirdly, at fifteen, she wasn't going to do any more necking. When she was at parties, kissing was never enough. Boys always wanted more. She knew now that the part of her that was so stirred by romantic thoughts and gentle touching was very bad. All she had been able to learn so far about sex was that it led to having babies and that it was against the law for a woman to sell herself for sex. Although prostitution, as it was called, had been around for centuries, it was still against the law. It also seems to be against God's laws. No wonder her father was so concerned about her well-being. No one would want his daughter to be a prostitute! That might mean that she would go to jail, and most assuredly it meant that she would go to Hell.

Jenny wasn't certain she believed in a real Hell, but on the other hand, it was a possibility. If she could imagine Heaven, she could also imagine Hell. Sometimes she was afraid for herself. She wondered what would happen to her, having all these thoughts and feelings with no one to tell them to. She remembered the night she had run away and gone in the wrong direction. She knew that she wouldn't have known what to do in Seattle. She had never even been away from home, except to go to a friend's house.

She looked out her window at the cold, dark night and wondered. *What if my parents were killed? What if they never came home? What would I do? How would I care for Adam? We have no one but ourselves, and because we keep moving all the time we don't even have any friends.*

When she had come home from running away, Reverend Wilkinson had talked to her a couple of times. He had wanted to help her, or so he had said. Jenny wasn't so sure she needed help, and if she did, she didn't know what kind. She was able to tell him that she hadn't been very happy. That even though she had good times at school, she kept wanting to run away.

Maybe she wanted to be someone else. But if she ran away and was still herself, she would be sad and lonely separated from her family. Who would she be? How could she run away from herself?

Once while she was sitting in church and praying for God to help her be a good person, she had thought she might tell Reverend Wilkinson how much she missed her father and how hard it was at home without him. She wanted to tell him, just as she told God, that her mother didn't understand her. It helped to talk to God, even if He didn't do anything. Maybe, just maybe, it was God who had made her father quit coming in her room at night. No matter how badly she wanted to get help, though, she couldn't take the risk of Reverend Wilkinson finding out about her and her father. He would probably tell her mother. He seemed to tell her mother everything. That was one of the main reasons it was hard to talk to him.

She wished she had someone she could talk to without her parents finding out. She had no idea what her father would say or do, but he had left no doubt in Jenny's mind that her mother would die if she ever found out what Jenny had done. Even if she didn't die, she might go crazy, and she would surely never speak to Jenny again. Even when Jenny was mad at her mother, she couldn't imagine never seeing her again.

Jenny decided that would be the third rule for her life. She would never tell anyone, ever, not even a teacher or a minister, about her and her father. It might be hard sometimes, but Jenny never broke her own rules. The truck driver and his sister had asked her a lot of questions, and the Sheriff had too. The safest answer for all those people was, "I don't know." And since Jenny wasn't sure, that didn't even seem to be a lie.

Adults always seemed to think she knew things she didn't know. When they asked her why she had run away, all she could say was, "I don't know". Her father answered back, "I know better than that, Jenny. What do you think you'll get from lying to us?"

She had told them she wasn't happy, that she was mad at her mother, but it didn't seem to be enough. Her father had told her that if she ever ran away again, he would take his belt to her.

As she brushed her teeth and got ready for bed, Jenny felt sad and lonely. She was reading Sinclair Lewis these days. She liked his writing, but she couldn't pretend the way she used to when she was younger. Not so very long ago, she could have lost herself in the pages of Elmer Gantry. She tried to imagine herself sitting in church listening to him preach, but it didn't work any more. No more.

Tears of isolation and uncertainty slid from her brimming eyelids, and she let them fall. She switched out the light to sleep, but instead she rolled over and let the tears express the deep hurting inside. As she sobbed, she became afraid of her own pain. She couldn't sleep.

She rose and went downstairs to make a cup of chocolate. When it was hot, she made a slice of cinnamon toast and sat down at the table. Hot cocoa always melted away her fears. It could solve almost anything, even feeling crazy.

Jenny felt like two people. One part of her was scared, sad, lonely, and confused. Another part had rules to live by that made everything simple and good. In that place she was happy and confident. For instance, she knew she could probably be on the debate team next year, even if they moved. And she knew she would make new friends because she always did.

As she put her cup in the sink, she made a rule for living in another town and going to another school. The part of her that made the rules would be in charge of the lonely, scared part of her. That felt like a good decision to

Jenny. In fact, when she went back upstairs, she forgot the sadness. Having rules really helped. *That must be why God gave rules to Moses.*

In her room, she picked up her Bible and marked another favorite verse: "Consider the lilies of the field and the birds of the air. God cares for them. Will He not care for you, too?"

Jenny was thankful to God for the rules she had made. When her parents returned tomorrow, she would be ready to move to a new town and begin a new life. God would help her, and she would help God.

---

1 A game designed for two players using the rules of Contract Bridge.

Chapter 23

Moving in the middle of winter was one of the worst things Jenny had ever experienced. There was no escape from the cold. It was much colder in Helena than it had been in Missoula. The day they moved into their new house, it was eight degrees below zero and the wind was blowing.

The worst part of all was that the new house was quite a disappointment after the big house in Missoula. It wasn't even a whole house; it was a duplex. There was a little kitchen in the back, a big room for living and eating, and three bedrooms. One was downstairs and two were upstairs, but they were all small.

The furnace didn't work, so the only heat was in the tiny kitchen. They huddled together around the kitchen stove, trying to stay warm. They made a big bowl of popcorn, and for once everyone wanted to move the iron skillet back and forth over the top of the stove to keep the kernels from scorching. They even had a game of bridge. Jimmy sat on Jenny's lap, and they played the same hand to keep warm. It wasn't too bad if you just didn't think about the cold.

Jenny remembered that sometimes in Spring Creek they had all three slept in the same bed to keep warm, and their mother had put warm bricks and flat irons, wrapped in towels, at their feet. Once Jimmy had wet the bed, and they had almost frozen to death before they got warm again.

Before long, everyone was ready to go to bed, and Jenny was thankful for her room alone, even in the cold. She had a headache, and her stomach hurt. She slid all the way under the covers, letting her body warm the space around her, and fell asleep. In the middle of the night, however, she woke with terrible stomach cramps. She threw up all over as she tried to find the light switch in the strange new house. Her mother heard her. After helping Jenny back to bed, she took her temperature. No wonder Jenny warmed her bed so fast; she was burning up with a fever.

After two days Jenny wasn't much better, so her mother bundled her up and took her to a doctor's office. Jenny didn't have much use for doctors. They were supposed to know so much, but it seemed to her they never did. The doctor assured her that she'd be fine. He said that she was probably just sick because she'd eaten too many goodies over the Christmas holidays. He and her mother talked about Jenny while she sat there, as though she didn't exist. Jenny felt as if her mother and the doctor were conspiring together. "Jenny gets sick like this whenever there is some sort of upheaval."

Her mother seemed to imply that Jenny got sick on purpose, or something. She was always saying things like: "You always get sick at the most incon-venient times," or "You deliberately overeat things that aren't good for you," or "Why would you get sick on holidays?" The one Jenny hated the most was: "If you would just relax you wouldn't get sick like this."

It was very confusing. At the same time that her mother criticized her and seemed angry, she brought her toast and cocoa, and washed her face and body with a cool washcloth to break the fever. Once during this particu-lar sickness, her mother asked, "Jenny, do you mind that you have to change schools in the middle of the year? I know you were doing well in all your classes in Missoula, and your teachers were sorry to have you leave. We had no choice, you know. I think you will like it here. They have a nice school."

Jenny just looked at her mother and said, "No, it's okay . . . I don't care. One school is the same as the next. I'll do fine."

"That's good, Jenny. There's no need to fret over things like that. Sometimes, I fear that you make yourself sick over things, and you must-n't do that. It's not worth it. I'm going to see if I can get a job; then you can have some new clothes, too. It is very cold here, and you'll need warmer things."

Jenny's mother had never had a job that Jenny knew of, so that sounded strange. Her parents had told her they were moving because her father had a good job, but now her mother said she was going to work so they would have more money. Confusing!

Oh, well. It doesn't matter. I'll get some baby-sitting jobs right away. There should be people right here in this neighborhood who need a baby-sitter. I could buy my own clothes like I did last fall. In the summer, I'll work again and save my money.

What she said was, "It's okay, Mom, really it is. I'll be fine tomorrow. I feel better already. I think I ate too much, that's all."

Three days later, Jenny registered for school. Her first semester English and Biology courses in Missoula were the same as the second semester courses in Helena. That meant she would have two semesters of grammar and no literature, and two semesters of beginning biology and no anatomy or lab work. In the process of getting all this down on paper, Jenny realized that she didn't really care. She could read all the literature and poetry she wanted, and she had dreaded cutting up a frog, anyhow. Everything would turn out fine.

Sometimes Jenny felt as if everything mattered passionately. But then, almost as quickly as she felt it, this passion disappeared, and nothing really mattered. Maybe there are more than two of me, Jenny thought.

She would find out about the debate club, and she would try out for concert band. That way she would begin to find some new friends. However, she would be more careful than she had been the last time. She had been too anxious, especially about boys. You couldn't trust them at all. She was smarter than she had been in the fall, and she had her rules.

On Sunday, she went to church, and in the evening, she went to the youth group. The group was going to go roller-skating in a couple of weeks, and she would get permission to go with them. She didn't have any friends yet, but maybe she didn't need any. That was one of the things that she used to think mattered a lot, but maybe it didn't matter either.

By the end of the first week, Jenny felt her new life had begun. And by the middle of February, it was as though her life had never changed. Her mother was working at the hospital, and Jenny had to come home after school to take care of Jimmy, but she didn't mind. Julie, the girl next door, was a year younger than Jenny and had a reputation for being wild. Most of the time, they walked to school together. It was a long walk, five miles or more past the Catholic college, over the tracks, and then past the armory. Once in a while, one of the boys on the debate team gave Jenny a ride home, but mostly she was alone those first months.

The second skating party was next week. True to her promise, her mother had made Jenny two new skirts, short, stylish ones with lots of pleats. Jenny was excited about wearing them at the skating rink. She planned to roll the waist band up a couple of notches. Jenny's mother insisted that her skirts should reach at least to the middle of her knees. Jenny didn't argue with her about it anymore, especially when her mother worked so hard. Most of the girls rolled theirs up, too, so it wasn't as if she was alone in that. She got lots of compliments on her skirts.

Jenny had also learned she could get lots of compliments by wearing her hair down her back, with just a ribbon or clip on the side. Most of the time she wore it in a roll or braids pinned around her head, but when she was skating, she loved for it to fall free. It fell way past the middle of her back, almost to her waist. It was soft and shiny and the most amazing blue-black color. Once someone had told her that her hair was the color of a black-bird's wing in the sunlight. Jenny was grateful for all the years of brushing her mother had insisted on. Her mother didn't think she should wear it down at school. One of her teachers actually said it was distracting. Jenny wore it down anyway, just to get attention. It made her different, and she liked being different. Part of that difference was being a stranger, but another part was inside.

Jenny considered being friends with the girl whose locker was next to hers. She had moved here after Christmas, too. But her parents were divorced. They had talked about classes and unimportant things, but Jenny was determined not to make the same mistakes she had made in Missoula. She stayed separate, not wanting to make friends too rapidly. Casual visiting with people, going skating, and joining the debate club gave her time to think more clearly about her life.

At the roller rink, Jenny found she could give up all this thinking and worrying. Only skating mattered. She wasn't a great skater, but she was good enough. Everyone knew who the best skaters were anyway. Sometimes during the night, they would just take the floor and perform fast and fancy.

A boy, Glenn, had asked Jenny to be his partner several times. She felt awkward and self-conscious, but he would just laugh and say, "I'll teach you. If you fall, I'll pick you up." He also told her, "Being afraid is the worst thing. It's bound to make you fall. Just skate with your heart like you know how, and you'll get better all the time." Jenny liked that kind of thinking. She hated being afraid, and she fought fear most of the time.

The skaters demanded her attention as they flew by, faster and faster.

Glenn went spinning by in a wide circle in front of her. Just as quickly, he reversed his direction and went spinning backwards. Over his shoulder, he called, "Wait for me. I'll take you home." Jenny had come with Julie and her brother, but she knew they wouldn't mind. She let herself feel the excitement inside of Glenn's invitation. As the skaters slowed, she imagined that before long, she would be flying around the rink beside Glenn. She would be his skating partner, and she would be really good.

Julie was excited for Jenny; with a girlish squeal, she gave Jenny a quick hug. They all agreed to meet for a Coke, and after some winding down from the intense physical energy, they all said good night. In the parking lot, Jenny slid across the seat of Glenn's `36 coupe and said nothing as he turned down Main Street in the opposite direction from her house. Glenn's car was very special; it had a rumble seat. Glenn told her they could actually get four more people in his car, six in all. Jenny had seen him picking up people after school, and had dreamed of being one of them. Glenn worked at the Western Union after school, so he had more money than most of the kids that Jenny knew. It made him seem older than some of the other boys, even though he wasn't.

They continued quite naturally up Last Chance Gulch until the town was just part of the darkness behind them. Glenn slid his arm around Jenny's shoulder and pulled her closer to him. She was both nervous and excited as she mentally ran through her list of new rules about boys. She would stay in charge of herself and Glenn with her rules. This time would be different than times in the past.

She remembered her rules, but she forgot her curfew. She liked Glenn, and she was sure he liked her. When he slid his hand onto places that made her uncomfortable, she said so, and he stopped. Once he even said, "I'm sorry Jen. You're just so great, I forget myself. Have you ever . . . gone all the way?"

Jenny felt her entire body flush, then tense. "No, never," she said.

"I'll be really good to you, Jen. I won't forget. Maybe, well, maybe you'd let me be first."

"Maybe," Jenny said, knowing she didn't want him to stop but also knowing she had to stay in charge. "What time is it?" she asked. "I have to be home by 12 o'clock."

"It's ten minutes to one, Jenny. I didn't know you had a deadline. I don't want you to get in trouble".

"Oh, I will be. I'll be in big trouble, but it's not your fault. I didn't say anything. My Dad will be mad, though."

"I'll tell him it was my fault. I didn't pay attention. I drove too far." He squeezed her hand as they sped along. "Don't worry. I know how to handle fathers. My old man comes down on me all the time, and I just talk him out of it, real fast."

"Oh, I hope so. He's been real strict lately threatening me and telling me he was going to strap me if I don't pay attention." Jenny didn't want Glenn to know about having run away, and she didn't want him to know anything about her father.

As they turned the corner of her street, Jenny saw that the porch light and front bedroom light were both on. It was now 1:30 in the morning. Jenny started praying. She wasn't sure why she was so scared.

Glenn held her hand as they walked toward the house, and just as they stepped onto the porch, her father opened the front door. He reached out through the open door, grabbed Jenny's arm and half-dragged, half-shoved her into the dimly lit hall.

"You can leave, young man. This is entirely too late for any decent girl to be out." He slammed the door in Glenn's face. As Jenny started up the stairs, he grabbed her arm again. "Oh, no you don't, young lady. I warned you there would be no more of this kind of behavior. Your mother told me you were completely out of control, but I expected more respect and obedience than this. It's after 1:30. There will be no whores in this family!"

Jenny felt like a trapped animal. She looked around furtively for her mother, but she was nowhere to be seen. Jenny's thoughts raced. *Why do I even bother to think of Mother and wish she were here? I have to deal with him by myself.*

Her eyes continued to dart, and she saw that although her father was wearing his bathrobe and pajamas, he had his pants belt in his hand. His fist was tight and his knuckles were already white. The belt was folded so that the buckle was in his hand. The double strap looked enormous to Jenny. Still holding her upper arm in a vise-like grip, he pulled her into the front room and threw her body face down across a straight-backed chair.

"You've been asking for this," he said as the strap hit her backside. Jenny felt stunned. A cry left her throat and pierced the room as another resounding blow hit her bare legs.

"NO! NO! NO! STOP!" she cried. As she thrust her body off the chair, the strap whipped around her leg and she fell back onto the floor. With his free arm, her father slammed her back on the chair, grabbed the hem of her brief pleated skirt, pulled it towards her head, and lashed her bare legs again and again.

In the midst of her sobs, Jenny saw an image of her bright red skirt twirling around and around at the skating rink. Something inside her stood still. Her body screamed and her voice sobbed, but somehow it was no longer her. There was only her mind, racing and racing.

How can I make him stop? He's not doing this to me because I was late. He's doing this because he hates me. He's doing this because I had a good time. He thinks I did bad things with Glenn, but I didn't. I am not a bad person. Why doesn't my mother stop him? She hates me, too. How can I stop him? I know! I know! I can pretend I'm not here!

She grabbed the bottom rung of the solid kitchen chair. With iron determination, she closed off her screams and sobbing. Closed off her stinging, hurting body. Closed off her throat, and gritted her teeth. Locked her jaw to keep the scream inside. She knew that her fingernails were cutting the palms of her hands, but she couldn't feel it.

As suddenly as it started, it stopped. Her father ordered her to bed. At first, Jenny wasn't sure she could move. Her head said to get up, but her legs seemed paralyzed. She jerked away as her father reached out again, only this time he was reaching to help her stand. In a quiet, gentle voice, as though he had not just raged at her, he said, "Let this be a lesson to you, Jenny. I did this for your own good. You must obey me."

In the still darkness of her room, Jenny removed her clothes and carefully hung her red skirt to keep the pleats straight. She smiled again at the memory of the wonderful time she had had. In the bathroom, she looked at the red blisters on her legs and buttocks, and studied the flaming belt marks that were all over the bottom half of her body. Some were already beginning to turn blue, and she wondered what she would wear to church in the morning so that no one would see. Blood trickled in a couple of places; she wet a cloth and sat on the toilet stool, gently patting her stinging wounds.

Back in her room, Jenny slid between the soft flannel sheets and thought about the only other time her father had ever hit her. She had been ten, but at this moment, it seemed like yesterday. It was the day her mother brought Jimmy home from the hospital after he was born. Jenny had stopped at the dime store instead of coming straight home. Once in the store, she had lost track of time looking at all the valentines on display. She had bought her mother a beautiful red and white handkerchief with a big "M" for Margaret printed on it. Worst of all, she had used the money she was supposed to use to buy a loaf of bread.

Her father had met her in the road that led to their house and whipped her all the way home with willow switches. When they reached their own front room, he took off his belt and whipped her more. Her mother had finally stopped him that time, but this time she was nowhere about. Tears slid from Jenny's tired eyes. She decided that her mother must not have hated her when she was ten years old, but she did now. Jenny's final thought, as sleep came, was of Glenn. Would he ever ask her out again after her father was so rude to him?

As the Sunday morning sun peeked around the window shade, Jenny reached down to touch her legs. They didn't seem to be too bad, even though they hurt and she could feel welts. She pulled back the covers and looked at them in the light of day. She gingerly outlined some of the bruises with her forefinger and wondered what she could wear to cover them. It became quite a project just to get dressed. She had to wear hose to cover up the bruises, but her garter belt cut across her backside in a very uncomfortable way. She managed to pull them over her legs with as little contact as possible.

If he ever does this to me again, I'll keep my legs crossed and I won't kick. That will keep the belt from going around my leg and cutting the inside that's so tender.

Somehow, it wasn't a question of Would there be a next time? She was certain there would be. As she checked her hem line, she was grateful that her mother insisted on those extra two inches. Today, they served a purpose; maybe tomorrow, too, if the marks still showed. She wasn't sure what she would do for gym class. Just be sick, she guessed, and go to the nurse's office. She had had enough headaches to get away with it. She had also had a pain in her side off and on all winter.

As she went downstairs for breakfast, she felt a familiar sickness in her stomach. She hoped her father wouldn't say anything, and he didn't. After church, Jenny spent most of the day in her room.

On Monday, she did exactly as she had planned about the bruises and gym. It was easy because she had a fever. She stayed in the nurse's office through lunch time and biology. Glenn was taking biology because he had missed it in the tenth grade, and she didn't want to see him. She knew he would ask her what had happened, and she was ashamed of what her father had done to her. No one must ever know.

As she lay on the narrow cot in the Nurse's office, she wondered, *How come I was born so bad? And how come I keep forgetting about going home on time and all the other things that get me in trouble?*

At the roller rink and on the ride with Glenn, she hadn't felt like a bad person. She had just felt like herself. But then in church and in school today, she knew that she was bad or she wouldn't have disobeyed her father. Anyone who saw her legs would know how bad she was and how severely her father had to punish her. He had accused her of lying when she told him she had forgotten the time, and now she wondered if forgetting was just another form of lying.

Later, as she stood in the lavatory brushing her hair, she stared for a long time into her own intense dark eyes.

Am I really two people? One who remembers the rules for being good and never getting in trouble, and another who is bad and gets in trouble all the time? Will the bad part break the rules in spite of my determination? If so, how can I ever be safe? Will I break my own rules and forget? How can I be sure which part is in charge of me?

Shaking her head and breaking the hypnotic gaze of her reflection, she turned and went back to the routine of the classroom.

Chapter 24

Jenny was going to Hennessey's department store after school to look at patterns for a new dress. Her mother was making the dress for her initiation into Rainbow Girls. Jenny had been afraid when they moved, that she wouldn't be initiated until her junior year. All the prettiest and most important girls were in Rainbows, and she wanted to belong. Her parents wanted her to belong too, and it felt good to be doing something all of them agreed on. That hadn't happened much lately.

She had been going to meetings with a committee and had learned all the secret rituals. Jenny loved them, and luckily she had a quick mind and could remember things with ease. She fantasized that next year she would be an officer. Rainbow Girls were asked to DeMolay dances, and Jenny had found she loved to dance. Dancing was like skating. Everything else could be forgotten at a dance. She was not bedeviled with tormenting thoughts and fears.

Weeks went by, and Jenny used all her energy to be good. Her homework was always done. She came home on time, did her chores, and felt good about herself. Her father forbade her to go roller skating for an entire month. Although she missed the fun and the excitement, she accepted her punishment and knew she deserved it. Glenn drove her home from school a few times, and neither of her parents objected. Once her mother went so far as to say, "He seems like a nice boy " Her father just grunted and said, "He's too old to be coming around here. Probably flunked out or he wouldn't be behind in school."

Jenny wanted to defend Glenn, to tell her father about how Glenn had to work to help support his mother and brothers. His father didn't have a job; he was sickly. But she didn't say anything. She disliked the part of herself that didn't speak up and tell her parents exactly what she thought and felt. She was very conscious of being afraid of her father and not wanting another whipping like the last one. Glenn didn't seem to care what other people thought, so why did she? The prom was coming up and she hoped he would ask her, but he hadn't. In fact, they hadn't been out since that night he brought her home late.

Ginger, the girl whose locker was next to hers, had asked Jenny to the movies a couple of times, but Jenny was reluctant to tell her that she was confined to her room. But her parents were eager for her to make new friends, so Jenny asked if she could break the punishment and go to the movies. Ginger was a Rainbow Girl, too, so Jenny thought her parents might approve. Much to Jenny's amazement, her mother and father agreed, with only one restriction: They must go early enough so that they could walk home before it got dark.

Jenny practiced all day saying to herself, *I will be safe. I won't do anything wrong if I am with Ginger. Unfortunately it didn't work out that way.*

At the theater, they ran into two boys who went to Jenny's youth group at church. Jenny liked Peter a lot. He was very short, even though he was older than Jenny, and really nice. He lived with his mother and sister. At first Jenny envied him, after what her father had done to her. But then she remembered how much she had missed her father when they weren't all living together.

After the movie, Peter and the other boy, Earl, asked her and Ginger to go have a Coke. Peter asked if he could walk home with Jenny. It seemed a good idea to Jenny, so she signaled to Ginger to go to the lavatory for a conference. She didn't know if Ginger wanted to go with Earl, and she also didn't know what kind of rules Ginger had. As they walked past the booths to the ladies room, Jenny wondered more about her new friend.

What kind of rules does Ginger have? And what kind of rules does her mother have? Does she have to follow the rules of the family she lives with? Does she make her own rules?

Jenny longed for someone to talk to about all these things She missed Mary Lou and Becky and even her old friend, Lois. They had shared everything, especially about parents, school, and boys. She opened her heart and her mind to the possibility of having Ginger for a friend.

In the ladies room, Ginger gave her a quick hug and said, "Oh, Jenny, Earl is so cute. I think he likes me, don't you?"

"Why, yes, I do. But why wouldn't he? You're so pretty. Does he want to walk home with you?"

"Yes. Yes! Are you sure it's okay?"

"Sure, it's okay. Peter has been wanting to take me home from youth group for several weeks. I think he really likes me, you know. But he's so short! He's very nice, but so short. Anyway, I don't think my father will care since Peter goes to our church."

"Oh, wonderful, Jenny. Is Glenn going to ask you to the prom? Do you think so, Jenny?"

"I dunno. I want to go, and I want to go with him, but I'm afraid to say anything. I don't want him to think I'm pushy. My mother says boys don't like pushy girls. I bet Peter would take me, but . . . you know."

"He's cute and nice too, but . . ."

"Let's say yes to splitting up and walking home anyhow, okay?"

Back at the table, the girls acted as though they had been discussing English literature or something, as they casually slid into the booth beside the two waiting young men. Jenny looked at the clock over the soda fountain and nonchalantly said, "I need to get home. My parents are angry at me for not getting home on time a couple of weeks ago. They only let me come to the movies because it started early. Shall we go, Ginger?"

Peter jumped up and interrupted, "Hey, I wanna walk you home, Jenny. It's okay with Earl. He'll take Ginger home. He doesn't mind. C'mon Jen."

Jenny looked at Ginger and demurely said, "Okay, if you're sure. Is that okay with you, Ginger?"

"Sure, that's fine. I don't mind. Our houses are on opposite sides of the town, anyhow, so one of us had to walk home alone. Are you sure that's okay, Earl?"

"Sure, it's fine with me. Peter and I weren't doing anything anyhow," Earl said casually.

As they left the soda fountain, Jenny grabbed her new friend's hand and gave it a squeeze. "See you tomorrow, Ginger." Their eyes met, a smile passed between them, and their friendship was secured.

Wow! How great it is to have a friend. I hope we will never, ever move again and I can have Ginger for a friend forever.

Peter wasn't all that important to Jenny. She actually forgot his presence as they walked through the City Park because she was so excited about her new friend. She was startled when Peter said, "Jenny, you're not listening to me. Can we sit down? I want to talk to you."

"I'm sorry Peter. I daydream a lot. My mother says it's a problem I have. Sure . . . we can sit down. What's on your mind? I'll pay attention."

"Well, Jenny, I've been thinking. I don't know you very well, but I sure do like you. You're very pretty, you're nice, and kind, too. I was wondering if you have a date for the prom? And, if you don't, would you go with me?" he ended breathlessly.

Jenny was aghast! Go with Peter to the prom? What would everyone think? He is so short! Like Ginger said, he's cute and he's nice but . . . Oh dear, what will I say? I mustn't hurt his feelings.

"Oh, uh . . . I don't know if my parents will even let me go. They're very strict, you know."

Peter looked right at her and said, "I know that I'm short, Jenny. I'm shorter than most girls, and I'm sure shorter than you. But I like you, and I want you to go with me."

Jenny didn't know what to say. He must have read her mind. No one had ever been so straightforward and honest with her. She respected and admired Peter for that, but she didn't want to go to the prom with someone shorter than her. Not that she was overly tall, but she wasn't short. Her mind whirled. If Glenn had asked her, she could just tell Peter no, but Glenn hadn't said anything. Maybe he wasn't going to go. It was all her father's fault. All the girls thought Glenn was the most handsome guy in school, and he had his own car! Peter's mother would probably drive them.

"Jenny. Are you listening to me?" Peter's voice reminded her of her immediate problem.

"Yes . . . yes, Peter, I hear you. I have to ask my parents. I truly want to and you're really sweet to ask me, but I have to ask them first. I don't even have a dress." She thought of the yards of peach-colored taffeta that were sitting by the sewing machine for her initiation dress.

"I'll ask them tomorrow, maybe. We'd better go. I was supposed to be home before dark."

"Okay, Jenny. Please say yes. I want you to go with me "

Holding hands, they walked past the tennis courts and the Civic Auditorium toward Jenny's house. As it grew darker, Jenny knew she had not paid attention to the time, and that dinner would be over when she arrived home. She hoped her mother hadn't done the dishes yet. She could hear her father's voice saying, "Your mother not only had to cook dinner but clean up, too, while you were out there ignoring your responsibilities to this family."

Sure enough, that is exactly what happened. Her mother was just finishing up at the kitchen sink, and her father glared when she stepped into the combination living and dining room. "I specifically told you to be home before dark, young lady. I told your mother we shouldn't let you go. You deliberately defy us with this growing disobedience. What do you have to say for yourself?"

"I came right straight home. It just gets dark really fast. I didn't mean to be late, and I didn't do anything wrong, either." Jenny knew her voice was raised, and that she wasn't safe with her father. But she just couldn't act like she had done something horrible when she hadn't. This whole thing was unfair, and she was angry.

"What on earth are we supposed to do with you? You're determined to destroy yourself." His voice was raised too. Jenny glanced toward the kitchen door, hoping her mother would stop rattling pans and say something. But she didn't. By now, her father was standing. Jenny turned toward the hall and, with a new defiance in her voice, said, "I have homework to do."

"I'll bet you do." He stepped forward, pulling his dining table chair in front of her. "Lie down over this chair!" His belt slid free from the last loop, and as Jenny took the few steps back to the chair, she felt the first crack. This time, she remembered to keep her legs together. What's more, she was determined not to let him think he could hurt her. She cried out for him to stop, but she didn't beg him the way she had the last time. She didn't say she was sorry, either. Why should she? She wasn't sorry. She knew she hadn't done anything wrong, so why was he doing this to her?

As with the first time, it stopped as suddenly as it began, and he became a different person. "Get something to eat, and do your homework. If you need some help with that geometry, let me know."

She went in the kitchen. Her mother was drying her hands and hanging up the towel. She turned to Jenny and said, "You must obey your father. I don't understand why you defy him this way. Is there some reason you can't do what he tells you? Do you just forget once you leave this house what you have been told? What happens in your mind that you don't pay attention?"

215

Jenny turned from the icebox and answered her mother the best she could, "I dunno. I didn't mean to get in trouble. I wasn't that late."

As her mother turned to leave the kitchen, a strange new thought came to her: *You're the one who makes him do this to me. You could make him stop, but you won't. I do my work. I'm not a bad person. You should tell him that and make him stop. I hate you! I hate you both! I should have run away to Seattle. You would probably be glad to be rid of me. I don't know why you ever brought me back. You hate me!*

With her plate in her hand and her books under her arm, Jenny walked toward the stairs and mumbled, "Good night," under her breath.

"Speak up, young lady. Don't mumble at your mother that way," her father said from behind his book.

"Good night, Mother," Jenny said. She hated him most of all.

Later, when the geometry was done and the welts soothed with a wet wash-cloth, Jenny drifted off to sleep. She was awakened by a quiet knock on her door. As her father entered her room, Jenny's entire body froze. "What do you want? I'm not doing anything. I'm asleep!" she said.

"I just want to tell you good night, Jenny." He sat on the edge of the bed. Jenny was so frightened that she felt sick. Her father had a can of salve in his hand. He took the lid off, reached over, and pulled back the covers.

"Jenny, I'm sorry that I had to whip you that way. You must learn to obey me. Let me put some salve on those welts. It will stop them from stinging so much, and they'll heal faster."

Jenny had stopped feeling. She lay there, paralyzed. He told her to roll over on her tummy, and she did. He pulled down her pajama bottoms and gently smoothed the strange smelling salve over her welts and blisters. She felt numb all over.

"Now turn over, and I'll do the front of your legs," he said to her. So she rolled over again, feeling like a puppet. Her body was lying there, but she wasn't in it. Some invisible force was pulling invisible strings to make the puppet work. One thing for sure, she wasn't going to act as if she cared what he did.

216

As quietly as he came in, he left, kissing her on the forehead and telling her again how sorry he was. Jenny just pulled up her pajamas, snuggled under the covers, and went to sleep. As far as she was concerned, this hadn't happened. It was far too confusing to try to figure out. It didn't matter. He didn't matter. Nothing really mattered.

Chapter 25

Glenn never asked Jenny to the prom. In fact, he never asked her out again, and neither of them ever said anything about that night. Once in a while, he drove her home from school. Jenny kept hoping he would say something, but he didn't.

She said "yes" to Peter; Ginger was glad because she was going with Earl. Earl's parents were letting him have the family car, so all four could go together.

Jenny's dress was beautiful. The girls at Rainbow couldn't believe that her mother had made it. She told them she could choose a dress or skirt from a magazine, and her mother would make one just like it.

When they first got to the dance, Jenny was a little self-conscious because Peter was so short. She was also embarrassed and ashamed for feeling that way. If she were a truly nice person, she wouldn't care about a person's looks if she liked them. Peter wasn't little, he was just short. He had a hard time finding a band uniform to fit. Tom Vincent, who was a smart aleck, had said once, right in front of everyone, "Hey Pete. You ever going to get out of that hole you're standing in?"

Jenny had been embarrassed for Peter, but she didn't say anything. Then she was ashamed of herself for not speaking up. She was also ashamed because even after she had accepted Peter's invitation, when girls asked her if she was going to the prom, she'd shrugged her shoulders and said, "Maybe, I haven't decided yet."

Peter was hanging around her at school, too, and she didn't want him to. He was a junior, so they didn't have any classes together. But he was one of the best debaters in the school. He was also the vice president of the debate club (next year he would be the president) and a class officer. He was very smart, even though he was short, and she did like him. What is my problem? she thought.

She even talked to Ginger about her embarrassment. She was ashamed that she had accepted his invitation because she wanted to go to the dance, not because she wanted to go with him.

Ginger had laughed at her and told her she was far too serious. It didn't make any difference, she said The important thing was that they were both going, and they were going together. She reminded Jenny that they were lucky to be going at all, since they had just moved here in the middle of the year. Ginger always made sense out of the things that Jenny worried about. She told Jenny that the other boys made fun of Peter because they were jealous of his intelligence. She had heard he would probably be valedictorian of his class. Just wear low-heeled shoes, Ginger said, and don't think about what any old snobs thought.

It was wonderful to have a best friend again. Ginger was right. They had a wonderful time. Jenny danced all the dances, and they went for a soda afterwards. Jenny's father had told Peter exactly when she had to be home, and Peter made sure they were there. They were even a few minutes early.

She felt it was okay to kiss Peter good night. After all, she owed him something: he had asked her to the dance, waited for her to make up her mind, and she'd had a good time. To her surprise, she enjoyed his kiss. In fact, she kissed him back. He didn't seem so short any more, although she did have to bend over a little. Earl and Ginger were waiting in the car. Jenny waved and said to Peter, "See you tomorrow."

221

She opened the door and stepped into the hall, hoping against hope that her parents would be asleep. No such luck, she thought, as she heard her mother's voice. "Jenny. That you?"

"Yes, Mother."

"Okay, dear. Be sure to hang up your dress. Did you have a good time?"

"Yes! Yes, everyone loved my dress. It's beautiful. Good night, Mom".

"Good night, dear."

Before she stripped the rustling panels of cloth over her head, Jenny twirled around her bed a few times, standing on her toes, dipping low, and twirling again. It must be wonderful to dance like Ginger Rogers, twirling and twirling for millions of people to watch. Jenny hadn't thought about being a movie star for a long time, but next year, she was going to try out for the school play. The last time she had heard from Mary Lou, she was thinking of being an ambassador or foreign policy maker, so they probably wouldn't be journalists together after all.

Ginger wanted to be a teacher, but Jenny didn't. She thought maybe her father was so strict because he had to teach all the time and make people do their work. He never seemed to stop. He taught only boys: trigonometry, drafting, and shop. The boys said he was very strict. She was glad that he was working with the National Youth Authority and not teaching at her school.

Jenny brought herself back to the business of hanging up her dress. After reading her dance program one more time, she pinned it on her bulletin board and went to bed.

Ginger was right. What a wonderful friend. The most important thing was to go to the dance. From now on, Jenny resolved, she would decide what was most important to her, and make her choices based on that.

I don't know why I feel so unsafe. I don't know why I have to think about things so much. It's a pain!

School would soon be out for the summer. Ginger and Jenny both had jobs at the hospital working in the diet kitchen. They had so many exciting plans. Jenny hated not being able to tell for sure when her father was going to whip her and when he wasn't. Sometimes when she thought he'd be mad and she didn't care, he didn't say anything. Other times, the slightest provocation set him off. Jenny learned to expect the worst. That way, when it didn't happen, it was great. And when it did happen, she didn't care.

Life seemed much easier since Jenny realized that what Ginger had said about the prom was true for everything. For example, there was a big party at the skating rink. Her father had decided the skating rink was a bad place and said she couldn't go. Jenny had become a good enough skater that she knew she could take part in the exhibition skating, and there were some boys coming from Saint Christopher's. So she lied to her parents. Her father called Ginger's house and found that neither one was there. When she got home, he was waiting for her with the belt in his hand.

Jenny didn't care anymore. When he asked her what she thought she was pulling, she just told him, "I wanted to go skating and you wouldn't let me, so I went, anyhow. I don't care if you whip me." And whip her, he did. It made him madder when she didn't scream, but she didn't care about that either. She was determined that he wasn't going to be the boss of her.

The welts always went away, and the bruises faded until the next time. Afterwards, he would come to her room and tell her how sorry he was.

Lately, her mother had taken to having long talks with Jenny about why her father had to punish her so harshly. She would beg Jenny to mind her father so that he wouldn't have to whip her. The part she hated the most was when her mother would ask her, "Why? Why, Jenny, don't you obey your father?"

All Jenny could say was, "I don't know." She wondered how her mother would react if she told her that she was actually two people: one who cared and one who didn't; one who hurt and one who was numb; one who loved and another who hated; one who was bad and one who was good. She knew her Sunday school teacher and her teachers at school would never believe how much she lied to her parents, because those people all thought she was a good person. She decided it would just confuse her mother to know about these thoughts. It confused Jenny. She couldn't always avoid thinking about it, but she tried to shut it out as much as she could.

223

When Jenny needed to think, she thought about how much fun she and Ginger would have this summer. Jenny could think weeks, even months ahead. Her parents liked Ginger and when they went fishing, Ginger was invited to come along. Ginger's little brother was the same age as Adam, and sometimes they went for long hikes together out towards Fort Harrison or up the hill with the big "H" on it. Other days, they'd go to the capitol building. One time, Jenny stood on the capitol steps and recited the Gettysburg Address. Ginger applauded, telling Jenny she would be a great governor or perhaps even president!

Summer was as wonderful as Jenny had imagined it would be. There were lots of picnics. Jenny missed camping in the woods, but she also liked working and being with friends. She liked time with her family, especially if Ginger came over. Two or three times a month they went fishing. Once in a while, her father asked Jenny to come along and carry his fishing basket, as he had when she was little. She was uncomfortable with him by herself. There was something about the way he smelled, now and then, that nauseated her. That and the way he touched her sometimes put her on edge. He didn't hug her or seem to even want a good night kiss. But outdoors, sometimes, he would squeeze her in an uncomfortable way.

Toward the end of July, he told her to come down to the river's edge to help him clean his catch for the day. Most of the time, they were silent, but when they were finished, he took his whet stones out of the creel[1] and said, "Here, Jenny, give me your knife. You need to keep it sharp if you're going to do a good job."

She gave it to him, rinsed each silver and speckled fish, and arranged them on a fresh bed of leaves in the bottom of the ancient creel. That creel had been in Jenny's life as long as she could remember. Jimmy wanted one just like it. She had saved most of her money for school clothes, but if she did a lot of baby-sitting, she could get him one for Christmas.

Her thoughts were interrupted by her father's voice. "Jenny, I want to talk to you about something. Are you listening?"

"Yes," she answered, not really looking at him, but feeling tense and watchful as she always did when she was alone with him.

"You know, Jenny, any time you want to change your mind about us, you can. I know you like what I can give you, and you know I'll never hurt you. You're older now and you're not fooling me about how you are with the boys. What do you say? Will you give your old Dad a chance?"

At first, Jenny didn't know what he was talking about. She thought he must mean the whippings, since according to him, they were all her fault. Her heart started pounding, and she couldn't speak. She had both hands clenched in the grass. When her father reached out to touch her, she jerked back, and her fist ripped out a whole clump of green grass.

"Don't be like this, Jenny, baby. I don't want you to be afraid of me. That's why I'm asking. I won't bother you if you say no."

Jenny swallowed. "No", she said. "I don't want you to do that." She wanted to add that she didn't do that with boys, either, but she didn't think it would matter. Her head felt hollow, like she might faint. This feeling scared her because she didn't want him to touch her and she needed to stay in charge.

He stopped, wiped her knife off, and gave it back to her. "I won't ask you again, Jenny, but if you change your mind, you won't be sorry."

Jenny snapped in the blade of her pocket knife and headed back to the picnic site. After a few steps, she wasn't dizzy any more, but thoughts were bouncing around in her brain like crazy. How could he possibly think she would change her mind about that? Never, ever! She avoided even thinking about what he had done. Why did he have to remind her? That was a long time ago. She had forgotten it, and her rules about boys had helped.

Even her mother was always questioning her and accusing her of things she wouldn't dream of doing. What was the matter with her parents anyhow? What kind of a person did they think she was? It was better to forget all this stuff. That was the only thing that made any sense at all. Forgetting.

---

1 A wicker basket, especially one used by anglers for carrying fish

Forensic League

The Helena High Forensic League this year did double duty in the field of contest speaking. The debate question on military training for youths under the present draft age was the topic for many interscholastic debates. April 24 saw Ron McCutcheon, senior, and Allen Johnson, junior, leave for Missoula. The National Defense Speakers' Bureau was organized in the school with 20 members.

Chapter 26

Jenny ended the summer by working two weeks at the Lion's Club summer camp as a junior counselor. It was an entirely new experience for her, and she loved it. Although her mother was there as the camp cook, Jenny slept in a cabin with an adult counselor and ten little girls, aged eight to eleven years old. It was wonderful to feel so important, planning hikes and adventures, helping with crafts, writing letters home to moms and dads, and hearing the counselors praise her for how great she was with the girls.

Jenny knew she was an excellent baby-sitter, and she always had more jobs than she could possibly do. But baby-sitting was like watching Jimmy and Adam. This was different. She liked the meetings they had with the counselors planning the days, and talking about the needs of individual campers. Mr. Wright, the head of the camp, praised Jenny to her mother as an unusual and sensitive young person. He hoped that she would consider a career working with children, and he wanted her to come back next year.

The experience and Mr. Wright's words made Jenny think about growing up. She would be sixteen in November, and in two years she would graduate from high school. What would she do when her parents didn't take care of her anymore?

Every time her father whipped her, she vowed to leave home as soon as she was eighteen, but she forgot her vow as soon as she wasn't mad anymore. Perhaps she would be a camp counselor or even a camp director, but then she would have to find something else to do in winter. Most of the counselors were teachers in the winter, and Jenny hadn't changed her mind about that.

When school started this year, she was going to take voice lessons from Mrs. Pierce, the choir director. Mrs. Pierce wanted Jenny to pursue her singing, and so did her father. One of his favorite stories was about hearing Madame Schumann-Heink sing "Madam Butterfly" when he was a young man. Jenny never tired of hearing him tell how the mezzo soprano's voice was as clear as a bell yet as soft as a butterfly wing.

Ginger played the piano, and they would play and sing for hours. They had frequently been asked to perform for Rainbow and other organizations. Jenny liked it more than she let on. Ginger thought she was great, and Jenny felt the same way about her. They were true friends.

A few days after camp, school started. It promised to be a glorious year. Ginger's locker was next to Jenny's again. She got to take English literature instead of more grammar, and she was accepted in the drama class, even though she had already taken the maximum number of classes. All she had to do was keep her grades up. Everything was easy but Latin II, and she had to make up a semester of geometry. Moving in the middle of the year had presented a challenge to her, but Jenny trusted her mind. It was one part of her that didn't let her down.

Early in October, the Forensic League, (Debate Club), held its first meeting, and Jenny made the school team. Last year, they had been second in the state, so there was a deep determination to be first this year. If they won the state competition, they would go on to the nationals, and compete with high schools their size all over the country.

Even in the concert band, where Jenny wasn't especially good, she was moved up three chairs. Jenny wanted a new clarinet, but they were very expensive, and she didn't expect she would ever get much better than she was. She had been playing since fifth grade. It was the same way with piano. She seemed to reach a certain level, and that was the best she could do. Her father said if Adam practiced as hard as she did, he would be a great pianist because he had musical talent. Jenny decided there were some things you couldn't do with only will power. It was a lot of fun, though. Music was always fun.

By Halloween, Jenny had quit trying to figure out why or when her father would go into a rage and use the belt on her. It didn't seem to matter what she did or didn't do. If she asked permission to do something, he said "No," so she had no choice but to do it anyway. In that case, of course, she got the belt. She finally reached the conclusion that it was better not to ask. Then it would look like she had forgotten, not like she had disobeyed. That seemed the more sensible course of action, even though the result was the same.

This Christmas, she was going to ask for ice skates so she could go skating at the college and the city rink. She had skated some last winter with her old clamp-ons, but she could do better with shoe skates. The city rink had lights, and no matter what her father said, she wanted to do what the other kids did. That didn't make her a bad person, either.

No matter how hard she tried to please her father, she ended up doing the wrong thing. She knew she loved him and he said he loved her. She wanted to believe him, but it was difficult at times. Her mother told her he loved her, and he whipped her to keep her out of trouble.

He was teaching at the high school this year, so it felt as if he was always watching her. Once, he came by the debate club meeting and talked to Mr. Greene, their coach. Jenny was afraid he was checking on her, but later, Mr. Greene mentioned they had talked about the war in Europe.

Everyone was concerned about the war and whether the United States would get involved. Adolf Hitler's armies were marching across Europe. She had seen Hitler on the Movietone Newsreel and believed her father when he said, "He is an evil and cruel man who has to be stopped." Her father believed if the United States didn't get into the war soon, it might come to American shores. Jenny didn't know how this could happen, but she respected her father's opinion. The dinner conversation was often political these days.

This part of her father made Jenny feel more than ever as if she had two lives. She loved listening to him talk and read aloud about Franklin Roosevelt and Winston Churchill, whom he admired greatly. One evening, he talked about Woodrow Wilson. He thought Wilson was a great human-itarian, but not an effective leader for the nation. Her father believed, how-ever, in the United Nations and the power of world politics. He would tell her, "One day the world will be much smaller than it is now because of avi-ation and communications, and our nation will have to provide leadership."

The more Jenny listened to him and asked him questions, the more confident she was on the debate team. Every year, there was a national theme for high school debates. This year, the subject was "Should There Be One Year of Compulsory Military Training in the United States at Eighteen Years of Age?". Jenny agreed with her father, who said, "If there is going to be a war, we should be prepared." But at the same time, she felt there shouldn't be a war in the first place, much less one that people had to fight in when they didn't want to.

Jenny had to study hard to gather the facts she needed to support her arguments, no matter which card she drew. (The cards determined which side of the argument each student was to debate.) She knew she was a better speaker when she truly believed something, but Mr. Greene kept reminding her that she must sound informed and forceful whether she agreed with her position or not.

Jenny and Carol, the only other girl on the debate team, had to work twice as hard to compete with the boys. They both believed that if there was compulsory training, girls should be included. Most of the boys disagreed because they didn't think girls could fight.

One day, Jenny got angry. She said she could fight and shoot a gun as well as any man. This was partly true. Jenny was good at hitting targets, like tin cans.

Jenny had shot a blue jay once, and she still kept his tail feathers in the lid of her yellow trunk. It was one of her saddest memories. Her father, who had taken her out to practice before pheasant season, had spotted the jay in a tree. As he pointed it out to her, Jenny took aim and fired. Every time she picked up the soft blue feathers now, she remembered how his body had sounded when it hit the soft earth beneath the tree. She had walked over to him and knelt down beside his motionless body. Stunned, she reached out and touched him. He was still warm. As drops of blood spilled from his body onto the ground, tears spilled from Jenny's eyes. He's dead. I killed him.

Jenny had killed plenty of gophers, but never a bird. She picked up three blue feathers, put them in her pocket, and ran to catch up with her father. Neither of them spoke about it. He must have known how she felt, because he never took her hunting again. She stayed in practice, in case of rattlesnakes, but she never shot a gun bigger than a .22 or .410, and she never killed anything again. So she knew her bragging was a lie. It just made her mad that boys thought they could do everything and girls couldn't.

"Oh, sure," Howard chided, "here comes Corporal Jenny Bennett with a battalion of prisoners! You will note that she is similar to the Brave Little Tailor: seven in one blow! Let's give her a medal for bravery, and be grateful that she had one full year with compulsory military training!"

Jenny blushed, but she didn't mind the attention from Howard. She knew it was all in fun, and she knew that sometimes she took things way too seriously. It puzzled her that some things affected her so deeply when most of her friends didn't seem to care one way or another. She would get angry, and more than once, she had cried over something. Mr. Greene told her in front of everyone that she'd have to save all those emotions for the drama department.

"Debate is a matter of argument, not emotions; a matter of facts and opinions, not feelings," he'd remind them when they became impassioned about their opinions. Jenny wasn't the only one who got carried away, but judges watched girls more closely, so they had to be extra vigilant. Mr. Greene said, "It's like being a woman lawyer: no one thinks she can carry it off, so they're waiting for one little emotional slip to prove their point."

Jenny's sixteenth birthday came just ten days before the state tournament. The team would drive to Missoula at noon on Wednesday and come home on Sunday. Although they were staying in the university dormitories, the trip would still cost extra money. So instead of birthday presents, she and her mother planned a special dinner with the family. They had selected a beautiful piece of plaid material for a new skirt, and she had bought a new sweater with her baby-sitting money. Ginger came for dinner. They had baked potatoes and meatloaf, one of Jenny's favorite meals, followed by chocolate cake with white fluffy icing and sixteen bright pink candles. Jenny could hardly believe that she was sixteen. It seemed like only yesterday that she was ten. Still, she could hardly wait to be eighteen.

Ginger stayed the night, and they went to church together in the morning. Ginger was Episcopalian, but since Jenny had to teach Sunday school, they went to her church. Everyone sang Happy Birthday to her, and Jenny was asked to choose her favorite hymn, which was "Just As I Am." She sang the words, which she knew by heart, "Though tossed about, with many a conflict, many a doubt, fighting and fears within, without, O Lamb of God, I come, I come."

Confidence filled her heart. God must know that she was good. Even if she did bad things, she was not a bad person. Her understanding of the Bible was that God forgave her. He understood. It continued to puzzle Jenny that people in church were so judgmental of others — or so it seemed to her — when the Bible taught forgiveness. Adults were as confusing to Jenny at sixteen as they had been when she was ten. She decided to dismiss the dilemma altogether.

Jenny wondered if she should pray for her team to win the tournament, but decided that it would be a selfish prayer. She did, however, pray that everyone would do the best they could, and that she would do especially well.

The week went by faster than Jenny expected and Wednesday, the day for driving to Missoula, faster still. There was an assembly in the morning. The team sat on stage while the teachers and the principal wished them well, encouraging them to do their very best. Some people mentioned the topic of the debate in relation to what was happening in Europe, but the focus was more on winning the tournament. Jenny was so excited, she wondered how she could keep her brain going in the right direction.

They arrived at the university dormitories just before dinner, in time to get room assignments and freshen up from the long drive. There would be a general meeting at 9 a.m. the next day. After the meeting, the order of the play-offs would be revealed.

233

Mr. Greene had assigned the teams according their scores from the last two weeks, and Jenny was debating with Howard. They were both pleased. Howard could get a little boring sometimes, so they were a good balance. There was probably nothing about compulsory military training that he didn't know, so he was a great partner. Jenny asked if it was okay with him to have her for his partner and he said, "Sure, I'm glad!" He and Gene were best friends, so she had thought they might want to be together. Jenny knew that Gene was probably a better debater than she was. He was a senior and had been on the second-place team last year. However, Mr. Greene stuck to his plan. Points were what counted. Gene sometimes goofed off, so he didn't win many rebuttal points. Everyone had both strengths and weaknesses. The team was well balanced and confident.

At the assembly, Jenny felt nervous. She hoped she wouldn't be sick. All the boys were dressed in suits and looked so serious. The other teams were like hers, one girl to four or five boys; so the girls rather tentatively smiled at each other. No one wanted to be disloyal, and everyone wanted to win. Even Jenny thought for a moment that everything was too serious. At a football game, a person could at least jump up and down and scream a little. Here, everyone had to shake hands and act as though the most important thing in the world was compulsory military training, not whether you won the debate or not.

One thing for sure, she and Carol agreed, there were a lot of cute guys at the tournament. Tomorrow night, the debate club at the college was having a dinner and dance for them. That will be fun, Jenny thought.

The first rounds were over Friday morning before 10:30. All four of their teams had won. By Saturday noon, the top eight teams would be determined, and by 3:30, the finalists would draw cards for their side of the argument. Points were posted after each debate, so everyone knew where each debater was weak and strong. Jenny was surprised at how well she did, especially when she had to debate NOT having compulsory training. But she and Howard were convinced by their own arguments, so they made a good team.

The party was wonderful! One of the sororities helped put it on, so there were lots of girls. The top team from last year was there, except for two graduates. Jenny thought their top person was the best debater there. He was certainly the most handsome. He had the bluest eyes and his tie matched them perfectly. He asked Jenny for the last dance; it was slow and they talked.

"Hey, I hear you're pretty good. Maybe we'll make the finals. How about that?" he said with a twinkle in his eye.

Jenny wasn't sure if he was flirting or teasing. She thought it would be safer not to mention herself. "We have a very good team. The best in the state."

"Maybe so," he said, "but we're going to win. We're not about to let your school have that trophy."

"We'll see," Jenny said, keeping it light hearted. He may be handsome, but he sure is arrogant!

She knew if they won, her team would probably debate him, but she didn't want to think about it. Dancing with him was like floating on a cloud. The debate didn't seem to matter, much less "The War and Compulsory Military Training." As the music stopped, he held her hand and firmly squeezed it as they walked across the dance floor to join the other girls for the walk back to the dorm.

"Can I walk you back?" he asked.

"No, thanks," Jenny said quickly. "I'm going with Carol. We're sharing a room. Good night."

When she told Carol what he had said, Carol agreed that he was very good looking. Jenny went to sleep halfway hoping she wouldn't win.

Saturday afternoon found Jenny and Howard in the final round. There were four teams left, and the winner of each team would debate for the outcome. So it was that Jenny, filled with terror, found herself competing with last year's championship debater, the one with the honeyed tongue and the eyes like sapphires. Howard was confident, and Mr. Greene had gone over almost everything he'd said all year long. Jenny prayed that Howard would draw "For," and he did. Then she felt confident too; too confident, maybe.

The biggest test of all was the rebuttal statement, and her opponent was pushing her all the way. Jenny felt backed in a corner on the issue of "The Certainty of United States Involvement in War." Before she could stop herself, she looked her opponent square in the eye, and said, "While so much time and attention is being paid to Hitler and the war in Europe, our entire Naval force is sitting in the Pacific paying no attention to the escalating military power in Japan. It is very likely we will be drawn into war whether we choose it or not."

235

The minute her mouth shut, she knew she was in trouble. Those were her father's words! Maybe her opponent would let it pass. Fat chance!, she thought.

"Miss Bennett, do you have any documentary evidence for such a statement? If it is as you say, does that have anything to do with eighteen-year-olds having a valuable year of disciplined education and career training?"

"No, sir," Jenny stammered, "that's just what I think."

"Time's up," the judge announced. As quickly as she could, given the etiquette of shaking hands and congratulating each other, Jenny ran from the room. She knew she had messed up, and she didn't want to be a dumb girl and cry in front of everyone. Carol found her in the lavatory. "Jenny, you have to come back. It was okay. He was just a jerk." Jenny knew Carol was right. She blew her nose, wiped her eyes, and slid in beside Howard in the assembly room. He was great. He put his arm around her shoulders and told her not to be worried. They didn't know the scores yet, but everyone knew it was very close. The announcement came: their team was five points behind the first-place team. Jenny was crushed. She felt it was all her fault. Mr. Greene said it was "an accumulation of things," but no one could convince Jenny.

"Why did you say that, Jenny?" Howard asked. "It was out of the blue and unrelated to anything anyone had introduced!"

"That's what my father believes," Jenny said defensively. "He thinks we we'll go to war with Japan. That's why the ships are in the Pacific. They have nothing to do with the war in Europe. There aren't any German U-boats in the Pacific Ocean!"

No one said anything. Then Mr. Greene broke the silence. "Well, Jenny. I respect your father's opinion, but I'm glad you didn't say that in there. Let's go have some supper."

On the way, they ran into the champions walking down the steps carrying home "their" trophy. They all shook hands again, congratulating each other and acting like good sports, but Jenny knew the other team were secretly glad that she had messed up. Mr. Blue Eyed Team Captain squeezed her hand again saying, "Tough luck, Jenny. Maybe I'll see you around."

The next day was Sunday, December the 7th. The kids in Mr. Greene's crowded car were doing everything they could to avoid thinking about going back to school with the news that they were still second in the state. Jenny cried some more. Just as she dozed off, she heard a voice on the car radio:

"We interrupt this program for an important news bulletin!" Everyone in the car went alert and still as the announcer said that Japanese fighter planes had bombed the Pacific Fleet at Pearl Harbor. Mr. Greene pulled the car over and stopped on the shoulder of the road as the announcer continued to speak. They had been talking of war for weeks now, pushing their young minds to understand as much as possible, and now the war had come.

Stunned, they began to ask questions, most of which had no answers. Someone commented that Jenny's father certainly knew what was going on, even though they had lost the debate. After assuring them that the immediate impact of war would be felt very little in central Montana, Mr. Greene drove home. It felt like a long way to Jenny, and she was grateful to be dropped off first.

Jenny's parents and Adam were gathered around the small table radio when she walked in the door. Her father rose to meet her and embraced her as he had when she was a child. "Jenny, have you heard the news? We're at war."

"Yes, Daddy, we heard it on the car radio. What does it mean? Who will have to go to war? Do you think the war will come here? How long will it last? Will we fight Hitler, too, like you said?"

Questions spilled out, most of which her father couldn't answer. But the reassurance in his voice calmed Jenny.

Her parents talked about World War I. Her mother told of a brother of one of her best friends, who had killed in France. Jenny hadn't thought of any of her friends dying. It was hard to imagine Howard, Gene, Glenn, or Peter going to war. Gene and Howard were going to be lawyers. Glenn planned to join the Navy, but he wanted to go to Officer Candidate School, not war. Peter's current passion was history, so he was talking about teaching it. None of the boys had any plans for going to war.

237

If she were a boy, would she want to go to war? Jenny remembered the blue jay and felt a knot in her stomach, but at the same time, she flashed on the piles of empty .22 cartridges she and Adam had collected from their target practice. One day, Adam had put a penny in the crack of a stump, and Jenny, kneeling on one knee, put a shot smack in the middle and bent it. If a rattlesnake came in view or earshot, she could kill it. After hours of newscasts, she went to bed thinking, "If a person is an enemy and is going to kill you, like a snake, then there is no alternative but to shoot him". She continued to ponder into the night. That must be the same as my father being forced to beat me when I don't obey him.

She knew he loved her; he said he hated the beatings and always felt sorry. It seemed stranger than ever that she kept doing things that angered him. Her mother couldn't understand why Jenny didn't obey him, either.

Why did the war make her think of her father beating her? She had heard enough about war and she had seen newsreels. Someone always got hurt. Innocent people got hurt; even killed. Having a debate about war and being in a war were very different.

Her parents asked about the debate tournament, but all Jenny told them was that they had lost by five points. She was ashamed of her part in that. Even if she was had been right about the Japanese, it hadn't helped them win the state trophy, and that was what their team and their school wanted.

In the morning, she halfway wanted to go to school and halfway didn't. Her world seemed upside down. At the breakfast table, they listened to more news of how terrible the attack on Pearl Harbor had been, how many ships had been hit, and how many men had been killed. "I'm glad you're a girl," her mother said, but now Jenny wished they drafted girls so she could fight for her country. She could lie about her age; she looked at least eighteen.

Ginger was waiting for Jenny at her locker. For some reason they didn't understand themselves, they held each other for a long time, crying about the war and the debate team loss. Then they walked arm and arm to the special assembly that had been called. As they slid into their seats, Jenny remembered how she had envisioned sitting on this same stage in front of the whole school while the principal acknowledged them as the State Championship Debate Team. For a moment, she could even hear the applause. Most kids didn't care about debate or the debate team, but they liked being winners and having a state trophy, no matter what the trophy was for.

There was a silence as they all stood to sing the Star Spangled Banner and repeat the Pledge of Allegiance. Jenny was in tears again; this time she didn't wonder why. She knew it was because of the war. Reverend Millhouse from the Episcopal Church said a prayer and asked for a moment of silence for the servicemen who had lost their lives and for their families. Jenny prayed with all her heart during that long minute. She was glad when it was finally over, and she could go to class.

Finally, it was announced that the student body should be proud that for the second year in a row, Helena High School had won second place in the State Debate Tournament. After a few more announcements, they were dismissed.

There were a lot of comments about Jenny's statement at the tournament that the U.S. was in danger of being attacked by Japan. The truth of that statement seemed to justify their loss, because telling the truth was more important than being a good debater. In her U.S. History class, the instructor asked if she or her father thought there was any likelihood of the mainland being invaded. Cities such as Seattle, Portland and San Francisco were certainly vulnerable. Jenny had never really thought about specific cities. In fact, she had never thought of Honolulu being attacked either. She had simply believed her father when he said there was a danger from Japan.

She hesitated, wondering if she shoould admit this or make up something that sounded more impressive. She kind of liked being a minor celebrity. In her best debate voice, she started talking about submarine refueling in the mid-Pacific, aircraft over the Bering Strait, and how rapidly the United States could arm themselves and retaliate. She wasn't sure if she had read this somewhere, if her father had said it, or if she was just making it up, but her words provoked a lively discussion.

For once, Jenny felt rewarded for her thoughts and opinions. One of the things Jenny didn't like about debate was that her opinions weren't considered legitimate unless she cited a lot of facts to back them up. Sometimes arguing to support her opinions felt like trying to make sense to her father. Her opinions didn't matter to him. When he was angry at her, he would say, "I'm not interested in your opinions or your feelings about this. Your responsibility is to obey your mother and me, and be a credit to this family."

Jenny wished she was eighteen so she could graduate and get on with her life. The future was becoming more and more important to her. Most of her friends would graduate this year, and the boys would go into the service. Shirley and Peggy, two of her friends from drama class and Rainbow, had signed up for nursing school. Jenny thought she might do that, although she'd never wanted to be a nurse. Everything would be paid for, and they would have uniforms too. It sounded like a good idea.

One afternoon, Jenny's mother tried to find out what was going on inside her. She sensed that Jenny was preoccupied and somewhat sad. Although they were usually unable to talk, Jenny shared with her mother that she wanted to graduate this year and that she felt like all her friends were leaving her.

When they had moved to Helena, the mix-up in her classes had meant that she went into some classes a year ahead. Next year, she would have to go back and catch up on the things she had missed. This meant that the first friends she had made were a year ahead of her in school. Jenny still wasn't used to going to such a big school, and these two circumstances made it even more difficult for her. She was glad her mother understood, instead of criticizing her for having foolish, ridiculous feelings.

She reminded Jenny of how many friends she did have and how much people liked her. She said Jenny was lucky that moving didn't bother her that much. Jenny didn't say a word. She didn't want to make her mother feel bad, but she still missed Mary Lou and Becky. Rachel had written that two of her older brothers had already joined the Navy and that her parents were upset because they wanted them to stay home and tend to the dairy. Jenny wondered if her mother ever missed her old friends, but she didn't ask.

In the silence that had come between them, her mother digressed from the subject of school and friends. She asked if Jenny had had any more headaches that she hadn't told her about, and if the pain in her side was still bothering her. Jenny almost always had a headache before her period, and the pain in her side seemed to come and go. However, she didn't particularly want to discuss it with her mother. For one thing, it didn't seem to be any of her mother's business, and for another, she would make her stay at home if she thought she was sick, and Jenny didn't like that. She just avoided the questions by asking if she could make a chocolate cake for supper. Her mother said, "That would be nice, Jenny . . . and don't worry, next year you'll be just fine." Her mother always said everything would be just fine.

240

As the aroma of chocolate filled the kitchen and Jenny halfheartedly read her history book, she wondered, *Shall I work at the hospital again this summer, or shall I work at the bakery?*

Her friend Evelyn's brother worked there, and lots of jobs were expected to open this summer because of the war. People were already moving to Seattle for better jobs. Ginger would continue working at the hospital to please her mother, but Jenny was sure her parents didn't care. She didn't even know if they cared whether she worked or not. They just took it for granted she would. The bakery paid more so she'd probably do that. It wouldn't be long before summer.

Chapter 27

Winter began to melt away, and signs of spring were popping out of the wet earth. Clumps of rock daisies, tender young dandelions and lambs quarters appeared in the sunny places. Everyone read and talked about the war, but in truth, it didn't change everyday life much.

Despite her determination to obey her father, Jenny continued to find herself disobeying him. Each time the fury of his belt snapped across her buttocks and legs, she made up her mind to listen more carefully and do as he said. By mid-March, however, it seemed there was no hope for the two of them.

If he told her to be home at 12 o'clock, something invariably kept her out until 12:30. If she determined not to talk back to him or her mother, one of them always said something she couldn't tolerate. She could hear her own words, but she couldn't seem to stop them.

Sometimes she was as surprised as they were at the things that set her off. They were unreasonable and unfair. They didn't want her to be like other kids. In fact, when she was in that mood, she felt they didn't like her at all and didn't particularly want her. She thought of running away again; but how or where escaped her. She started saving her money, and then spent it on a pair of spectator pumps her mother hated. She wasn't old enough for high heels according to her mother.

One day as she walked to school, it occurred to Jenny that there was one sure way to get out of all this. She began to think a lot about dying. She guessed her parents would be sorry if she was dead, but they might also be relieved that all their trouble with her was over. Once the thought of dying entered her head, she couldn't stop thinking about it.

Jenny went through town one day with Evelyn, and they decided to go to the bakery and get applications for summer work. Evelyn didn't have a Social Security number yet, so they went from the bakery to the Social

Security office. While they were there, they decided to go to Evelyn's house and fill out the applications. The lady had said they might even get after-school work if they wanted. Intent on her project, it wasn't until Evelyn's mother came home from work that Jenny realized how late it was and that her mother didn't know where she was. She ran almost all the way home, but after dinner, she got a whipping. She hated not knowing and waiting. Sometimes it was worse than the whipping itself. That night, she decided to find a way to kill herself.

After school the next day, she went to the library and did some research on suicide. She knew it was a sin, but she shrugged that off since she seemed to already be a sinner of considerable stature. She considered guns, but a rifle was pretty complicated. Her mother had told her the story of a neighbor who tried to shoot himself, and all he did was shoot holes in the kitchen floor and break a chair. Hanging sounded fairly easy, but you needed to fasten your rope from a high enough place so you could either break your neck or dangle until you died. Most hangings, people broke their neck. That sounded scary to Jenny, so she decided on poison.

The only poisons she knew about were rat poison and iodine. They were both labeled "Poison" on the container with the warning "Not to take internally." The rat poison was in little squares that looked and smelled really bad. She didn't see how she could possibly chew them up and swallow them. She also didn't have any idea how many squares she would need to kill herself. Would she have to eat the whole box? The iodine seemed easier. She didn't feel particularly brave, just desperate to be done with her idea.

She thought a long time about leaving a note, and she wrote several. But the more she wrote, the sadder it was to think about being dead and leaving her family. Her father would be glad, but she was afraid her mother would be very upset. She decided against a note because it made her feel too sad about dying.

Her parents were going to play cards the night Jenny decided to drink the iodine. In her mind, it was a good plan. By morning, she would be dead in her bed. But it was much more difficult than Jenny imagined it would be. Iodine was the worst stuff Jenny had ever tasted, bitter and yukky. It made her mouth pucker just to put the bottle to her lips. She couldn't make herself pour it in. She kept her tongue stuck in the neck of the bottle.

Oh, dear. I'll have to mix this in water. So she sat on the bathroom floor, and drop by drop, in glasses of water, drank the entire bottle. Several times she felt like vomiting, but she managed to keep it down. When she finished, she put the stopper back in the bottle and replaced it on the shelf in the medicine cabinet.

She was feeling sicker and sicker. In a panic, Jenny hurried to her bedroom so she could die in her own bed. Just as she lay down, she had to bolt for the bathroom. She reached the toilet stool just in time. Quarts of fluid came surging out of her body. It felt like her whole insides were coming out through her throat. Iodine water even came out of her nose. When it finally stopped, Jenny automatically cleaned up the mess that had missed the stool and crawled back to her bed on her hands and knees. She lay down exhausted. *By morning, I will be dead.*

But morning came, and she wasn't dead. Without saying anything, she took her place at the table.

"Jenny, are you sick?" her mother asked. "You look pale."

"I was sick last night. I had a headache, but I'm fine now. I just need to eat something," Jenny answered, her eyes on the table.

"You'd better have some toast with that. Don't drink that cold milk. I'll make you some tea."

Not much food reached Jenny's stomach before she had to charge up the stairs to vomit again. When her mother entered the bathroom, the smell of iodine permeated the air. Jenny quickly explained that she had knocked the bottle out of the cabinet and spilled it. Her mother helped Jenny back to her bed, gently rubbed her forehead, and encouraged her to fall back to sleep if she could. Perhaps she could eat something later.

Jenny slept most of Sunday. Though she didn't feel well, she went to school on Monday and Tuesday. Tuesday night, she threw up again, and on Wednesday she ended up in the nurse's office. She had a temperature, and the nurse called her mother. When her mother came to get her, she took Jenny directly to the doctor's office. Jenny had already been there a number of times for these eruptions with accompanying fever. This time, however, there were excessive white cells in the blood stream. The next thing Jenny knew, she was lying in a hospital bed, dressed in a white hospital gown. She was scared. Her mother had called her father from the doctor's office. She explained to Jenny that she would pick him up from school, feed

246

Jenny's brothers, and come back to see her before she went to sleep. They would operate first thing in the morning. Jenny didn't feel well, and they said she couldn't have any supper, so she decided to go to sleep.

She wondered about the iodine. *Did it make me sick, or was this my regular sickness? It doesn't matter. If no one said anything, I certainly won't.* In all this fuss, she had forgotten about being dead. Then it occurred to her that she might die on the operating table.

Her mother kept her promise, came back with some of Jenny's things, and talked with her about waking up from the operation. She said that Jenny might hurt and feel sick, but afterward they hoped she would be finished with the headaches and throwing-up spells. She had even stopped at Hennessey's drug store and bought Jenny a present, a cologne of her very own. It was to be Jenny's favorite for years. The smell made her feel loved, wanted, and very beautiful, a kind of fragile beauty that could lie beneath a white sheet and be totally cared for. Her mother said it was very exotic for a sixteen-year-old, but that sometimes, Jenny was very exotic. Before she left to go home, she took Jenny's hand and told her not to be afraid. Jenny truthfully assured her that she wasn't. She felt very special and attended to. Now she hoped she wouldn't die.

247

When her mother left the nurse came in and began to do all kinds of strange things. She shaved Jenny's tummy, her legs, and everywhere. Jenny started shaking. It was scary being touched down there. The nurse was kind and told her not to be afraid. They would give her a shot soon, and she would be fast asleep. Then another nurse came in and gave Jenny a glass of orange juice, advising her to swallow it quickly. It tasted like it had been shaken in a malted milk shaker, and it had castor oil in it. Jenny was sure she would throw it up. When it was finally all swallowed, she started shaking again. Again the nurse patted her and told her not to be afraid. She would be right back with some pills and a shot.

Jenny was still frightened. If it wasn't scary, they wouldn't be constantly telling her not to be afraid. That's what her mother did. When things felt bad or scary, or she was very angry, her mother would always tell her not to pay any attention to how she felt. Everything would be okay. Most of the time, things did turn out okay. Jenny closed her eyes and decided to forget how she felt. She was good at forgetting. In fact, she had almost forgotten she was in the hospital when the nurse came in and gave her a shot.

It was the next afternoon before Jenny had to remember where she was and what had happened to her. Suddenly, she had to vomit. She wished she didn't constantly feel like throwing up. She heard her own voice as though it was a million miles away.

"Mom! Mom! I have to throw up!" Her mother's hand was right there, and her soft voice soothed Jenny's fears as the wrenching pain took over. Tears came, and the shock of physical pain hit Jenny's awareness.

"Oh, Mommy! I hurt! I can't move!"

"Lie as still as you can, dear. The doctor had to make a big incision in your stomach, and you have a lot of stitches. The quieter you are and the more you sleep, the easier it will be."

Jenny put her hand on her tummy. It felt like her whole body was one big bandage.

"Why is the bandage so big? I thought my appendix was little."

"Don't worry," her mother said. "The doctors thought perhaps there was something else wrong in there, so they took a big look. You're completely healthy. That's good to know. Sleep as much as you can, and try not to move."

"Why would something else be wrong with me?"

"You don't understand, dear. There's nothing wrong. Your appendix was very inflamed and would probably have burst if it hadn't been removed. I saw it myself. Because of the headaches, the doctor thought you might have some . . . female problems. But everything is normal. You just have to get well, now. Tomorrow will be much better."

"Okay. But I can't move; it really hurts. Can I have a drink?"

Her mother lifted the straw to her lips and in a few moments, Jenny went back to sleep.

Each day, to Jenny's surprise, she did get better. It was slow and painful, but she admitted to herself that she liked all the attention. Her teachers sent homework, and everyone sent cards and wrote letters. Her mother came every day and brought little things, fussed over her, and read her cards to her. It was ten days before she went home. Even though it was hard to walk, she was glad to be out of the hospital. Adam and Jimmy were happy to see her, and although her father had not visited her in the hospital, he seemed glad that she was home. She was eager to return to school, but it would be a couple more weeks, the doctor said, before she could go up and down stairs and walk from class to class.

On her first day home, Jenny went into the bathroom and opened the medicine cabinet. There on the shelf was a new bottle of iodine, with its skull and crossbones on the label. Jenny touched her abdomen. *Maybe? No. I'll never do that again. I'm glad I'm not dead. I have a lot of things I want to do. I want to see my friends again! It was stupid to want to die. Your whole life is over when you die, and you don't get to do anything!*

Chapter 28

Jenny and Ginger sang "The Old Rugged Cross" for Easter Sunrise Service on the steps of the Capitol Building, and Jenny felt her heart filled with springtime. She was caught up on her studies, she had a part in the spring play, *A Murder Has Been Arranged*, and Howard had taken her to the movies twice. He wasn't as exciting as Glenn, but her parents liked him and he was very nice to Jenny. He didn't expect a lot, and he never bothered her. Besides, he was a DeMolay, and although he didn't have his own car, he could have his parents' car whenever he wanted it.

Things went well at home after the operation until one Sunday afternoon just before school was out. Jenny was doing her homework at the card table, and her mother was making Jenny a summer skirt. She asked Jenny to run upstairs and get a skirt with a length she liked for her mother to measure. No one was more surprised than Jenny when she heard herself say jokingly,

"Well, why don't you go? You're younger than me. I went last time."

Although her mother didn't object, Jenny's father said, "Young lady, that's no way to speak to your mother. You're getting too big for your britches. What you need is a good whipping to keep you in your place."

Jenny knew she should stop herself, but she didn't seem to be in charge of what came out of her mouth. "If you think it will do any good," she said, "why don't you go ahead?"

That was more than her father could tolerate. Jenny hardly had time to fathom what had happened when she found herself holding the rung of the chair, clenching fists and jaw while the all-too-familiar strap left its mark. This time, she kicked, bolted from the chair, and darted for the door to the hallway. But he grabbed her and continued beating her until his rage was spent. Once Jenny thought she heard her mother's voice tell him to stop, but maybe she had just imagined it.

Upstairs in her room, she felt hurt and angry. *I was only kidding. Why did he do this? It doesn't change anything.* She took some aspirin and washed herself, thinking again of running away. There was one girl at school who lived at the YWCA. Jenny didn't know her or how she paid for it, but she knew she lived there. It was an idea.

Long after her mother had finished the supper dishes, she heard her father's footsteps on the stairs. It was only a few steps past the bathroom to Jenny's room. Jenny wished with all her heart that she could disappear. but when he sat down on the edge of her bed, she hadn't gone anywhere. She was right there.

253

He picked up her hand and placed a silver dollar in her palm. "Jenny, I'm so sorry. You mustn't fight me the way you do. I can't help myself. Let go of the covers, and let me put some salve on your legs."

Jenny threw the coin on the floor as though it were burning her hand. She grabbed her sheet and blanket and held them up to her chin. She had never before been so angry and so scared at the same time. A voice from inside her that she had never heard before said,

"Don't you ever, ever touch me again. If you do, I'll leave, and you 'll never see me again as long as you live."

Jenny's eyes were like flames as she looked directly at him. He said nothing. He stood up, and as he turned, picked up the dollar and placed it on her dresser.

"I don't want your dumb dollar," Jenny said. But he left it there and walked slowly from her room with the can of salve in his hand.

Oh, well. I can always use a dollar.

BOTOM

B-17's

Chapter 29

Summer was a glorious time of hiking, picnics, and basking in long, lazy days. Jenny went to work at the bakery, but so many of her friends were there that it didn't seem like work. Her family moved into a bigger house with a big yard and planted a huge Victory Garden. Jenny didn't particularly like working in the garden, but she loved her own little plot of flowers. Her favorite flower was the sweet pea. She planted a row of them along the entire garden fence. She planted baby's breath to put in bouquets and made sure she kept them cut so they wouldn't stop blooming. The nasturtiums she planted in front were the same; if she kept cutting them, they bloomed all summer.

On Sundays, she would often go with the Rainbows or church group out of town to the Masonic Home to visit and sing with the old folks. She would take bouquets of sweet peas, which they loved. There was one very old man there, named Jake, who was in a wheelchair. She would bring him flowers for his room and push his chair around the grounds, chattering and visiting with him all the while. He carved tiny objects out of wood, and every now and then he would slip one into Jenny's hand. Her favorite was a little fan that actually opened and shut. She carefully stored the wooden treasures in their own box in the tray of her yellow trunk. Jenny felt like a good person doing good things.

A division of paratroopers had moved into town and was staying in the Masonic Temple, which also served as a civic center. They were supposed to be staying at Fort Harrison, a few miles out of town, but it wasn't ready for them. There were about 300 men in all, mostly French Canadian. With their French accents and combat boots, they made the war seem very close at hand. Before long, the skies above the fertile green valley surrounding Last Chance Gulch were filled with what seemed like billions of white parachutes. The sight was breathtaking and frightening at the same time. The war, once an abstract event, took on new meaning.

Along with the excitement and romance of foreign soldiers, there came another change to the tranquil summer. A significant number of the men had already been to Europe. They were back in the States for voluntary training, and they lived life on the edge. Drinking was prevalent; the once quiet main street with its three or four bars was now a playground for rowdy young men who expected to die soon anyway. After dark, women weren't as safe as they used to be. Some of the restaurants and shops in town put signs in their windows that read, MEN IN THE ARMED SERVICES NOT WELCOME. Jenny thought that was terrible, but her father was adamant in his support of the shop owners. Everywhere you went, people talked about what could be done. Although only a few rowdy men made it bad for the rest, no one was prepared for the fallout of war to be so close.

257

Just as the first contingent was established out of town at the resurrected fort, a company of Negro soldiers took their place. Jenny's parents were Southerners, and although she didn't recall her mother ever saying much about it, her father was outspoken about his views: Negroes, half-breed Indians, and Catholics were all in one category: Not Good. Jenny hadn't seen more than half a dozen Negroes in her life so it fascinated her to walk by the building in which they were housed. Sometimes one of them said "Hi" to her, and she would say "Hi" back. They seemed like ordinary people to her. More signs went up in town: NEGROES NOT ALLOWED. Some people in town thought that was unpatriotic; others said it was for the protection of the townspeople. The signs didn't stay very long, and the Negro soldiers didn't go out to the Fort, either. They were transferred out of the area.

In the meantime, her mother joined a committee to form a USO so the soldiers would have a place to go when they came to town. Much to her surprise, when Jenny asked if she could be a hostess and help, her mother said she didn't see why not. However, it would be several months before the plans would be implemented. They were to start out at the YWCA, giving support and help on weekends with individual family matters, and offering writing materials, soft drinks, and cookies. In the fall, they would probably have a dance, and Jenny could go. Her mother would be a chaperon.

"It's the least we can do for the war," her mother said. During the first world war, she had wrapped bandages and knitted mufflers. She said it made women feel more useful to be doing something. Jenny had begun to realize something about her mother: she was always doing something. Then Jenny noticed that she was the same way; always busy, always coming and going, always planning what to do next. The part that puzzled her about all this activity was that her mother scolded Jenny about being too busy. She would say, "Jenny, you're doing too much. You'll be sick again. You burn the candle at both ends. You never relax. You must slow down."

Jenny never knew how to respond. She would assure her mother that she was fine, and she'd rest on Sunday or next week or whatever time came to mind. That seemed to satisfy her mother until the next time. Jenny couldn't think of anything she was doing that she could stop doing. Her life had become very precious to her, and she was grateful she hadn't died.

Ginger had gone to visit relatives for the end of summer, and it was a great day for Jenny when the phone rang one Friday night and she heard a familiar voice that she had missed.

"Hi, Jen. It's me. Can you go on a picnic tomorrow? My cousin has a new boyfriend from out at the airport, and he has a couple of friends that want a date. Can you go? Then we can talk and catch up too. Ask, okay?"

Jenny turned her head around to the kitchen and asked her mother if she could go with Ginger and Maggie. After a brief conversation about chores, her mother agreed.

"Yes, she said yes! Shall I meet you at your house? What shall I bring?"

"Maggie is bringing everything, and we can pay her later. Is that okay with you?"

"Sure, sure. I saved a lot of money. I spent most of it on school clothes, but I still have some leftover. Do you think the boys are cute? I've never been out with an Air Cadet. Did you know my dad is going to teach the cadets at the college instead of teaching at the high school? I hate it. He'll know everyone."

"Oh, Jenny, your dad is so sweet and you're so lucky. You shouldn't feel that way. What I think is, the guys will like him, and you'll be sort of In. Know what I mean?"

"That's not the way it is at school. Guys always ask me if my old man is as mean at home as he is in class. I bet some of them might ask me out if it weren't for my father."

"But they're only high school boys. They're so stupid and immature, anyhow. With the Naval Air Force taking over Saint Anthony's College and the Air School and all the soldiers at the Fort, who cares about high school boys? I don't."

"You're right about that. My mother said I could go to the first USO dance. She's going to be a chaperon. You can get a form from her and have your mother sign it so we can go together."

"A form. What for?"

"Oh, it's nothing . . . rules about guys. For instance, you can't refuse to dance with someone who asks you, and you can't leave with anyone. Just dumb rules so your mother knows you're safe." As if anything would happen, Jenny thought.

"How exciting. I can't wait to see you. Come early. Good-bye."

"Bye, Ginger. I'm sure glad you're home. I missed you."

"I missed you too, Jen. Bye!"

The phone clicked and Jenny stood a while just holding the receiver. She had missed Ginger, but it seemed she missed her more now that she had heard her voice. It is wonderful to have a best friend. Ginger's father had been killed in an accident. Usually Jenny tried to remember not to mention her father because it always seemed to make Ginger sad. Her father was nice to Ginger. He liked her to come over, and Jenny could take her wherever they went if there was room in the car.

The next day was a perfect Indian summer day for their picnic. Leaves were starting to turn, and winter would soon be here. But for today, the sun covered the earth with a blanket of warm air. Once in a while, a breeze would warn of chilly nights, but it was a perfect way to begin your senior year in high school.

The guys were great. They explained about the Navy taking over the school for an officer candidate program. The Airport School would be training them with small planes, and then they would go to Seattle or Tacoma and fly fighters and bombers. They were all from Southern California, which sounded like a fanciful world to Jenny, and they had all been to Hollywood. One guy had worked in a grocery store in Beverly Hills. Sometimes it was hard to believe that all the places on Jenny's map were real.

They roasted hot dogs and marshmallows, sang dumb camp songs, and promised to get together next weekend. Jenny hadn't told her parents there would be boys on this picnic, so she couldn't make a promise for next week. She just went along. Jenny's house was on the way to the college, so Maggie drove her home first. Jenny's date walked her to the door, held her hand, and asked for her phone number. Jenny's heart skipped a beat as he leaned down and gave her a quick but gentle kiss saying, "This was my lucky day! See you, beautiful Jenny." And he was gone.

Jenny slipped quietly into the house, more floating than walking. Her parents were listening to the radio and working on a jigsaw puzzle.

"You're a little late, young lady," her father commented, not looking up.

"I know. I'm sorry, Daddy. We just had such a good time. We drove all the way to Gates of the Mountain. We haven't seen each other for a whole month, you know."

"Yes, well, get to bed. Church is in the morning," he said.

Jenny involuntarily stiffened, but kissed them both good night and went to her room. It had been so long since she had had a whipping, she had almost forgotten how they felt. In fact, she thought as she undressed, *I think I HAVE forgotten!*

School started on Thursday, and it was wonderful to see everyone. Jenny missed her friends from last year, but being a senior seemed to make up for it. They had an assembly, and Mr. Greene read the names of the boys who had enlisted. There was a big plaque in the hall by the library, and all their names would be posted there. There were thirty-eight names in all. Glenn's name was one of those he read, and Jenny thought of the small pack of letters she had in her trunk, postmarked from somewhere in Texas. She had promised to answer him every time he wrote, and she had kept her promise all summer. She had also met a soldier from Jersey, named Joe, and told him she'd write to him, but he hadn't written yet.

They recited the Pledge of Allegiance and sang the *Star Spangled Banner*. Jenny was in tears again. She wondered why the war made her cry. *Because war means killing, and killing is sad*, she figured. Ginger was in tears, too. Although they never talked about it, they knew they both felt the same way. They would write to any servicemen who asked them. When the dances started, they would go to every one and dance with whoever wanted to dance.

Maggie had graduated two years ago, and she had gone out with some of the paratroopers. She said, "You never know if your letter will be the last one they get before they are wounded, or even killed. That's why letters are so important."

The classroom bell startled Jenny from her reflections, and she left the assembly. She decided to stop at the office and see about joining the Civil Aeronautics Association and becoming a cadet. She could be a navigator, or perhaps even a pilot. She picked up the literature, but you had to be eighteen, and Jenny wasn't even seventeen yet. Age qualifications always made her mad. She signed up for a special Red Cross First Aid class and switched her physics class to aeronautical engineering. There, she could study weather, instrumentation, and plane identification and have field trips to the airport. Her parents had to sign, but she knew that was no problem. The war had become everything, and you did whatever you could to help. As Jenny went to English class, she felt good about her decision. Girls could join the Navy, and she just might do that. Even if she couldn't be a pilot, she would help the best way she could.

The first USO dance was even better than it had promised to be. Jenny's mother took Ginger and Jenny, so they knew they would have to go home with her. But that didn't matter; all that mattered was dancing. There were three or four guys to every girl, so it was pretty easy to avoid anyone you didn't want to dance with. In the crowd, you could duck behind someone if you saw a guy you didn't fancy coming toward you. Or you could accidentally bump into some unsuspecting uniform. The guy you bumped could be counted on to take your cue and dance with you.

There was a Sergeant from New Jersey who held the girls so tight they couldn't breathe, so they would help each other out and duck for the ladies' room when they saw him coming. Girls could complain to the chaperons, but no one wanted to do that. No matter how much you didn't like a guy, no one wanted to get him in trouble.

It was great fun to talk to soldiers and air cadets from all over the country: Texas, Florida, Nebraska, Jersey, and California. The girls agreed that Californians were the best dancers.

All the servicemen were homesick and admitted they were afraid to go to war. Sometimes they talked about their girlfriends at home and showed pictures. Emotions flowed like warm honey and sometimes like cascading waterfalls. No one dance partner was like the last, so every moment seemed special.

The future that Jenny had dreamed of for so much of her life didn't seem important anymore. The only thing that mattered was the music, and dancing with one stranger after another. Jenny and her friends felt exceedingly beautiful as a result of all the attention. Their mothers, however, hovered and watched and worried.

Their little town had finally begun to take part in the war. Everyone adjusted to food stamps, and women became adept at trading sugar coupons for canned food coupons. Tables soon held more beans and pasta and less meat. Roast beef was more of a treat than ever, and your grocer was the most important person you knew. Mr. MacDougal always called Jenny's mother when something that had been missing for a long time came in, and Jenny would go right to the store and pick it up. But except for dancing and rationing, the day-to-day lives of families went on pretty much as usual. They were as yet untouched by the personal tragedy that war brings.

Chapter 30

Jenny was going to a party at Thelma's house. She and Thelma weren't exactly good friends. Thelma was just a sophomore, but they did walk to school together occasionally. They had moved from the other side of town last year. The party was for her brother, who had been in boot camp. Jenny didn't know Thelma's brother, but she had seen him around school.

She had not been to a party in a long time. Somewhere along the way, she had decided parties weren't safe for her. She was frequently invited, but she always backed off by saying she had to baby-sit, or that her parents wouldn't let her. Thelma's party seemed different because her brother was a serviceman, and Jenny had no real reason not to go.

She asked Thelma if she needed any help before the party and agreed to come early and bring a chocolate cake with fudge frosting. She chose a new white sweater to wear with two long strings of red beads that went with her red pleated skirt, perfect for dancing. Although it was November, it wasn't too cold, yet, so she wore her white ankle sox and saddle shoes. She liked what she saw in the mirror, and hoped she would like Thelma's brother's friend.

Thelma hadn't said so, but she was counting on Jenny to make sure he had a good time. Jenny was older than most of Thelma's friends, and she was a very good dancer. She glanced at the clock to make sure she wasn't too early, picked up her cake in the kitchen, and walked the half block to Thelma's house.

It was a wonderful party. None of Jenny's best friends were there; it was a different crowd. They knew who she was and that she lived down the street, but they recognized that she was there because this was a special occasion.

Thelma's brother, Jim, introduced his friend, Buddy, to Jenny, and they got along right away. He was from Texas, and had a Southern way of talking that was part drawl and part cowboy. He was cute, too, and a great dancer.

Jenny knew there was beer in the back yard and probably something else, but she didn't go out to see and she didn't ask. Sometimes it was best not to know what was going on; then she didn't think about any of her rules. The rules kept her out of trouble, but they made life difficult at times.

Just before one o'clock, Buddy walked her home, and they stood on the front porch kissing for a long time. Jenny knew they were kissing more than she should allow, but she didn't stop him. Old feelings stirred in her that she hadn't let herself feel for a long time. It felt good to let him hold her close and to feel his hard strong body against hers. He slid his hand up under her soft wool sweater. Goose bumps slid across her skin, and they weren't all from the cold. She listened for the click of the porch light and hurriedly made a date to go for a ride and a movie on Sunday. One more kiss good night and he was gone.

Jenny folded her sweater and hung up her skirt. She felt excited all over. She wondered where the old fears and anxieties had gone. She suspected it had something to do with her father, but wasn't sure how. He was different these days. There seemed to be something about her he didn't like, but most of the time he left her alone.

Buddy was cute and nice. He would be leaving at the end of the week, so why not spend Sunday with him? She would walk down to Thelma's, and her parents wouldn't know she wasn't going to stay there all day. They were always nervous about cars.

At breakfast, she told her parents of her plans to spend the day with Thelma and her brother. She was surprised that this seemed fine. She could still hear her mother's voice saying, "Jenny, I just don't understand you. If you would just do as your father says and not provoke him you wouldn't always be in trouble."

Jenny knew it was dishonest to let her parents think she was going to Thelma's to be nice to her, when actually, Thelma had nothing to do with it. She didn't want to get in trouble. The part of her that didn't want trouble thought it was wrong to be dishonest. The other part knew that being dishonest was the only way to stay out of trouble. Her mother was right, in a way. When she avoided her father, she didn't have trouble. The voices

267

presented a constant dilemma, and trying to figure it out only made it worse. Forgetting stopped the confusion. How great to be able to forget!

Everyone was waiting outside Thelma's house when Jenny arrived, and they all piled into the car. They had barely said hello when Buddy started where he had left off the night before, putting his arms around her and kissing her in broad daylight. Jenny knew she was letting Buddy go too far, but she liked it, so she just kept necking with him and letting the voices talk to each other.

Thelma had to baby-sit later in the day and couldn't go to the movies, so they rode around for a couple of hours, then took her home. Jenny and Buddy got in the front seat with Jim, and they headed out of town. Buddy and Jenny were still necking. Jim didn't seem to pay any attention. Every now and then, Buddy and Jim would laugh and talk a while about things back at camp. Jenny felt so grown up, not like a high school kid but really part of the war, as she listened to their stories about the barracks and drill sergeants.

Buddy finally said, "Hey, where you going anyhow, Seattle?"

"Yeah, why not? It feels so great to be driving my car again, I just wanna drive and drive and never stop. I feel like driving all the way to the Pacific Ocean and never stopping."

"Great with me, old buddy. How about it, Jen, shall we run away with Jim to the Pacific Ocean?"

"Sure, why not? I've never been there. Once I started out to Seattle, but I got only part way." Jenny volunteered, not wanting to feel as if she had never been anywhere.

"Hell, we got a whole ten days, and you still got that bottle of sloe gin in the trunk. Let's head for the coast." They both laughed, and Jim pulled over on the shoulder of the road and made a quick trip to the trunk. "Better stop and get a coke to go with this stuff."

They headed west over the mountains. Rather than give any thought to her parents, Jenny took a drink from the open bottle that was handed to her. It was strange tasting and sweet, not at all as she thought it would be. She remembered trying a cigarette once back in the eighth grade and how awful it had tasted. She had assumed that anything with alcohol in it would taste as awful as a cigarette in her mouth. It wasn't so; it actually tasted good.

By the time they had been on the road a couple of hours, they were all three laughing and talking crazy. They stopped somewhere, had hamburgers, and shared some French fries. They just tossed all their cares to the wind. Buddy was driving now, but he kept leaning over to give her little pecks on the neck or take a nibble of her ear. Now and then, he would slip his hand over on her thigh and squeeze.

Once, Jim hollered at him and said, "Hey, Buddy, if you're going to pay more attention to the chick than the road, I better drive. Better still, maybe I better keep the babe hot." With that, he pulled Jenny over against him and planted his wet, gin-flavored lips against hers. Jenny didn't think it made a whole lot of difference who kissed her at this point, but Buddy told Jim to knock it off. Jenny liked that; she gave a playful shove to Jim and moved back over toward Buddy. She was conscious of how much she enjoyed the tension between them, which she believed had solely to do with her.

By midnight, Jenny didn't have any idea how far they had come, but she knew she was a long way from home. She had fallen asleep. "Where are we?" she asked. "What time is it?"

"Oh, hell, I don't know. We're in the mountains. No town for miles, not even a service station. There are some houses and some summer cabins. Maybe we can find a place to stay. Most of the cabins are empty."

Buddy pulled off the highway onto a remote mountain road. There were a couple of mountain houses with lights on, but as they went farther and farther from the highway, there were no lights and they were lost in the darkness of the forest.

"Where are we going?" Jenny asked.

"We're gonna spend the night in one of these places. Maybe they'll even have a bottle sitting around. There's only a round of drinks left in this." He held the bottle up and suddenly stopped before an isolated cabin.

Jenny sat up as the ramifications of these actions began to dawn on her. "We're going to stay here? But it's not ours. How will we get in?" You can't stay here."

Jim was already out of the car, checking doors and boarded-up windows. "Sure we can. It's perfect. Way off the road. No one for miles. They won't even know we're here. This is great! This must be the kitchen. Get the tire iron, Buddy. I can pry this loose." Buddy did as he was ordered, and in no time they had the window pried open. Jim reached over and took Jenny's hand, pulling her out of the car and over to the open window.

"Here, Jen, I'll lift you up, and you can crawl in and unlock the door. There's a bolt on the inside."

"Oh, no! No! I can't do that. We shouldn't be doing this at all. This is wrong! I don't want to do this. I can't do this!"

"Sure you can," Jim and Buddy chorused, and she found herself boosted to the window ledge and crawling through the small window, sliding into a kitchen sink. "It's dark," she whispered, not knowing for sure why. "Its real dark. I can't see anything."

"Just stand still for a while; your eyes will get used to it. Then follow the wall around to the front. I'll knock on the door so you'll know when you're close."

"Don't be scared, Jen. You're the greatest," Buddy encouraged her.

Jenny's heart was pounding. For the first time since she started this adventure, she wanted to go home. As she felt her way along the short countertop, she thought of her mother and how worried she would be. *I'll never be able to explain this. It's the middle of the night!*

"Ouch!" She ran into the edge of a table and stumbled across the chair set underneath it. It was strange, dark, and scary. *Don't think, don't feel, just find the door.* Eventually she reached the sound of Buddy's reassuring voice. She got the door open, and by the time Buddy held her in his arms, she was shaking.

"This isn't ours, and we shouldn't be here," she said in a small child's frightened voice.

"C'mon, Jen. Have some fun. We'll find a light and see if these folks have anything to eat or drink. Then we'll get some sleep."

"Right. Take it easy!" said Jim. "We're just going to borrow it for a while.

The owners won't mind and in the morning, I'll fix the window. Oh, great! I found a lamp." He had been searching with the light of a match. "Hey, this is great! Too bad we can't build a fire. Might attract attention." He carried the lamp into the kitchen. There he started opening cupboard doors and deciding what they should eat: Campbell's soup or macaroni.

"Well, we'll have to build a little fire. No one will notice at this hour," he said. Jim was definitely in charge. Jenny decided to sit down at the kitchen table and not think about any of this, just sit.

"Get the gin. We'll finish that off," he ordered Buddy, who headed for the car. It wasn't that Jim was bossy, it was just that someone had to take charge, and he was doing it. They ate their meal and talked about how far they would get tomorrow. Actually, Jim and Buddy talked. Jenny just listened and worried about her mother. Finally, she worked up the courage to say out loud, "I need to go home."

"What do you mean, go home? I thought you were with us all the way . . . all the way to the Pacific Ocean!" Jim admonished.

"Well, no. I guess I can't do that. I ran away once, and my parents called the police. I'm real sorry. I don't wanna cause any trouble, but I think my mother will be very upset."

"What'd you run away for?" Buddy asked.

"I dunno. Just a dumb thing I did. Mad at my mom, I guess, for not letting me have my own way."

"Jesus! I never thought they'd call the cops, for one stinking night! Let's get some sleep and talk in the morning. Check the beds. They got such a great place, the beds are probably made."

Jim picked up the lamp, and they walked through the front room to a small bedroom. It was so small, there was just a dresser under the window and an old-fashioned iron bed. There were blankets, pillows, and an extra blanket at the foot of the bed. Still in charge, Jim sent Buddy and Jenny to bed together, while he took blankets to the couch. Jenny took off her shoes and slid between the covers next to the wall. Buddy reached over and pulled her to him.

"C'mon, Jenny. Let's make the best of this. I won't hurt you. Let's undress, and I'll get you warm," he said softly as he began kissing her neck and ears.

"No, no, no! I mustn't do this. I have to sleep . . . I have to go home. My parents are going to be furious at me!"

He kissed her and caressed her, gently persuading her to surrender to the passion of the moment. She was bewildered and physically drained. She felt herself sinking, sinking as though into a dark, deep abyss. Her head was swirling; if she hadn't been lying down, she would have fallen. There seemed to be only one place to fall and that was into Buddy's strong and waiting arms.

They kept necking, heavily. She knew he was undressing her, but she couldn't seem to say or do anything except hold on to him. She felt that if she didn't hold on, she might fall and fall and never stop falling. The only time she wasn't falling was when he was kissing her. All there was in the world was kissing. His lips on hers, his tongue touching hers, his body moving next to hers.

A thought drifted past her like a ticker-tape banner, that maybe she wasn't falling. She was flying, and she liked that, so she kept holding on tight, falling and flying. As movement was somehow suspended in space, she was aware of being warmer and warmer, and although she was not alone in this crazy mixed up place, she felt alone. One moment, an eagle flew high above a rugged mountain peak. Then she soared down, down, down till there was no eagle, only waves crashing and moving beneath the surface of the sea.

Once she thought she cried out, "*Mother! Mother! I need you. Where are you?*" Then there was quietness and tears. Tears flowed soundlessly from Jenny's eyes, down her nose and cheeks, against Buddy's shoulder.

"Jenny, Jenny. You okay? Why are you crying? I didn't hurt you, did I?" Buddy asked.

"No, no . . . I dunno. I'm sleepy." Gin and fatigue consumed her. Jenny dropped off to sleep, unaware of her journey.

Dawn came pouring through the window at about the same time that Jim grabbed hold of Buddy's foot.

"C'mon, old buddy. We better get out of here. If her old man is going to call the cops, the sooner we get her back, the better," said Jim, still in charge.

Jenny hid her nakedness, feeling shame and fear and confusion. Since she seemed to be the cause of all this anxiety, she pulled the blanket around her and slid off the bed. Buddy had already left the room, and that made it easier to find her clothes and slip them on. She shivered in the cold and decided she should at least make the bed. What she really wanted was to stay hidden in the bedroom. The day was feeling too difficult already.

Buddy called, "C'mon, Jen. We have to get out of here. It's late!" They met about halfway across the small front room and he gave her a quick squeeze. "You okay, Jenny?"

"Sure. I just thought I should straighten the covers," she mumbled. She wondered why she didn't want him to touch her. She guessed Jim and Buddy were mad because she was getting them in trouble. She decided that when they got in the car, she would tell them how sorry she was.

Jenny stayed inside to lock the front door and then climbed out the way she got in. Then Jim fixed the boards back on the kitchen window. Jenny had a headache and felt sick to her stomach. She hoped she wouldn't throw up. People didn't usually like it when she did that, and she thought it wise not to cause any more trouble.

273

Buddy kept giving her little hugs and asking her if she was okay, but her feelings weren't the same as they had been yesterday. The car hadn't been moving very long before Jenny knew she was going to vomit. They stopped none too soon. After she got back in the car, Buddy put his arm around her and laid her head on his shoulder.

"It's okay, Jenny. Just too much gin. We're going on home. We weren't going anywhere, anyhow. We have to go back to camp. I sure don't want any trouble with the Army, any more than I want trouble with your old man."

Jenny swallowed and then said, "I'm sorry. I didn't think we were really going this far. My parents are very strict, and I should have told you. I hope you won't get in any trouble. I'm dreadfully sorry."

Buddy brushed back her hair as she lay her head on his shoulder. "Don't worry, Jen, we'll think of something. Get some rest."

Jenny slept. It seemed the best place to be, asleep. In fact, Jenny acted asleep long after she woke up and wondered what was happening at home.

When they turned the corner of her street, they didn't have to wonder very long. There was the Sheriff's car, right in front of her house. Jim slammed on the brakes and turned around.

"Jesus! You meant it when you said they'd call the cops. We sure messed up! The last thing I need is trouble." Jim headed straight out of town to the old cemetery, where he could think.

It was now about four o'clock on Monday. School was out, and it would soon be dark. Jenny decided it was her problem, not theirs, and convinced them to drop her off close to her house. She would just walk home and say she had gotten lost. She would make it clear to her parents that it wasn't Jim and Buddy's fault that she'd been gone. They could say that they had looked for her until dark, and then assumed she had gone home.

Yes, that's what they would say. That they went for a ride, went hiking, and then got separated from each other. Jenny had gotten lost, and they could-n't find her anywhere. They thought she must have found a way to go home. It was dark by then, and they had slept in the car. In the meantime, Jenny had slept in an old shed, and in the morning she started walking towards home. She was worried sick because her parents didn't know where she was. She didn't know what to do but just keep walking.

Jenny didn't think her father would believe her, but if they told the same story, he would surely believe Jim and Buddy. In their fear and desperation, their story made sense.

When she got out the car, Buddy gave her a hug and said, "See you," but they both knew he wouldn't. All Jenny felt was fear. Buddy didn't matter; she didn't even know his last name. All she knew about him was that he was from Texas.

When she turned down her street, the Sheriff's car was not at her house anymore, but down the street at Thelma's. Jenny's heart seemed to stop. *Oh, what have I done. I can never go home again.* She turned, walked away, and just kept walking.

Chapter 31

Night came. Jenny got colder and colder. She looked for shelter under the bridge by the college, but there was a small fire burning by an abandoned car in the ravine, and she was too scared to go closer. She thought about going on the highway again, but then she remembered the last time she ran away. She didn't know where else to go. She knew she would eventually get caught, so she just kept walking.

A patrol car came by, and she ditched behind a clump of shrubs with bare branches. They weren't much cover, but her fears told her she had better hide until she figured out what to do. She was getting frightfully cold. Ahead of her was the National Guard Armory with its cement walls and unfinished foundation.

That's a good place. It's dark, and no one ever goes there because it's not finished. She ran the rest of the way and found a covered place to crouch down, away from the now chilling breeze.

Huddled up in a corner, she began to feel warm and kind of dizzy again. She realized she hadn't eaten all day. A few tears fell. She didn't think about being bad or good, just about being hungry, cold, lonely, and scared. She dozed off. She had no idea how much time had passed when a gentle voice spoke her name"Jenny? Jenny?"and an equally gentle hand touched her shoulder. She opened her eyes to see a state trooper looming over her. His flashlight flooded her entire body.

"Is your name Jenny?" he continued in his strong, gentle voice.

"Yes." Her teeth chattered as she crouched further into the corner.

"Jenny, do you know your folks are clear out of their minds looking for you? What are you doing here? Who the hell left you here, and what are you afraid of?"

He lifted her to her feet, and Jenny noticed that another officer was with him. They took her to their car. It was warm and safe inside. Jenny slid into the corner as far as she could. She was thankful and scared at the same time.

She wanted to go home, so she was glad when they turned her corner. She was also filled with terror about going there. She knew her mother would be worried sick. The officer kept telling her, "Your mother is out of her mind with worry about you!" He also assured her that all she needed was a warm soft bed and she'd be okay. She hoped he was right.

It wasn't far to her house. They went in, and her mother took her in her arms. Jenny wanted to cry, but she couldn't.

The officers asked if she had been with Jim and Buddy and she said "Yes." She forgot the story they had made up.

"Did either of those guys do anything to you?" they asked. "Screw around with you?"

"I don't know," Jenny said. It was the truth.

They all agreed that what Jenny needed now was warm food and sleep. No one said anything to her about how bad she had been. When her mother asked if she had eaten today and Jenny said, "No," and her mother made her milk toast and cocoa, Jenny's favorites. She even asked if Jenny needed help bathing, and although Jenny declined, she didn't mind her mother asking. Adam kissed her good night, and said he loved her and was glad she was home. Her father gave her a hug and a kiss, and said they would "deal with all this in the morning." Jenny wasn't sure what "all this" meant, but she was finally home and it felt like the best place in the world.

After breakfast the next morning, her mother announced that they were going to the doctor. Jenny wanted to ask why, but thought it best just to do as she was told. On the way there, her mother asked her, point blank, if she had had sex with one of those men. Jenny could tell her only what she had told the police. "I don't know. I don't think so."

"What do you mean, you don't know? You have to know. How could you not know?"

"I dunno. I just don't know."

Jenny felt the same way at the doctor's office as he explained to her that no one was going to blame or hurt her. They just needed to know if either of "those men" had hurt her or had sex with her.

She answered that she had slept with Buddy in a cabin that they had broken into. She said Jim had told her to sleep with Buddy, but she didn't know if he "did anything."

The doctor examined her and told her what he was doing as he went along, but that didn't make it any better. Her mother held her hand and acted worried. The doctor left, and her mother patted her and told her not to worry, everything would be all right.

When the doctor came back, he nodded to her mother as though Jenny weren't there and said, "Yes, the hymen is broken, and there is semen in the specimen I took. There are also traces of blood. Of course, if she has been impregnated, we'll take care of it immediately. There'll be no problem there."

Her mother looked more worried than ever. She told Jenny to get dressed and meet them in the doctor's office. On the way home, her mother told her, "You will say nothing about this to anyone. No one! If you are pregnant, we'll take care of it immediately, so let me know about your period."

Jenny hated her mother asking about her period, but she knew she didn't have a choice. *How could this have happened when I don't remember it? How can the doctor be sure? Maybe he was wrong. I ought to know, and I don't know. I want to remember, and I can't!*

At home, no one said much to her except to rest and not to worry. So she slept, woke up, and slept again. She told the Sheriff everything about going for a ride: not knowing where she was, not wanting to climb in the window, and wanting to come home. When he asked if they had drunk liquor, she said, "Yes," and told him what it tasted like. She couldn't remember what it was called.

Her father said she was to stay home from school and not to talk to anyone about this. He had spoken to the principal, and her teachers had given him her homework. Jenny kept expecting him to be angry, but he never was.

She slept most of Tuesday and did her homework until Ginger called and asked how she was. She said she was sick, as her mother had told her to say. She said it might be contagious so Ginger couldn't come over. Jenny didn't know why she wasn't supposed to tell Ginger, but she wasn't about to rock the boat. There was still no anger, which amazed her, and no one had said anything about punishment. It was confusing.

On Wednesday, her father woke her and said they had to go to court. "Just tell the truth," he said at breakfast, "and this will be all over. Don't worry at all as long as you're honest."

By the time they reached the court house, he had said it a dozen times. In the court room, she and her parents sat at a big table. A man introduced himself to her, but she didn't register his name. There were other men there and a woman who wrote everything down. When the judge came in, everyone stood, and then he began to read the papers in front of him. He asked Jenny her name and told her he had to ask her some questions. He said she could sit with her parents and didn't have to stand up, but she had to tell the truth. He said her answers were very important. One of the men brought a Bible over, and Jenny swore to tell the whole truth and nothing but the truth.

The Judge asked her about the party and how well she knew Thelma and Jim. He asked if she had ever consumed alcoholic beverages before, and she said, "No." He asked why Thelma had gone home instead of staying with them, and if Jim had made any advances towards her. He said that there was medical evidence that Private Calvin J. Gibson had had sexual relations with her. He asked her if Buddy had forced himself on her or hurt her in any way. By the tone of his voice, Jenny thought the truth was not going to be what he wanted, but she stuck with it and said, "I don't think so, but I don't know."

The Judge cleared his throat. "No one is going to hurt you or blame you about any of this, Jenny. These young men are members of the Armed Services, and they were very aware that you are a minor. Now, do you recall either of them forcing you to be sexual with them or in any way doing you harm?"

Jenny took a deep breath. "No, sir. I don't think so. Jim told me I had to sleep with Buddy, and I did."

"Did you undress or behave in a sexual manner towards this" he looked at the papers, "Calvin-Buddy-man?"

"No sir. I left my clothes on. I was scared."

"Did he make advances toward you?"

"Yes, he told me to undress."

"Did you?"

"No, not really."

"Did he then have sexual intercourse with you?"

"I don't know."

Silence.

The judge shifted a little in his chair and looking directly at Jenny, he said, "Young lady, you are very fortunate to have such wonderful, caring parents. Do you know that?"

"Yes sir."

"Then, do you have any idea how you got yourself into a mess like this?"

"No, sir. I don't know." And she didn't. She wasn't even certain what the mess was.

When she left with her parents, she saw Jim and Buddy in the hall with some other soldiers. She looked away quickly. They didn't appear to want to see her either. Jenny had a lot of questions, but she decided it was wiser not to ask anything.

Her father dropped her and her mother off at home and went on to work. Jenny went upstairs to bed. Bed seemed the best place to be these days. She didn't feel sick anymore, but everyone kept asking her if she was okay. Even Jimmy brought his book up to her bed, and as he climbed up beside her he asked, "Jenny, are you sick? Are you okay?"

At dinner on Thursday, her father told her she was to stay home all week-end and go back to school on Monday. She could go to church, but she was-n't to make any other plans. No one wanted the truth to get out, so she was to stay home "sick".

As an afterthought, her father said to her mother, "That Jimmy's father is one fine man. He understands our position and says he'll give us any sup-port he can. This going in the Army has been rough on his boy, and they didn't think anything about it when he asked to bring a stranger home with him. He and his wife feel very bad about what happened."

Jenny's mother had that look on her face that meant not to talk about it, so he didn't say any more. Jenny sensed it had to do with Jim and Buddy. She wasn't getting punished because it was their fault. She guessed Thelma wouldn't be her friend anymore, but they weren't very good friends anyway.

Jenny changed the subject by asking someone to study her airplane identi-fication cards with her. She had made drawings of all the planes on five-by-seven-inch cards and written all the statistics she needed to know on the back. Her father said when the dishes were done, he would test her. With his new job at the airport, he needed to know these things too. It was the first normal evening in their house for several days.

Jenny was thankful when Monday morning arrived. She and Ginger were going to meet early and catch up. Jenny's mother had said to tell everyone they'd thought Jenny had the measles, but it turned out to be bronchial pneumonia. It felt strange that her parents should be telling her to lie. If it was Jim and Buddy's fault, as it seemed to be, why couldn't Jenny just say so? But her mother had said that if Ginger's mother ever found out, Jenny might lose her for a friend. So Jenny never breathed a word to anyone, and no one ever asked.

"Remember Buddy, Jen?" Ginger said many weeks later. "He got a dishon-orable discharge from the Army for what he did to you. My mom said he deserved it. I've never told a soul, though, and I won't."

Jenny just looked at her, half listening, and said, "Oh, that's good. My mother said not to mention it, either."

That closed the door forever. The whole experience disappeared into the world that was forgotten.

Chapter 32

Shortly after Thanksgiving and Jenny's birthday, she came bursting in the front door after a trip through town, bubbling with excitement. "Mom! Mom! I have seen the most beautiful dress in the whole wide world. I tried it on, and it fits me perfectly. I have to have it!"

"Slow down Jenny, just slow down. If I'm going to hear about this dress, you have to slow down."

"It's this soft material they call 'jersey,' and it's the most beautiful color of red you ever saw. Around the neckline is tiny red and golden embroidery, and when I walk, it swirls and moves like . . . like . . . like . . . oh, I dunno, just beautiful! You have to come and see it. Pleeease? I can wear it to the Senior Banquet and Rainbow AND the Valentines Dance for DeMolay."

"Well, how much does this incredible garment cost? Perhaps I can make it."

"No, no, no! You can't, you see, because of the material and the embroidery. Besides, I want that one. Ginger was with me and she thinks I should have it, too. The lady in the store said it was made for me. Will you come see it? Please?"

"Well, Jenny. Don't go setting your heart on something you can't have, but after school tomorrow, we'll go look at it. It's dinner time now."

At dinner, Jenny repeated her pleading conversation with her father, proclaiming the rare beauty of this particular dress, and how advantageous it would be for her parents to buy it for her. She promised to wear it and wear it and wear it.

The only other store-bought dress Jenny had ever had was in the sixth grade, and her mother was quick to remind her of how she had begged and begged for that particular dress, too. That time, her parents had finally bargained with her that if she won the county declamatory contest, she could have that dress for the Regionals. It had been red and proudly displayed in the window of J.C. Penney's. The tragedy about that dress was that Jenny wore it only a few times. When her mother washed it, the material frayed so badly, the seams pulled out. It couldn't be fixed because it had also shrunk. It had cost her parents a lot of money, and her mother never let her forget how badly she had wanted it and how worthless it turned out to be.

It seemed to Jenny that her mother never forgot anything, especially if it was bad. And whenever anything bad happened in the family, it seemed to be her fault. As far as Jenny knew, or according to her mother, she hadn't even been born right. The doctor wasn't there, and she was all red, covered with black hair, and screaming. She didn't learn to walk right, either. They had also thought she would never cut any teeth. (Jenny was never sure who "they" were.) These stories had been accumulating her entire life. Her mother never forgot them, and never let Jenny forget them.

But this new dress was not like the old one. Jenny just knew it! This dress would last forever.

Her mother went to see it, and even let Jenny try it on again. Jenny felt hopeful, but her hope was dashed to the ground when her mother saw the price tag. "Jenny, this is out of the question. There is no possible way that we can afford this."

"But I can help. I have some money."

"But you'll have to have shoes, too. It's just too much. I'll see if The Mercantile has any material like this, and if not, perhaps my friend, Madge, has something you can borrow. She's offered many times."

Jenny swallowed her tears. She didn't want to make her mother feel bad about not having the money. She dressed while her mother gave the garment back to the clerk. When she came back, Jenny said, "Can we go to the yardage store now? If they don't have that material, maybe I'll just get something different. Everyone saw that dress in the window, and I don't want to wear any old borrowed dress."

"No, we won't look at fabric today," her mother said. "It's too near dinner. I'm sorry, Jenny. You shouldn't have gotten your hopes up. You knew it was entirely too expensive."

"Well, I just thought . . . It's okay." She swallowed tears again.

I don't know what I'll say to Ginger . . . just the truth, I guess. As she rode home beside her mother, she realized that she didn't know very much about money. She didn't understand why they never seemed to have enough. Teachers must make a lot of money, and she knew they weren't poor. But it felt as if whenever she wanted anything, there wasn't enough money. She thought she might ask her mother about this, but looking at her mother's silent face, she decided not to.

Her mother still wanted Jenny to confide in her. Part of Jenny wanted to, but when they tried, it didn't usually work out. Her mother would pry and Jenny would clam up, that's what her mother called it. A lot of the time, she asked questions that Jenny couldn't answer, so Jenny would reply, "I don't know." Her mother didn't seem to have any tolerance for that at all. She always acted as if Jenny knew but wouldn't tell her. Sometimes that was true, but most often not. Jenny had no answers about a lot of things.

One day when they were baking cookies, she had thought of asking her mother if she ever felt like more than one person. But the more she thought about it, the more ridiculous it seemed. And after the day in court, Jenny was sure there was another part of her that got her into trouble. *It wasn't me. That's why I didn't know the answers to the judge's questions. It wasn't me. That's why it was easy to forget.*

It sounds kind of crazy. Maybe there are two of me, or another person who isn't me at all. Better not say anything about that, ever.

When they got home, she was surprised that her father remembered where they had been and asked about the dress. Jenny didn't look at him but mumbled towards the floor, "It cost too much money," and went straight to her room. She could hear her parents talking but she didn't try to hear their words. If she couldn't have it, what difference did it make what they said about it? Probably her father would come in and explain to her what she already knew, and he would ask her, "You do understand, don't you, Jenny?"

And Jenny would reply, "Yes, Father," even if she didn't.

She lay down on her bed. Sure enough, in a little while, the doorknob turned, and her father came in to explain why she couldn't have the dress. From the moment the knob turned, she wanted him to leave. She hated having him in her room. She didn't even want him to open the door. She was getting very good at giving him the answers he wanted so that he would leave quickly. This time, she told him she understood about the dress, and it didn't matter. She added that she had better help her mother with dinner, and scooted past him down the stairs and into the kitchen. She was relieved to have the whole thing over with and glad it would never be mentioned again. She could count on her family not to mention unpleasant feelings.

On the Saturday after Thanksgiving, Jenny turned seventeen, and the whole family went to the Chinese restaurant for dinner. Jenny loved going there. From the moment they stepped through the double doors, and Jenny smelled the mixture of spices and incense and cooking odors floating through the long corridor to the kitchen, she could imagine she was in China. On both sides of the corridor were little rooms with the most exquisite curtains over the doorways, dark crimson with gold embroidery, and one of cloth that looked like gold. Inside the little rooms, over each table, was a Chinese lantern with pictures on all sides and tassels hanging from each corner. If you touched it gently, it would twirl around and around, and the figures on the sides would move and dance in their own separate movements.

Ginger joined the family at Jenny's house for ice cream and cake. Ginger had turned seventeen in the summer, and it felt good to them to be the same age again. More than ever they wondered what they would do when high school ended. It seemed to Jenny that she was expected to have her future all planned out. It was enough for her just to live from one week to the next, with Christmas coming, ice skating season, and then the Senior Banquet coming up right after New Year's.

She hadn't told Ginger she couldn't have the red dress for the banquet. As a matter of fact, she wasn't even getting a new dress; she was wearing one of Madge's. It was actually very pretty, so Jenny put the red dress out of her mind and agreed with her mother. "It is lovely, dear, and we're so lucky to have such a generous friend."

Her mother was right, Madge Hendricks was generous. When Jenny babysat for the Hendricks, they always paid her well, and if she spent the night, she got an extra five dollars. In the spring, Madge was going to have another baby, and Jenny had agreed to stay there for an entire month. Jenny loved babies, and she was very good with them. That was partly from having Jimmy for a little brother, she figured. As soon as the baby was born, she was to go there after school, prepare meals for the children, and put them to bed. Mr. Hendricks came home around ten or eleven o'clock from his job, but he would help in the morning so she wouldn't be late for school.

Jenny started when she heard her mother saying her name. "Jenny, Jenny! Didn't you hear me? Where on earth do you go, anyhow? Set up the card table; we'll start that new puzzle . . . the one of the London Bridge and the tower. You've been wanting to start it."

"Oh, I'm sorry. I don't know where I went. Somewhere, I guess. It's exciting to be seventeen and a senior. Before long, I'll be grown up."

"What do you think will be so great about being grown up?" her father asked.

"Oh, I don't know. It just feels different, I guess. There was a lady at school from the hospital, and I signed up to go on a tour. Maybe I'll be a Navy nurse."

"A nurse!" he exclaimed. "Last time anyone mentioned nursing, you thought that would be the worst profession on earth."

"Daddy, that was before the war. It's different now. They need nurses. I could start when school is out. I wouldn't have to wait till I'm eighteen if I went in the regular Navy."

"I don't think you need to be considering signing up for the Navy or the Army."

"Come on, you two," her mother interrupted, "eighteen is a whole year away. Let's just have a good time being seventeen, okay?"

Later that night, cuddled up together in bed, Ginger and Jenny promised to be friends forever. Jenny told her about the dress, and Ginger was wonderful. She gave Jenny a big hug and said, "Jenny, you'll be just beautiful, no matter what you have to wear. I think you're the prettiest, smartest friend I have ever had."

"Thank you, Ginger. You're my best friend, too. And thank you for spending my birthday with me. If you go away to school, this might be the very last birthday we spend together."

"Don't say that, Jenny. It's a long ways away."

"It's for sure I can never go to Colorado to school. We don't have any money. I brought home the catalogues from Northwestern and UCLA, and my mother said I ought to stop thinking those thoughts right now. But Miss Tucker, my drama teacher, said to send the applications in anyway. My mother says California is no place for a decent girl, anyhow, so they would-n't let me go to UCLA."

"If you can't go to California, you can come to Colorado."

"The truth is, I think I'm just pretending, because I always thought I'd go away to school. But my dad says no place is safe for a girl since the war. Towns aren't the same. Schools aren't the same. And if I'm going to school, I had better plan on State Normal College. My dad went there. I guess it would be better than staying at home."

"Something will work out, Jenny. Don't worry."

"Hey, you two! You'll be late for church if you don't get some sleep," Jenny's mother called from the dining room door. "Quiet down in there. The birthday is over. Good night now."

Giggling like little girls, they covered their heads with blankets and spent another hour whispering about dates for the Valentine's Dance. Jenny knew Harold would ask her, and she'd probably say "Yes." But it was more fun to pretend that at least six boys she liked would ask her, and she'd have to choose. Finally, they slept to dream the dreams of teenage girls, partly in yesterday and partly in tomorrow.

Time always went fast at Jenny's house between her birthday and Christmas. First she and her mother baked fruitcakes, with all those special candied fruits and nutmeats that you never got to eat any other time of year. The cakes were carefully wrapped in cloth and stored in air-tight tins. Then cookie baking began. Jenny loved this special time of year when she felt as if she had as much authority in the kitchen as her mother. They had been saving sugar and sugar coupons, and all her mother's friends were trading recipes with wartime substitutions.

On the Saturday night before Christmas, her mother was in charge of the refreshments at the USO, and they were making everything as special as they could. Someone had mailed them pecans from Georgia, and another friend of her mother had given them some walnuts. Jenny was also going to make an angel food cake. If they had enough sugar for fluffy white frosting, she would make a chocolate cake, too. All the guys at the USO were grate-ful for home cooking. It made Jenny feel very special and worthwhile.

Snow fell, and the ice-skating pond froze solid. It was a storybook Christmas, and on Christmas morning, she couldn't wait to see everyone open the presents she had given them. Because of Jimmy, they still had Santa Claus, and secretly, Jenny hoped Santa would always come. She loved her little brother, and the best part of all was that she knew how much he loved her. When she woke, she heard his voice in the front room and waited for him to play the game of waking her.

"Jenny, Jenny!" He burst through the door. "Come quick and see what Santa left you. You have brand new skates! White ones with long laces!"

She shot out of bed and without slipping on her robe, ran with him to the tree of splendor.

"Look! Look, Jenny, I have skis! Real skis, and they're brand new!" Adam shouted.

There was a flurry, and then Jimmy thrust the beautiful white skates into her hands.

"Look, Look," he continued, "I have skates, too, and mittens and a hat that matches! You can teach me! You can teach me!"

It was almost too much for Jenny. Tears welled up, and she looked at her parents, who were sitting on the couch, watching. She and Adam knew that Santa had nothing to do with this, and she acknowledged it with a big hug for each of them.

"Thank you, thank you, thank you! I love them! I just love them!"

Her mother smiled, but she admonished Jenny, "Jenny, you can't go around loving every inanimate object in your possession. Love is for people." Then she added, "They're nice skates, and I'm glad you like them."

"Yes, and they're figure skates, too. You wait and see. I'll be able to write my name in ice. The church is having a skating party next week, and I can practice every day. I can teach Jimmy, too. Thank you, thank you!" and she turned to admire Adam's new skis as he slid across the living room floor.

"Adam, you look like a real skier. I'll hike up the hill with you. You can start today. A lot of my friends ski and they'll help you. What a wonderful Christmas! Let's open our stockings now."

Her father interrupted with a reminder for them to put on their robes and slippers before someone caught a cold. When everyone returned, they sat down for the Christmas ritual of emptying stockings and exchanging gifts. There was one present with red tissue and silver ribbon that Jenny hadn't seen yesterday, and when Adam, who was "Santa" this year, handed it to her, she thought he had made a mistake. But there it was on the red and white tag, "To Jenny, From Dad." This was strange. Her father had never given her a separate gift before. She looked over at him and felt an old feeling, strange but familiar at the same time, sink into her stomach. He smiled and said, "Well, open it, Jenny!.

Jenny opened it, and there before her very eyes, in white tissue paper, were folds of gorgeous soft red jersey. She gasped, "Oh, no. It can't be! The red dress!" and she lifted it out of the box. "Oh, no. I don't believe it!"

She held it to her shoulders and floated around the room in ecstasy. Then she threw herself in her father's arms, the dress still draped around her, kissing him and thanking him profusely. Then, jumping to her feet, she twirled in front of her mother.

"I really, really, really do love this dress, Mom. More than the whole, wide world. I love it!"

"Okay, Jenny," her mother allowed. "This one thing you can love, just not everything. Let's put breakfast on the table."

On the way to the kitchen, Jenny wanted to give her mother a hug, but she sensed it wasn't quite okay. It didn't matter. Nothing mattered. She had the red dress for the Senior Banquet.

Chapter 33

Spring came. The Hendricks had their baby and Jenny moved in, as had been planned. She hadn't decided what she was going to do at the end of May when school was out, but it was becoming clear to her that her mother was right about daydreams. They didn't get you anywhere. Nothing that Jenny had ever dreamed of being when she grew up seemed to be coming true.

Part of the problem was the war, but she couldn't even do anything to help because she was too young. She had visited the hospital, and even though the uniforms and the idea of being a Lieutenant in the Navy were exciting, she didn't want to be a nurse. She got a knot in her stomach just thinking about all the yukky things nurses had to do. And any college except State Normal was out of the question financially. But she would make good money at the Hendricks doing something she loved to do, and she would try to forget tomorrow.

Jenny liked Mr. Hendricks as well as she liked any man, but it was strange being in the house with him by herself. One day, when she was cleaning up the bathrooms from bedtime baths, he leaned on the door frame, smiling, and said right out, "My boys are pretty lucky. Sure would like you to give me a bath and sing me to sleep."

She guessed it was a joke, but Jenny felt uncomfortable and embarrassed. She blushed and rushed by him with the dirty clothes and wet towels. "I have to do a tub of clothes. I can hang them up before I go to school." As a last minute thought she added, "Then I have to finish my homework."

Mrs. Hendricks had an automatic washing machine. It was amazing to put the clothes in with the soap and have the whole thing work by itself. The only thing Jenny had to be careful of was not to put in too many clothes or too much soap. One day when she was helping before the baby came, she had put in too much soap, and bubbles had come out all around the door, across the washroom floor, and clear out the back door. Jenny was horrified at her mistake, but Mrs. Hendricks just laughed and said it happened all the time.

Mr. Hendricks was listening to the radio and reading the paper when Jenny came back from the washroom, so Jenny took her books to the kitchen table. He smiled, and Jenny wondered why she felt so strange inside. It wasn't as if she didn't know him. He'd go upstairs to bed pretty soon, so Jenny just kept studying, way past any work she had to do. She reminded herself to go to the library tomorrow and get an extra book to read.

She was startled to feel Mr. Hendrick's hand on her shoulder. It gave her the creeps. "I won't be home for dinner tomorrow. I'll go by the hospital and visit Madge and the baby and then go back to work. I should be home about 2:30 in the morning. You lock the door, though, and I'll let myself in."

"Yes, Mr. Hendricks, I'll be fine," Jenny said, trying to slide her shoulder out from under his hand. He squeezed it, though, before she could get away. *Oh, yuk! I wish he wouldn't touch me.*

"I'll check the kids," he called to her as he walked upstairs. Long after Jenny went to bed in the little room off the kitchen, she thought about how funny he made her feel. She had never felt this way before, so she guessed it was because they were here alone. She thought she should listen for the children, so she left her door open. Then it occurred to her that with their father there, perhaps she should shut the door. When she crawled back in bed, she fell right to sleep.

The next two days went very well. Mr. Hendricks didn't come home until the middle of the night, and even though Jenny heard him rustle around in the kitchen, she wasn't bothered by him as she had been.

On the fourth night, Ronnie had a nightmare, and Jenny lay down next to him so he wouldn't wake everyone else. His favorite song was "Irish Lullaby," which he called "The Lu La Song." Jenny stroked his soft little shoulder and sang to him. She hadn't even heard Mr. Hendricks come into the room when suddenly he lay down on the bed beside her. She stopped singing, and he asked her to sing it again. He began to stroke her arm, and they all went off to sleep in a few seconds.

When Jenny awoke, she was uncomfortably aware that Mr. Hendricks had his hand over her breast.

He must be asleep. Otherwise I'm sure he wouldn't touch me that way. But I'm trapped between Ronnie and Mr. Hendricks. Maybe I can just roll over on my side.

She did, and Mr. Hendricks woke up. He kissed her on the cheek. "Thank you, Jenny. That was real nice." Saying good night, he went to his room.

Jenny went back to her room, feeling scared and sick to her stomach. Mr. and Mrs. Hendricks were two of the nicest people she knew, and they both liked her a lot. Otherwise, they wouldn't have wanted her to stay with the children while Mrs. Hendricks was in the hospital. The baby was doing great, but Mrs. Hendricks was having some complications and would probably be in the hospital the rest of next week. Jenny didn't mind. She liked not being at home; it made her feel grown up.

This being nervous and afraid of Mr. Hendricks is silly. I'd better just forget it and go to sleep.

Chapter 34

The next day at school was very exciting, one Jenny had been looking forward to. Seniors didn't have any classes in the afternoon because there was a special Career Day set up in the gymnasium. Ginger had already been accepted at Colorado State. They both knew that's what she would do, even though they often imagined other more exciting adventures together. Her mother had gone there and expected Ginger to go there, too. There was insurance money from her father to pay her way.

All her life, Jenny had expected to go away to college. When she had started high school and had to decide between Latin and French, her father had told her, "Regardless of what course of study you decide on in college, Latin will be good for you."

So she had taken Latin. Now that she was graduating with all the right courses in language, science, and literature, she was suddenly faced with a new reality. She didn't have any money. She pretended to her teachers and friends that she was going away to college because she didn't know how to tell them the truth. It seemed it was something she should have known, but she hadn't. When the applications came back from UCLA and she told her mother about the high out-of-state fee, she was surprised at her mother's startled response.

"Jenny," she said, "I don't know where you get these notions. We don't have that kind of money. If you want to go to State Normal, you can do that, but anything else is out of the question!"

"But, Mom, all my friends are going other places. At least they're going to the university."

"Well, I can't help that, dear. Your friends have considerably more money than we do. School teachers don't make that much. You know that."

"Yes, I guess so. I just thought . . . Oh, well, maybe I'll just get a job somewhere. It doesn't matter."

Jenny felt this must be her own fault, even though she hadn't figured out how. The immediate problem, however, was how to tell her friends she was not going away to school. Lying to her friends made Jenny feel bad.

Something would happen today to help her decide what to do. She just knew it. There were booths in the gym from the Air Force, the Marines, and the Navy. If she were eighteen, she would join the Navy, but she wouldn't be eighteen for six more months. What should she do in the meantime?

The State Department of Education had a booth, and a man from the department had spoken at the assembly. She remembered having a lump in her throat when he explained what was happening in small towns and in the country. So many teachers were being called into the Army that many schools across the state were being closed. This meant that parents would either have to teach their own children or find places for them to live in larger towns. Some ranchers could afford to move in winter, but very few.

Jenny couldn't imagine not going to school.   School was the most important thing in her life. The man from the State Department had said every child in America had a God given right to learn to read and write. Therefore, the State Department had decided to grant temporary certificates to graduating seniors to help out in this wartime crisis. He had invited anyone interested to talk to him that afternoon. As with anything related to the war, Jenny had gotten all choked up with emotions. She wanted to do something to contribute.

Maybe it wouldn't be like being in the Navy, but it would be helping out, she thought as she walked over to the State Department of Education's booth.

"Hello, young lady," the man said. "You interested in helping out with this crisis in education?"

"Yes," Jenny heard herself say. "My father doesn't want me to go away to school, not with war and all. Maybe I can do this. I'm a very good teacher; everyone says that."

"Well, great!" he said with a broad smile. "Here are the papers for the application. All you have to do is submit a transcript of your grades, attend a ten-week course at State Normal, and pass the written examination. I have no doubt you can do that!"

"How would I get a job, and where would I have to go?"

"That shouldn't be a problem. You can choose some schools that aren't too far from home and let them know you're interested. Their own school boards will do the actual hiring."

There was a big map of the State of Montana on the wall, sprinkled with little red flags. Each flag represented a school that would need a teacher by fall. Jenny made her decision. She had determined never to be a school teacher, but this was different because of the war. It wasn't as if she would teach forever, and she had to do something. School was almost over. She took the papers and slid them inside her notebook with a resolve to think this through, then tell her parents her decision. Everything would work out just fine.

Jenny had been looking forward to leaving home, so she was surprised that making concrete plans made her very anxious. When Ginger interrupted her with something about Saturday night, Jenny chose not to share her decision with her friend.

When school is over, it won't be the same for us. Even if Ginger doesn't think so, I know it won't. It's never the same. It's like moving around. Your friends are never the same. That's why it's important not to get too close to friends and feel as if you can't live without them.

That's the way she felt about Mary Lou. She hadn't written to her since Christmas. She knew Mary Lou was going back East to Stevens College, and for a fleeting moment she wondered why she wasn't doing any of the things she had always thought she would do. Life was so difficult. She turned to Ginger and suggested they go to town and have a soda.

That night before she went to bed, Jenny filled out the papers for State Normal School and the application to take the state exam. A representative from the Department of Education would come to the Normal school and administer the examination. Afterward, the names of everyone who passed would be mailed to the schools that needed teachers.

Jenny had enough money for the application fees and almost enough for ten weeks of room and board in the dormitory. She was sure her parents would take her to school since that's what they wanted her to do anyway. If not, she could take the bus.

She felt scared by her decision, but excited too. It might be fun to teach, and she would be helping her country.

Chapter 35

Jenny had a week left at the Hendricks. It had been fun, but she was anxious to get on with her life. After dinner and home-work, she went upstairs to check on the kids and decided she would go to bed too. She went to sleep imagining how it would be this summer to really and truly live away from home.

In the wee hours of the morning, she stirred when she heard the back door, but knowing it was Mr. Hendricks, she didn't fully waken. She was sound asleep when he sat on the edge of her bed and touched her shoulder.

"Don't be afraid, Jenny. It's me. I'm not able to go to sleep, and I thought maybe we could talk a little while."

"Huh? Oh, Mr. Hendricks. Do you want me to get up?"

"No, no. You stay here. I'll stretch out beside you. Why don't you call me Don? I'd much prefer that to Mr. Hendricks. We've known each other a long time, and aren't we more like friends?"

"Yes, I guess so, Don. What do you want to talk about? Mrs. Hendricks is okay, isn't she?"

"Yes, she's doing fine. I just feel very lonely by myself. It's been lonely for me all year. Madge has been so busy with the children, and being pregnant again. I don't know . . . I'm so lonely. I think we just don't love each other anymore."

"Oh, that must be terrible, Mr. Hendricks. I mean, Don. That must be just terrible. I know Mrs. Hendricks loves you. Maybe you just think she doesn't because she's so busy."

"I shouldn't be telling you my troubles like this. I've already said too much.

Why don't you just sing to me. You have such a lovely, sweet voice. It's no wonder my boys love you the way they do."

So Jenny sang lullabies to Mr. Hendricks, and it didn't feel as strange as she thought it would. He lay close to her, stroked her arm while she sang, then got up to leave for his own room. He thanked Jenny, said he felt better, and kissed her very lightly on the mouth. To Jenny's surprise, she kissed him back. He said, "That a girl, Jenny. I knew you had some of the same feelings I did. I'll see you tomorrow. Good night."

The next two nights, Mr. Hendricks came to her room. On the third night, he crawled between the covers and stroked her all over as they kissed. Part of the time Jenny just lay there, and part of the time she didn't. She knew it was wrong, but it felt very good. She sang to him and thought how sad it was that he was such a nice man and so lonely in his own house. Mrs. Hendricks was to come home in a couple of days, and Jenny would go home by the end of another week. *It couldn't possibly do any harm if it makes him feel better. It feels good to be held and stroked and told how wonderful and beautiful I am. It can't be too wrong.*

That day at school, as they talked over their plans for the weekend, and Jenny told Ginger about her decision to join the Emergency Teachers Program. To Jenny's surprise, Ginger was elated for her. She said she wished she could do that too, but her mother expected her to go to Colorado in the fall. They mourned about not having the summer together, but vowed to spend every day they had doing something special. Confiding in Ginger and having her for a special friend reminded Jenny of Mr. Hendricks. She concluded that she must be special to him since he confided in her in his secret way.

When I have a baby, I'll be extra, extra loving to my husband so he won't feel lonely and unloved. How could Mrs. Hendricks be so thoughtless?

The more he shared, the more she understood. Jenny wanted to tell Ginger. But Mr. Hendricks had told her it was their secret, and that made her feel special.

That night, Mr. Hendricks asked her if she would make love with him "all the way." Jenny knew she couldn't do that. It would be wrong, and besides, she didn't want to. He kept kissing her and then he kissed her breasts. Jenny panicked. This wasn't fun any more. Something was going to happen to her over which she had no control. She started to cry and pushed him away from her, and he stopped. He said he was sorry; he wouldn't do that again. But she was still frightened.

She didn't do well in school the next day. Something about last night had made her sick to her stomach and created a restlessness in her that she hadn't felt for a long time. She didn't like the feelings, so she kept trying to figure out what to do. She was so distracted that she didn't hear her name being called in literature class.

Ginger was coming over for supper, and they were going to study together, so at least the time would pass faster. It wouldn't help any when Mr. Hendricks came home, but she would have to deal with that when the time came.

As it turned out, Mr. Hendricks felt as bad as she did. He told her he hadn't been able to think of anything else all day, and he was so sorry. He assured her he wouldn't do it again. He asked Jenny to sing to him, and when she had sung a few songs, he kissed her and went to bed. Jenny was so relieved she went right to sleep.

Mrs. Hendricks was coming home with the baby on Sunday. One more week, she thought, and I'll have plenty of money for room and board. She still hadn't told her parents about her plans. It could wait. On Saturday, she cleaned the house, changed all the beds, and did the laundry. Before he went to work Saturday night, Mr. Hendricks was going to take Jenny home to spend Sunday with her family. Little Ronnie wanted her to stay and live with them, and she admitted to herself that she would miss them. It was nice to feel needed and important. She knew Jimmy thought she was important, but no one else did, that's for sure.

However, when she and Mr. Hendricks got in the car to take her home, he didn't turn in the direction of her house. Instead, he drove the car toward the old cemetery road.

"Where are we going? I thought we were going to my house," Jenny asked, puzzled and anxious.

"I just thought we could take a few minutes together one last time. I'm going to miss you so much, Jenny. You don't know what a wonderful feeling you've brought into my life," and he reached over and took her hand. He pulled off the road under some shade trees, leaned over Jenny, and opened her door.

"C'mon, let's get in the back seat. It'll be more comfortable to talk."

Jenny did just as she was told. Once in the back seat, something inside of her said, No, No, Mr. Hendricks! But she wasn't sure if it came out of her mouth or stayed in her throat somewhere. There was darkness and fear, yes's and no's, and then just darkness.

The next thing Jenny knew, Mr. Hendricks was outside the car zipping up his pants and fastening his belt. He leaned in and kissed her, smiling. "I knew you'd be good, Jenny. You better pee before you put your panties on."

Jenny did as she was told. I should be feeling something, but I don't. She sat quietly all the way home. When Mr. Hendricks said good-bye at the door, she told him good-bye and took her things to her room. She was glad no one was home. She sat on the edge of the bed for a while. Her head was a little dizzy, she thought she might vomit, but she didn't feel anything else.

I guess I'll take a bath, she thought and slowly and methodically undressed, leaving her clothes on the floor. Once in the tub of warm water, she rubbed the warm soap suds over her body again and again. When the water began to cool, she washed her hair, too. When it was all clean, she lay back in the tub and watched the long black tendrils float on the surface of the water. Holding herself, she stroked her upper arms and wondered what it would be like to be a mermaid, and if there really were such creatures.

Finally the water was cold. She dried herself and went to her room. It wasn't dark, but all she could think of was going to sleep. She shivered for a few minutes in her fresh clean sheets. Then, hugging her pillow and glad to be home, she slid into a peaceful sleep.

Just after dark, her mother opened her bedroom door and woke her. "Jenny, wake up and set the table. Dinner's almost ready. I went by the Hendricks to get you, only to find out Don had already brought you home."

Jenny felt as if she must be returning from another world. "Huh? Oh, hi, Mom. I'll put my robe on and be right there." Jenny picked up her clothes and put her check in the top dresser drawer. She felt good about the amount she had earned. She reminded herself to talk to her parents about her plan to go to State Normal and teach school next year.

At the dinner table, there was much chatter about the new baby at the Hendricks and how long Jenny had been gone from home. Her mother suggested that Jenny should stop by the YWCA and give her name to the placement office for Mother's Helpers. Jenny felt proud as her mother praised her abilities with children.

"Well, I've decided to go to State Normal this summer," she said.

"You what?!" her mother exclaimed in surprise. Jenny told them about the man from the Department of Education. As she expected, both of her parents were pleased at her decision. By the time the table was cleared and she and her mother were doing the dishes, the entire plan was in place, including making her some summer clothes. Jenny felt a great sense of relief to have plans for the future. It was exciting to be going away from home, even if it wasn't to any of the places she had dreamed of. She felt very grown up and in charge of her life.

Chapter 36

The next few weeks were a constant flurry of activity: parties, dances, exams, sewing, and a lot of baby-sitting to pay for it all. Jenny chose to have graduation night with her family, and Ginger came over for cake and ice cream. Ginger's mother had to work very early the next day, so she went back to her place after the graduation ceremony. Graduation itself was exciting but somber. There were empty chairs for the graduating seniors who had already left for war. By fall, more than half the boys would be in some branch of the armed services. By Christmas, all but a few who were not physically fit or whose family needed them would be gone. Jenny wished again that she was a boy, but she wasn't, and she was definitely helping by joining the Emergency Teaching Forces. Women had to help in whatever way they could.

That night when Jenny undressed, she folded her new dress and slip, and put them in the open suitcase. The next day she finished packing, and on Friday her parents took her half way across the state to her summer home in the school dormitory. Jenny was much more excited than she wanted to let on. Jimmy and Adam were excited too, although Jimmy wasn't at all certain he liked the idea of leaving her there. It was like the old days when they went on camping trips. They hadn't done that for several years.

The dorm matron, Miss Greer, was expecting her. She took Jenny and her mother upstairs to her room at the end of the hall, right across from the shower room. When she reached Jenny's room, she turned to Jenny's mother and nodded toward the end of the hall where big double doors were shut beneath a sign that read "Boys Dormitory." "The doors are shut between the Boys' Dorm and this wing, but of course there aren't any boys here, what with the war," she said. It didn't seem important to Jenny, but obviously it was to Miss Greer.

She opened the door to Jenny's room for the summer and said that the bed on the right was Jenny's. Two desks sat side by side in the middle of the room, and at the end of each bed was a three-drawer dresser. Big double windows looked out on the sprawling green campus. Everything else was in the compact storage closet unit at the opposite end of the stark cubical.

317

"Your roommate's name is April; she'll be here late tonight. Here's your key; don't lose it. There's a one dollar charge for a new one," Miss Greer said. "On your bed is a list of the dormitory rules, which were also in your packet. They are strictly enforced. I owe that to your parents. They entrust you to me." She addressed this remark to Jenny's mother, not to Jenny.

To Jenny she said, "But I'm certain you won't have any problem adhering to the rules, Jenny. I remember when your father graduated. Dean Morris will be so happy to see you. Next Sunday is the President's Tea, and you are expected to attend. Leave your things here, and I'll show you the parlors and the dining room. There will be a light supper at 6:30 for the girls who have arrived."

"We're staying over," Jenny's mother volunteered. "Jenny will eat supper with us."

Downstairs there were two small private sitting rooms where girls could have guests. There was a big, rather splendid room known as the parlor, with a huge stone fireplace at the end and deep velvety couches and chairs arranged in groups. There were a couple of mahogany tables that could be used for study, and directly opposite the fireplace was an ebony grand piano.

"Girls can sign up to use this piano for practice during school hours. It has a beautiful tone. I'm very proud of this room. My girls spend a lot of time here. It makes the starkness of the dormitory life more like home," Miss Greer said.

What a strange lady, Jenny thought. *She acts as if she's my mother or something, but all she really does is run the dorm.*

They followed her down the wide stairway to the dining room where large round tables were set with ten places each.

"This room is built to accommodate both the Boys' and Girls' Dorms, so it will be half empty all summer. It's hard to say how it will be in the fall. Mostly girls, I suppose. Some local ranch boys will be continuing in school because they're needed to keep the sheep and cattle ranches operating, but they won't be here," she rattled on.

338

Jenny concluded there must not be any men left in this town. At least in Helena, there were Air Force cadets and soldiers. After going dancing every weekend, this could be a strange experience, she thought.

Her father took them all out for supper, and when they returned to the dormitory, Jenny kissed everyone good-bye. When she pushed the buzzer on the front door, a voice promptly asked, "Yes?" and as instructed, Jenny said her name into the adjoining speaker. The buzzer unlatched the door, and when it was shut behind her, Jenny walked to the little window that looked into Miss Greer's office.

"Hello, Jenny," Miss Greer smiled. "Sign your name and the time that you returned. Any time that you are not on campus, you must sign in and out. That's for your protection. Have a good sleep and remember, I'm always here if you need me. There's a buzzer on my apartment next door."

I can't imagine what I would need her for, but I guess it's good to know such things.

She had been asleep for some time when she was awakened by Miss Greer's now familiar, drippy-sweet voice. "Jenny, your roommate is here. April, this is Jenny."

"Hi," Jenny said, trying to wake up as little as possible.

"Hi," April answered. "Sorry to wake you."

"Oh, that's okay. You don't smoke, do you?"

"No," April said, rather startled at the abruptness of the question. It was the last thing Jenny's mother had reminded her. Jenny was allergic to cigarette smoke, and her mother had said it was best to say so right out before they got to know each other.

"Oh, that's good. I'm allergic and my mother said I should ask."

"Oh, that's okay," April said.

By the end of the week, Jenny knew who her friends would be. Juanita and Glenda, who roomed together, were in her chorus and art classes. They really liked each other There were six rooms downstairs, and most of them housed older women who were already teachers. Everyone else was there to get a certificate and go in September to some new place to teach school. It created a common bond.

On Friday, a whole group went roller skating together; and on Sunday, they decided to try out one of the three main Protestant churches close to campus. Because the course was designed especially for the emergency certification, there was a lot of homework. By the end of the first week, everyone was settled in.

April was in Jenny's health science class but not in any others; they tended to study with their classmates. When Jenny and April were together, they chatted mostly about their families. April said she had only come to get away from home; she hated her mother. Jenny had thought at times that she didn't like her mother, but she certainly didn't hate her, or her father either. April's father had left them when she was about ten, so he didn't matter that much to her. Everyone had a different story to tell about her family.

One of the girls next door had a twin brother who had gone into the Navy. They had never been separated before, and she wrote to him several times a week. No matter what they were doing, she would say good night and go write to him. One night, Jenny went back to her room with her and offered to write to him, too. Jenny loved writing letters, so it was no problem writing to a stranger. She hoped he would answer.

During the third week of school, Jenny should have had her period. It didn't come. It was the second one she had missed. She wrote a letter to Mr. Hendricks, leaving her name off the envelope. She prayed that Mrs. Hendricks wouldn't open it.

About ten days later, she got a package with a letter saying, "Take these pills and if they don't work, call my brother at this number." Jenny took the pills and they made her sick but she didn't start her period. She kept praying it would come.

The days went by quickly. In addition to her regular classes, she had signed up for piano practice and swimming. By the middle of July, however, she knew she had to call Mr. Hendricks' brother. She had missed her third period and fainted in chorus class. She had been dizzy a lot, but the school nurse had assured her it was the high altitude. When Mrs. White asked if she had had a recent period, Jenny said "Yes." She had resolved not to lie anymore, but in this case she didn't feel she had any options. Mrs. White encouraged her to go home for a couple of days, and that fit in with Jenny's plans.

320 Mr. Hendricks' brother, Ray, had returned her call. Jenny was to meet him at the end of the week to have an abortion. Everyone at school thought she was just going home for the weekend, although Jenny thought Mrs. Greer seemed suspicious. Perhaps it was because Jenny felt guilty.

The next afternoon, Juanita walked with her to the bus stop and waited until Jenny boarded. Ray was waiting for her in Silver City. His brother had showed him a picture of Jenny and told her that Ray had a limp and used a cane.

As the bus rolled out of town, Jenny told herself that everything would be okay as long as her mother didn't find out. She thought the best thing to do was to pray all the way there. So to the rhythm of the wheels, Jenny prayed.

It was dusk when she walked into the red-carpeted lobby of the hotel. With its velour wallpaper and wooden panels, it seemed like a set from a movie. Even the man at the desk looked as if he might have a gun belt around his mid-section. She walked to the center of the room, clutching her bag, and scanned the room.

He's not here. She felt both relief and terror. *What will I do?* She was startled by a voice beside her.

"Jenny? Hi, I'm Ray. Let's have a drink."

"Oh, I don't drink."

"Are you hungry?"

"Yes." Paralysis seemed to be setting in. "Yes, I'm hungry," Jenny said in a choked voice she hardly recognized as her own.

"Good. Let's relax and get acquainted. Then tomorrow, we'll take care of your little problem. Everything is going to be just fine."

Dinner wasn't so bad. Ray asked a lot of questions and seemed to be a nice man. He talked about his brother and how he had been getting Don out of trouble most of Don's life. This was the third time he'd had to do this. He had told his brother straight out, it cost too damned much money. "Don would have come himself," he said, "but with the new baby and all, Madge would have been real mad."

"That would have been nice, but I really appreciate you helping me. I've been really sick at school."

"You want coffee?"

"I don't drink coffee."

"Oh. You don't mind if I do and have a cigarette, do you? You look tired."

"No, no. That's okay. I'm not tired."

They left the hotel dining room and crossed the Gold Rush Lobby to the elevator. At the third floor it clanked to a stop, and Ray guided her to Room 308. In its time, it had been an extravagant hotel. At this moment, all it was for Jenny was a bed, a dresser, a chair, and an adjoining bath. Her only hope lay in this strange man. He was completely in charge of her, and she felt lonely and cared-for at the same time. She wished that Mr. Hendricks had come, but he hadn't. Not that she blamed him. What if someone found out?

"You can change in the bathroom. I'll wait here." When she came back into the room, Ray was sitting on the bed in his shorts. Jenny had never seen anyone but her father in his undershorts. Furthermore, Ray was unbuckling his leg right below his knee!

Ray laughed. "You've never seen one of these before? Well, it's not so bad. I lost my own leg in a farm accident when I was a kid. Been using this one ever since I grew up. Don't let it bother you. I never wear it to bed. It's easier that way. Lately my knee has been bothering me, so I use the cane, too." He switched out the light, pulled back the covers, and slid between the sheets.

Jenny was shaking all over. Suddenly The Voice, which she had not heard for a long time, spoke in her mind.

Oh, my God. I hope my mother doesn't find out about this. Just lie still, Jenny. Everything will be fine. Just do what you have to do.

As she lay down, she felt Ray's heavy hand slide across her waist and move up to caress her breasts. *Oh, God! Oh, God! What will I do? I have to do what he wants! I don't know what to do without him tomorrow!*

322

She was startled to hear her own voice. "Oh, no! Please, please, don't do this to me!"

Oh, my God! I said it out loud! I hope he doesn't leave me!

"Hey, kid. What's the matter, anyhow? I'm not going to hurt you. C'mon, loosen up. Don was right. You sure are pretty. C'mon now, don't cry on me. How old are you, anyhow?"

"Seventeen."

"Jesus! I thought you were older than that. How long has Don been messing around with you, anyhow?"

"I baby-sit for them. I stayed at their house when the baby was born. My mother is a good friend of Mrs. Hendricks."

"How did this happen to you?"

"I don't remember. Mr. Hendricks came to my bed at night, and we just sort of started necking and kissing and stuff. I liked it at first and he would ask me to sing to him. Mrs. Hendricks was in the hospital, and the kids all slept upstairs. My room was off the kitchen. He told me he didn't really love Mrs. Hendricks anymore but just stayed there because of the kids. It didn't seem so bad because he was lonely, but then I wanted him to stop. When it was time for me to go home, he took me in the car, and this happened. I didn't know what to do, so I called him." Through tears she said, "I don't want you to do that to me, too."

"I won't, kid. Jesus! I just figured you were like the others. I don't wanna hurt you. You get some sleep, and we'll take care of you tomorrow. Jesus! That God damned fool! Leaving me with a kid, and I've got to get back home tomorrow. Never get my money back, either, I'll bet. This is the last time I bail him out! Enough is enough!"

Chapter 37

In the morning, they caught a cab. It seemed like a million miles before they stopped in front of an old, worn-down, white frame building. Ray opened the front door for her, and they walked down a long, dimly lit hall. At the end of the hall, they went upstairs and knocked on the first door. Jenny wasn't shaking anymore. She was numb. She didn't seem to be Jenny anymore, but someone else.

A heavy-set woman in a white uniform came into the room where Ray and Jenny were seated. She said to Ray, "You have the money . . . in cash?"

"Yes," he said, and added, "she's real scared."

Her voice changed to something like warm honey. "C'mon, sweetie. This won't take long, and it won't even hurt. You should have come sooner, you know. You girls just never learn, do you? Well, lucky I'm here and this gentleman is willing to make good his mistake. Some girls aren't that lucky. Just slip off your panties, and get up here on this table."

Why does she let Ray watch? She thinks it's him! I didn't know it cost so much. No wonder he's mad.

"Now, sweetie. I do real good work, and my girls don't get in any trouble. It takes a little longer, but it's worth it. Especially since you waited so long. Go to a movie or something, and in three or four hours you'll start having real bad cramps. Don't panic. Just go to your room and stay there. By five, maybe six hours it will be all over. If it's not, pull real gentle on this string. Wait till the pain comes, then pull. Don't make any noise in that hotel. And don't call me unless nothing happens or you get real sick." She turned to Ray. "You get the newspaper like I said?"

"Yeah, it's in the room."

"Don't get any blood in that hotel room. Dunno why you didn't put her up somewhere cheaper. I don't trust that place." She turned back to Jenny. "You take all that comes out of you and take it to the bus depot. Put it in the trash there. You hear me?"

"Yes."

"And I don't wanna see you here again. You're a real nice kid."

Ray dropped her off at the hotel, and Jenny went to a movie as she had been told. All day she did as she had been told. The pain got worse and worse. She bit her lip to keep from crying; then she bit the pillow and cried in loneliness and anguish. Finally, about dusk, it was over. She had followed all instructions. She walked down to the elevator, out the lobby, across the street, and the few blocks to the bus station.

Thank God there's no one around. Jenny dropped her package in the trash bin. Turning to leave, she noticed a phone on the wall. In a daze, she found the change and asked the operator, "Can I have long distance? I need to place a collect call to Helena. This is Jenny."

The wait was forever. Then the tears came. "Mom, this is Jenny. I'm at the bus station in Silver City. I'm real sick. I wanted to come home, but I didn't make it. I'm real sick."

"Jenny, what's wrong? Do you need me to come?"

"No, Mom. I'm okay. I guess I just had a bad period. I fainted in the bus depot and had to stay here. I was scared the school called you. I wanted to come home, but I'm okay."

"Do you have money?"

"Yes."

"You stay there tonight, and take the morning bus back to school. You'll be just fine tomorrow. The altitude there is really high. You'll be just fine."

"Okay, Mom." Silence. "I love you Mom."

"Okay, Jenny. Now you call me when you get back to school."

"Yes, Mom."

Tears spilled from Jenny's eyes as she hung up the phone. She picked up her bag. She had about twenty minutes before the bus came. More than anything else, she wanted to get out of the bus depot. *What if someone had seen her drop the newspaper in the trash? She had done a terrible thing. What would happen to her if someone found out? Busses came and left. I'll never take another bus anywhere as long as I live. I have to forget this. It has to be like it never happened. I'll just forget it. That's what I have to do.*

The bus came and Jenny boarded. She was thankful there weren't very many people on board, and no one sat beside her. Praying hard had helped her on the way to Silver City, so she prayed all the way back to school.

Thank you, God, for Miss Greer not calling Mother.

She must never know what I have done.

She would be so ashamed.

And please, help me forget this, forever and ever.

Please help me forget!

Epilogue

Jenny forgot for thirty-three years.

She taught school for one year, in one of the last frontier citadels, the one-room school house. There were three other buildings on the schoolyard property, a small but adequate teacherage and two outhouses. The school was the social center of the sprawling ranch community, and Jenny became a part of all that happened there. For the first time in her life she lived alone, and she liked it. Her heritage made her comfortable with the wilderness, although she carried her .22 rifle to and from school in case of rattlesnakes. She was confident she could use it and did on one occasion, when a lazy six-foot rattler decided to take a nap on the school house porch.

The following year, she joined the great army of women who went to work in the factories and shipyards. She became a riveter and repaired the wings of B-52 bombers so they could return to the Pacific theater. She kept on dancing, two, three, four nights a week and she wrote letters to many of the soldiers and sailors she met. In its own confusing but intense way, it was an exciting time for her. She felt as if she were participating in something bigger than herself. Her world was still small, but she had meaning and purpose in her life, and that was important to her. It became a theme throughout all her future experience.

One soldier was different from the rest. He fell in love with Jenny and asked her to marry him. She said "Yes," and when the war was over, her mother made her a beautiful white satin dress, and Ginger came from Colorado to be her maid-of-honor. Her father walked her down the aisle, and Jenny began a new life in California.

A year and a half after she left her family, a tiny, dark-haired bundle in a blue blanket was placed in her outstretched arms. He was the first of five children Jenny and her husband raised. In the arms of her own new family, she began to learn about love all over again; about fun and laughter; nights of fevered foreheads and upset tummies; parks, beaches, museums and zoos. Motherhood became a playground of safety for Jenny, and she devoted her life to her chosen role.

In the summers, she took her new family to visit Grandma and Grandpa. There her children learned a new kind of love with uncles, aunts, and cousins who came on fishing trips. Summer birthdays were celebrated with fried chicken and corn on the cob. Best of all were Grandma's raspberry bushes with their plump, juicy berries and the bright ruby-red currants that simmered from bubbly kettles to jars of mouth-watering jelly. There had always been a close attachment to nature in Jenny's family, and away from the sprawling suburbs of Los Angeles, an entire world was shared with her children. In the out-of-doors, Jenny and her parents and brothers had always been close and had a lot of fun. The love that she had experienced there was shared with her children. In a strange way, Jenny's lost memories allowed her children the rich experience of grandparents.

When her father died, Jenny was at his bedside. Although she wondered at the strange sense of relief she felt, she mourned his passing. She missed him in her life. No word had ever been exchanged between them about what he had done to her. It was forgotten. Once, he admitted to her that he had spanked her too severely as a child. He felt, in the long run, it hadn't helped anything. Jenny agreed with him. It hadn't helped anything.

Jenny's life was not without internal stresses, and sometimes they took their toll on her family. She continued to have violent and terrifying nightmares, sometimes accompanied by migraine headaches. Her husband would hold her and assure her there was nothing to be afraid of, and she would fall back to sleep in his arms. There were strange little things that caused her to panic. If anyone turned out the lights in a room and she wasn't prepared, she became alarmed. As long as she was alone she trusted the dark, but never with anyone there, not even her husband. This seemed like a strange contradiction to her family, but they learned to live with it. She also had a compulsion to open and shut doors to the rooms she slept in. It didn't make any difference whether doors were open or shut; she just had to feel that she was in charge of the door. This extended to cupboard and closet doors. Sometimes in someone else's house she would walk across a room full of people and shut a door. It became a joke with friends and family and pretty soon it didn't seem strange. It was just something Jenny did.

Inside Jenny, though, there was a deep inner darkness that she shared with no one. Many nights she would waken with chills of some deep fright, and she frequently wondered if she had some form of insanity. She would become overwhelmed with guilt and shame, and make long lists of things that would help her move toward perfection and away from shame. Nothing was ever enough. No matter how hard she worked or how long the lists were, she could not be the perfect wife and mother she wanted to be.

In the night when she was alone, she would face the terror of her childhood that she was a bad person. The source of the terror remained hidden from her, and reinforced her conviction that if people knew who she really was, she would be condemned. All this she held as a secret, never sharing it with anyone.

By good fortune, her husband was a kind and gentle man, but although he tried to intervene at times, no amount of reassurance could convince Jenny that she was fine the way she was. She knew she was a failure. If a meal turned out badly or the bank account didn't balance, Jenny would blame herself for hours and days. In the night, she would weep in her husband's arms and admonish him for marrying her, telling him that if he only knew how bad she was, he would leave her. He was puzzled yet patient. Once he asked her, "Jenny, what have you ever done that makes you feel so bad about yourself? Everyone who knows you knows how wonderful you are, and they say I'm the luckiest guy alive to have you for my wife."

"I don't know," Jenny replied. "I just know that inside, I feel like a bad person." One night, she shared the contents of a recurring dream: a huge dark shadowy male figure would stand over her, chase her and shout at her, "You must be destroyed. You are bad." The figure never caught her in the dream, but Jenny would run and run from him, looking for a place to hide. In all sincerity she asked her husband, "What if I really am a bad person and you just can't see it?" In his efforts to comfort her, he couldn't hear the extent of her pain and terror. Jenny was like a small child with a monster in her closet, and all the grownups were saying, "The monster isn't there."

After a particularly bad episode, they would plan an outing in the nearby mountains or the beach, and Jenny's usual sunny and loving personality would somehow be restored. Although it was clear that her home was a safe place, Jenny never felt completely safe there. Leaving always felt safer.

Early in her third pregnancy, a soft-spoken, persuasive man knocked on her door and invited Jenny to come to his church on Sunday. For the first time since moving to the sprawling Los Angeles basin, Jenny found a home. The familiar Bible stories of her childhood took on new meaning, and Jenny subconsciously began to work off her guilt in the heart of the church community. There she was able to expand her natural talent for and love of children by teaching. She invited herself to sing again. She made friends.

Babies were born and baptized. Potlucks became a way of life and holidays were shared with other displaced families from all points east of California. More importantly, Jenny began to reconnect with the God of her early childhood. He was someone she could trust; someone who knew about mountains and about how beavers built their homes. God became someone she could talk to in the middle of the night. She even began to write again: thoughts and ideas about scriptures; feelings and prayers; even some poetry.

It was so wonderful for Jenny to have a place to discover herself as a creative, loving, giving person that she eventually became a professional in Religious Education and Youth Work. For nineteen years, she remained in the bosom of the church. Her faith and joy touched the lives of many children and young people, as well as the adults who worked with her. God and God's love were a very personal experience for her, and the man, Jesus, was her teacher and friend.

Just as in her childhood, though, Jenny hated the inconsistencies and hypocrisy in the church organization. She was puzzled by prejudice and piousness, and troubled by the nonacceptance of individual lives. For example, there was a big dispute in the church over whether Alcoholics Anonymous should be allowed to meet in the church building. Some staunch and powerful members didn't want "drunks" in their building. And many church members didn't think boys with long hair should be allowed to participate in any part of the liturgy of the church.

For Jenny, the turmoil of the Sixties became a forum for liberation, as she began to take public stands on racism, farm worker's rights, abortion, and the Vietnam War. Her own sons reached draft age, and she joined them and many others in the process of making painful decisions about themselves and war. Jenny knew these social changes were placing a demand on her to make new decisions, but she wasn't aware of how deeply those decisions would affect her life.

335

In 1972, her husband's employment brought them to the San Francisco Bay area. Although Jenny had made a home for herself in Orange County, she welcomed the opportunity to move to a less conservative and congested place. The Sixties had given her opportunities to look inside herself in a new way. She saw that there was more to her than wife, mother, and church worker, and that she had a right to find out who that was. She had also given back to God the problem of healing all the wounds of the universe and accepted His blessing to find out what else she could do. Along with many others in the feminist movement, she began to consider that perhaps God was female, and that the culture she had grown up in was not necessarily always "right."

Her children felt abandoned, and her husband wondered who this selfish person was who had replaced his wife. Nonetheless, she went on changing. She returned to college full-time and reclaimed some of the energy of her adolescence. She wanted for herself the opportunities she had helped to provide for her children, opportunities for college and career. By returning to school, Jenny opened her imagination to her own possibilities, her own potential. In the competition of the classroom, she laid claim to the power of her mind. She was excited about just being herself. The focus began to shift from what she did for other people to who she was. And there remained, always, the need to have a meaningful life.

One day in a women's study class, a young woman shared, in a powerfully moving presentation, her experience of being raped. Jenny swallowed tears over and over, and finally left the classroom crying. It didn't occur to her that her tears were not all for the young woman As she was to discover, they were also for herself. During the next few days, she began to have flashbacks about her father. There was nothing particularly dramatic about the memories, only that they were accompanied by pain and tears. She felt haunted by her father, who had been dead for many years. After about a week, she sat down one evening with her journal and began to write. By four in the morning, she had spontaneously recalled and written the secrets of her childhood. Tearful and exhausted, she fell into bed, knowing that she had written the truth.

Jenny continued to remember for the next sixteen years. She remembered in individual therapy at a time when therapists wanted to believe it wasn't true. The therapists who did believe her told her all she had to do was forgive her father.

She remembered in philosophy classes as she studied about the nature of man and the nature of good and evil. Why had her father done such things to her? If she could just understand what had gone on in him, she thought it would help. What she gained was a deeper understanding of herself. She became a stronger person, a person who began to understand more about what it meant to be a human being. She recognized that there was nothing inherently bad about her. She was human and her experience of herself was just that: human.

She remembered in Gestalt groups and reclaimed her lost pain and unfocused rage at being raped and betrayed by the man she loved. Her life became a kaleidoscope of uncovering deep, dark and hidden feelings. She recognized for the first time that the anger she felt at social injustice was anger about the injustice perpetrated on her. The pain she felt was her pain, and the tears she shed were for herself. She could now weep for the separation of her self in childhood.

She remembered in body work as she melted the blocks in her muscular and neuro systems. She began to acquire a new knowledge of her forgotten body. She felt again the pain of rape and physical abuse. She mourned the loss of joy in childbirth. In their ignorance, doctors had measured and x-rayed her, explaining that she should have no problem giving birth. But she had. Her pelvis was rigid and inflexible, and her babies were born with ether and forceps. In fact, her body had been numb for most of her adult life.

She remembered as she began to transform her childhood wound through loving service to hundreds of girls and boys, men and women, as a therapist, teacher, and trainer in the field of treating child sexual abuse. She made a conscious decision to work with a group of girls aged eight to twelve. She shared her truth that she was their age the first time her father touched her. They learned by her example how important it is to tell their truth and to be believed. She had a magic about her in adolescent groups, a magic of acceptance. She never denied their pain and rage. She affirmed that the process of forgetting had been necessary for their survival.

She remembered in writing the pages of this book. Through all this remembering, Jenny's life has been restructured, and a life-giving force has been set free in her. That force is the God-given right of every child to live and breathe in a safe environment, and to love and be loved without abuse or betrayal. No longer a victim of her parents' lack of attention and ignorance, a reflection of the ignorance of their time, an ignorance that still exists, she can fully claim herself without the painful denial of childhood abuse. She can feel herself as a whole person, not one part split off from the other. She is free to fully claim the curious, creative, joyful little girl who moves through the pages of this book. This truth is reclaimed in Jenny's spirit, which was loved and nurtured in the same family that wounded her.

Alice Miller calls incest "soul murder" and all too frequently it is. But for many thousands of boys and girls like Jenny, the soul simply oversees the separation of the psyche. To forget is necessary to survive. To remember is to move beyond survival, beyond existence, to the full transformative potential of human life. There is fear and pain in the remembering, and it is equally true that healing and hope lie in the remembering. Jenny's soul is not dead. She lives each day, moment by moment, inviting the lessons of the past to walk with her into her future. As a child, her fear and shame immobilized her in a world without personal power. When the forgetting and the remembering no longer had power over her, she could experience her freedom of choice. One of the most difficult choices was to act on the knowledge that no one, today, must walk this journey alone.

If Jenny's story is your story, reach out. And if some other Jenny reaches out to you, believe her, support her, and invite her on the joyful and painful road to her own recovery from childhood abuse.

Note: This particular story is Jenny's, from girlhood to womanhood. Sex abuse is not, however, limited to girls, and sex abusers are not exclusively male.

Epilogue

Resources

The Healing Woman
POBox 3038, Moss Beach, CA 94038
tel (415) 728-0339; fax (415) 728-1324
The national newsletter for women survivors of childhood sexual abuse. Each month, The Healing Woman reaches out to survivors and offers them a wise, warm, and loving community where their voices can be heard — and where their issues will be understood.

Parents United International, Giarretto Institute
232 East Gish Road, San Jose, CA 95112
tel (408) 453-7616
International treatment and support groups for victims of child sexual abuse and their families: Daughters and Sons United, Adults Molested As Children United, and Parents United. Write for information on groups in your area.

VOICES (Victims of Incest Can Emerge Survivors) in Action
POBox 148309, Chicago, IL 60614
tel (800) 7-VOICE-8
National network for incest survivors: literature, therapist referrals, conferences, and more.

359

LEONA S. TOCKEY, MFCC (*Marriage, Family & Child Counselor*) maintains a private practice in Newark, California. She is a nationally recognized expert in the treatment of sex abuse survivors of all ages and their families. Leona is a dedicated healer who communicates power: the transformation of life's tragedies into meaningful living.

For the past ten years, Leona has studied indigenous cultures as a pathway to healing grief and loss, claiming personal power and community building. She has a visible passion for life which is shared in speaking, teaching and through workshop and seminar presentations.

Leona can be reached at *Life Arrow*: 2464 El Camino Real, Santa Clara, California, 95051.

RICHARD MARTIN is an artist and award winning designer living in San Francisco. The "Family Album" illustrations in this book were realized using computer enhanced photography. Various faces were composited for expressive purposes and to protect the identities in the original photographs.